the GRUMP next door

BRIGHTON WALSH

Edited by Lisa Hollett of Silently Correcting Your Grammar, LLC
Cover Design © Brighton Walsh
Illustration by Newton Henrique

The Grump Next Door is a work of fiction. Names, characters, places, and incidents are either products of the author's imagination or are used fictitiously, and any resemblance to actual persons, living or dead, business establishments, events, or locales is coincidental.

Digital ISBN: 978-1-68518-047-8
Paperback ISBN: 978-1-68518-048-5
Special Edition ISBN: 978-1-68518-053-9

CONTENT NOTES

Please be advised that this book contains content that may be upsetting for some readers. Should you prefer detailed information in order to have the best reading experience, please visit the author's website or scan the QR code below to view a full list of content notes.

CHAPTER ONE

ATLAS

IF THERE WAS one thing I hated more than people, it was talking to people. And talking to people while my oversized frame was stuffed into a monkey suit was seventh circle of hell territory.

Didn't have much of a choice, though.

The sooner I made my appearance at the annual charity gala my former team held, the sooner I could make the rounds, and the sooner I'd be back here in my hotel room.

My *empty* hotel room.

I could shower off the stench of jersey chasers, jerk off to a faceless woman in peace, and fall into a restless sleep. Then I'd head back home in the morning.

This was my least favorite way to spend an evening, but even though I'd been out of the league for five years, I hadn't missed one of these events. And despite my disdain for the attire—and events in general—I didn't plan to start anytime soon.

I tugged on my dress shirt, buttoning it up with as much care as I could manage. Which wasn't much. After a glance in the mirror verifying I hadn't misaligned the buttons, I grabbed my cuff links engraved with my number—a retirement gift from the team owner—and slipped them through the holes before securing them into place.

I'd tied enough bow ties in my life that I could do it without thought. The problem was, if I didn't have anything occupying my mind, it tended to wander to places I'd rather leave in the rearview mirror.

Halfway through tying the bow, my phone buzzed from its place on the nightstand. I abandoned the knot and strode over to glance at the screen. My youngest brother's name flashed, along with a string of call notifications I'd missed while in the shower.

I pressed the button to accept the call. "Yeah."

"Nice of you to finally answer, dickhead," Lincoln said.

"I'm a little busy, Linc. What's up?"

"We've got a Mom Situation," he said without preamble. The clinking of glasses and the loud hum of voices carried over the line, telling me he was at One Night Stan's. "And since I can't be both there and covering the bar, we've gotta tag team."

I froze on my path back to the mirror, my steps halting as a dozen different scenarios flew through my mind, each one worse than the last. "What kind of Mom Situation?"

"Nope. I'm not gonna spill so you can pick and choose. Just tell me which one you can take care of—Mom or the bar. And hurry the fuck up. Who knows what she's gotten into while I waited for your ass to answer."

"I didn't answer because I'm a little busy here. Why didn't you call Declan?"

"Uh, because I actually wanted someone to show up?"

Fair enough. Dec wasn't exactly reliable. And Xander was a plane ride away, so he couldn't just swing by the family bar to lend a hand.

"Well, I can't show up. I'm out of town." I scrubbed a hand across my mouth. "Jesus Christ, does no one look at the family calendar?"

Lincoln snorted. "What am I, a soccer mom? No, I don't look at the fucking calendar."

"Well, if you had, you'd know I'm in Portland."

"Maine or Oregon?"

"Maine."

Not that it mattered. Even though I was in the same state, it might as well have been another country for all the good it did me. This was the first time I'd left our small town all year —since the last time I'd come to this exact event, actually. But of course, shit would hit the fan on the singular day I wasn't in Starlight Cove.

How bad would it *really* be if I missed the charity gala? And how quickly could I charter a private jet?

"I don't buy it," Lincoln said. "You never leave this place. Barely leave your house unless you're here, at the school, or at an away game for the team. So stop fucking around, quit giving me excuses, and help me handle this."

With a muttered curse, I hung up on him and navigated to the camera app.

Group text with Atlas, Xander, Declan, and Lincoln

7:27 p.m.

LINCOLN:

Why did you hang up on me, asshole?

I sent him the picture of myself glaring at him in reply.

ATLAS:

Team charity thing in Portland. Just like last year. Just like next year. Just like I put in the fucking calendar.

DECLAN:

Am I supposed to be impressed that you jetted off somewhere in your $10k tux?

ATLAS:

Linc needs you at the bar or to check on Mom. Your pick.

DECLAN:

I'm busy

I ground my molars, biting back the string of curses I wanted to release. How my brothers still acted like fucking children even though they were all in their thirties was a goddamn mystery.

ATLAS:

Unbusy yourself, shithead. I'm four hours away and can't exactly pop over.

LINCOLN:

Guess it'll forever remain a mystery why I didn't call Dec first.

DECLAN:

One of you assholes fill me in on what's
going on.

LINCOLN:

Mom Situation

DECLAN:

Dire or standard?

LINCOLN:

Anyone's guess. Her faucet's been dripping.
Instead of waiting for one of us to handle it,
she started watching YouTube videos. She's
attempting to be her own plumber.

"Motherfucker," I muttered. I began typing out a reply when another text notification popped up, this time from the woman in question. I clicked over to the thread with just her and me.

MOM:

I know your brother has sent out the bat
signal or whatever, but I'm FINE. I'm a fully
grown, independent woman and don't need
my sons to come to my rescue all the time.
Have fun at your gala! And send me
pictures!!! I'll take care of this myself, no
need to worry. These videos are very
informative!

ATLAS:

Mom. Just leave it alone for now. Don't
touch anything.

MOM:

I'm perfectly capable of handling things in
my own house, Atlas.

ATLAS:

I know you are. But just wait for one of us,
will you?

MOM:

Your brothers are welcome to help me once
they get here. Unless I've already finished
by then.

Group text with Atlas, Xander, Declan, and Lincoln

7:36 p.m.

ATLAS:

Jesus Christ, one of you needs to get over
there right fucking now. She's diving in
without waiting for us.

LINCOLN:

I've got the bar to handle, and we're two
deep because Mabel's offering half off a sex
toy if people buy her a drink. I'm going to
have to roll her out of here by last call.

ATLAS:

Dec. That means you're up.

DECLAN:

Goddammit. You fuckers have no idea what
I'm passing up for you.

LINCOLN:

Not for us, douchebag. For Mom.

DECLAN:

Yeah, yeah. I'm on my way.

XANDER:

Sorry for the late reply. Looks like you got it
handled, but lmk if otherwise.

LINCOLN:

Convenient, Xan.

XANDER:

I can't do shit when I'm 1k miles away, dickweed.

ATLAS:

Someone keep me up to date.

LINCOLN:

Enjoy the fancy party. Word on the street is there are a whole lot of thirsty women ready to pounce.

ATLAS:

What's that supposed to mean?

LINCOLN:

When's the last time you looked at your Instagram?

ATLAS:

I have an Instagram?

LINCOLN:

Yes, idiot. You got tagged in a bunch of promo pics for the event. The ladies are going feral. Including Cara Preston. She's happy to be your date or—and I quote—whatever you need, anytime. So your next game should be fun.

"Fuck me," I groaned to my empty hotel room and scrubbed a hand down my face.

I tossed my phone on the bed and finished tying my bow tie, my mind properly occupied this time. That woman might as well have taken out a billboard for how subtle she'd been in her interest since I'd moved back home.

Problem was, I didn't date my players' moms. Or women who lived in Starlight Cove. Or in general.

I'd come to realize that returning home—or to my hotel room—alone and jacking off to a faceless woman held a lot fewer headaches for me. God knew my family proved enough of a challenge that I didn't need to add any more to my list.

CHAPTER TWO

SUTTON

ON ANY OTHER SATURDAY NIGHT, my big plans for the evening would've been to spend it in an empty house with my current read and my vibrator. Possibly at the same time. Okay, *probably* at the same time.

Unfortunately, moving across the country thwarted those plans. Being stuck in a hotel room with my teenage daughter meant there was absolutely no fun in my future. Especially when that teenage daughter was cursing my very existence for dragging her away from the *favorite city she's ever lived*—never mind she'd said that about literally every place we'd ever called home.

Laurel groaned as soon as we walked into our room. "Seriously? We have to share a bed?"

I walked past her, rolling my suitcase behind me, and glanced around the space. With its crisp, clean lines and modern touches, this hotel was a step up from our last one. But it did, in fact, have only one bed. "I thought we loved when that happened."

"Ugh, in *books*." She fell back onto the bed, her eye roll loud enough for me to hear. "Not with my mother."

Sixteen-year-old attitude was going strong with this one.

"You heard the guy at check-in—with the event happening, we only managed to snag this room because of a last-minute cancelation."

And thank god for that because if I had to spend even five more minutes in a car with Laurel, I wasn't sure both of us would make it out alive.

Bracing my hands on either side of her shoulders, I leaned over her on the bed and shot her a mischievous smile. "You wanna crash whatever fancy sportsball thing is happening in the ballroom?"

"We hate sportsball."

"All the more reason to crash it. I'd be willing to bet gala plus sportsball equals good food."

"Silence plus solitude equals a good night."

Becoming a mom at sixteen hadn't been easy, but I loved my daughter more than life itself. Would crack open my chest and rip out my own heart if she needed it. But spending two days in a car with her and her shitty attitude was pushing me to my limit. What I wouldn't *give* for a roll of duct tape right now.

"Hey, I have a great idea," I said with false cheer as I pushed to stand. "I'm gonna head down to the bar for a while and give you some privacy for your existential crisis. Sound good?"

"Still living in Atlanta would sound good."

"Great! I'll work on getting that time spinner up and

running while I'm enjoying a lemon drop." I hooked my oversized purse over my shoulder and strode toward the door. "Lock this behind me."

"I *know*, Mom. *God*. I'm not a child."

The look I shot her screamed more than my words ever could. Unfortunately, her attention was focused solely on her phone, so the effect was wasted.

I stepped out into the hall, the door shutting behind me, and leaned against the wall. Breathing out a deep sigh, I let my head fall back and closed my eyes, waiting until I heard the lock click into place.

"Mouthy little shit," I muttered, sidestepping a guy coming out of the door across the way. "Sorry, not you."

Without waiting for him to reply, I hooked my bag higher on my shoulder and strode toward the elevator. I might not have been able to have any fun with my vibrator tonight, but at least I had my book with me. Getting lost in a fictional world for a while was exactly what I needed.

I'd park myself at the bar for an hour or two, give both Laurel and me some breathing room, and head back up to try to get a good night's sleep. We had several hours in the car tomorrow before we'd arrive at our new home. And then came the unpacking. My daughter was just going to *love* that.

While moving wasn't new for us, her attitude definitely was. And I couldn't say I was a fan. I also couldn't blame her. Switching high schools halfway through wasn't ideal, but I didn't have much of a choice.

As a travel nurse, I had to go where the job was, and I couldn't always choose where I wanted that to be. I was just lucky a good friend from college had been looking to hire a nurse when my last contract ended. It was serendipitous.

Yeah, Starlight Cove, Maine, was a far cry from Atlanta. And yeah, it was smaller than any other place we'd lived... ever. But I wasn't sure that was so bad.

I wouldn't mind a slower life for us. One where it didn't take an hour to drive ten miles. One where I didn't have to wonder what part of the city she was lost in on a Friday night. One where I could enjoy these last two years of having her home with me before she flew the nest for good.

It'd been just the two of us for so long, I wasn't sure what I'd do when I no longer had that. I wanted to soak up every second I could.

"What I'm *not* gonna do is cry tonight," I mumbled to absolutely no one as the elevator dinged and the doors opened.

As I stepped inside, I tugged my book out of my purse... and somehow managed to fumble a move I'd done a hundred times before. The corner of the paperback got caught on my strap, flew out of my hand, and landed on the floor, skidding to a stop in front of a pair of polished black men's dress shoes.

"Shit, sorry. I don't usually assault people with books. At least, not at the first meeting."

The man reached down and picked up the paperback, flipping it so the title faced him before extending it to me. "*Fake Dating Her Ex*...good choice."

His voice was deep, just a low rumble that somehow perfectly matched his appearance. Dark hair, harsh brows slanting over whiskey eyes, and a short beard that did absolutely nothing to hide his sharp jaw or those full, sinful lips.

Taking the book from his outstretched hand, I raised a brow. "Read a lot of romance, do you?"

"Depends on what you define as a lot."

Uh...for this man? Anything more than zero would be a lot. He wasn't exactly the poster child for a smut slut.

I stepped to the other side of the elevator and took him in. He was huge, with shoulders roughly the width of a truck and thighs the size of tree trunks, all encased in a fancy suit that probably cost more than a nice used car.

It didn't take much to deduce he was more than likely on his way to or from that sportsball thing happening tonight. I glanced at the floor panel to his right, noticing the bar/ballroom level was lit up—to, then.

He was going to be as out of place there as I would be, considering I was still wearing my standard driving uniform that basically amounted to pajamas. Tuxedo or not, he looked like he belonged in a secluded cabin in the forest, being pissed off about all the wood he had to chop rather than attending a gala.

And he *definitely* didn't look like he read romance.

"More than three?" I asked.

He lifted his gaze to mine, and *jesusfuck*. I felt that all the way to my toes and every single forgotten inch in between.

That was...new.

I didn't usually have that sort of reaction to a man. Not after mere minutes. And certainly not after coming out of a spectacularly shitty relationship where just the thought of men pissed me off.

"In a week?" he asked.

My brows lifted. "Um...I was thinking in a year."

"Then by that definition, yeah." He pressed himself against the far wall, hands tucked in his pockets, face impassive. Though his gaze...it kept straying to mine. Almost as if he couldn't help himself.

Even standing slouched as he was, he positively dwarfed the space. There was no denying just how imposing this man was. But something about the way he was holding himself told me he was trying very hard not to be.

I cleared my throat. "Well, Mr. Seven Foot Tall, it's not very often you meet a guy who looks like you who happens to read romance."

"Six-six." His lips twitched—there and gone so quick, I wasn't sure I hadn't imagined it—and he glanced down at the book I held. "And, to be fair, I haven't read that one. But my mom loved it."

"Your mom, huh?" I couldn't keep the surprise out of my voice. "You guys have book club?"

"She's a librarian. And a great cook. Sometimes I don't have a choice."

The way he said it, all business, no inflection, brought a smile to my lips. It'd been a long time since a man had been able to disarm me long enough to do that. Even longer since I'd felt regret over not being able to see where this could possibly lead.

Alas, it wasn't in the cards.

The elevator came to a stop, and he reached out, holding the doors open for me. "Enjoy your book."

"Enjoy your gala." I laughed as his scowl only deepened,

and I stepped out of the elevator, shooting him a smile over my shoulder. "I bet the food will be good, at least. Eat something delicious for me."

Then, without a backward glance, I headed toward the bar. I was ready for a drink. And to get lost in a world where a woman like me would've spent the night with Mr. Tall, Dark, and Grumpy instead of by herself with only a book boyfriend for company.

APPARENTLY THE UNIVERSE had taken my silent desire as permission that I didn't want to be alone and dropped the worst of mankind in my path.

I'd been at the bar for fifty minutes, and this random guy had been on my ass for forty-five of them. I hadn't even gotten a chance to open my book before he'd sidled up to the stool next to mine, shooting me a leering smile and diving straight into a single-sided conversation.

One I'd tried subtly and not so subtly to put an end to.

Normally, I'd just up and leave—I wasn't in the habit of allowing men my company if I didn't want to—but this wasn't a normal situation. It hadn't taken me long to realize he was the same guy I'd seen in the hallway outside Laurel's and my room. Because of course he was. My one talent in life was my ability to attract some real losers.

Since my teenage daughter was in our room, alone, I had no intention of leading him back there. Which meant I was stuck.

The bar was about half full, scattered with an eclectic

mix of people—a few in jeans, several who'd obviously escaped from the gala...and exactly no one dressed in pseudo pajamas, save for me.

Unfortunately, even that hadn't stopped Chief Creep from descending.

I'd kept a napkin over my drink the entire time because I didn't trust that he wouldn't slip something into it if I even blinked. I was giving him the coldest shoulder known to humankind, but he just would not take the hint. And I was really damn tired of this game.

I'd been down this road before, and I had no intention of returning so soon.

"C'mon, you know you wanna come back to my room." He gave me a slow perusal, the sweep of his gaze like slime coating my skin. "A pretty girl like you shouldn't be alone tonight."

Fuck *me*. While all his other talk amounted to please, *please* come home with me, this was the first time he'd laid it out so clearly. I needed to be done with this, and I needed that *now*.

Unfortunately, the bartender was otherwise occupied, and the closest patron was four stools away, so I didn't have any hope of catching their attention.

I was on my own.

I scanned the bar as Chief Creep leaned closer, his rancid breath sweeping across my skin. My mind was spinning a thousand miles an hour as I darted my gaze around the space, trying to find a way out of this. Preferably one that didn't end with my body being found on the ten o'clock news. There were a few men in tuxedos clustered together who I assumed to be sportsball players, but I wasn't about to dive into a group.

And then I spotted *him*.

Mr. Tall, Dark, and Grumpy stood at the entrance of the bar, an imposing sight even from across the room. Had he somehow gotten *bigger* in the hour since we'd met in the elevator? Or was it just the air he was putting off now?

He surveyed the room, a scowl firmly in place, mouth set in a hard line, brows drawn down. His tuxedo was still impeccable, save for the tie now hanging loosely around his neck, the top couple buttons of his shirt undone. But even those helped in broadcasting a silent, *stay the fuck away from me if you know what's good for you.*

The problem was, I *didn't* know what was good for me.

Even surrounded by other hulking players, he was, without a doubt, the biggest, meanest-looking motherfucker in here. And he was exactly what I needed.

"Who says I'm alone?" I barely spared Chief Creep a glance before grabbing my bag, sliding off my stool, and heading straight for the man I'd been certain I would never see again.

This might be a mistake. This *probably* was a mistake. But my internal alarm had been blaring from the moment Rancid Breath Douchebag had sat down next to me, when it hadn't so much as beeped while in an enclosed elevator with Mr. Tall, Dark, and Grumpy.

Besides, a guy who listened to his mom dish about her latest romance novel couldn't be all bad. Could he?

I'd taken only three steps toward him when his gaze

landed—and stayed—on mine. He watched my approach with an intense focus I felt all the way to my toes.

And I had absolutely no business liking that as much as I did.

I didn't slow my steps, worried if I did, I'd second-guess just what the hell I was doing and be right back at square one —or worse, with Chief Creep following me to my room. I had pepper spray somewhere in my bag, but I'd rather not have to spray a random guy outside my hotel room and deal with the cops tonight.

The space around Mr. Tall, Dark, and Grumpy was sparse, as if no one else had the audacity to step too close.

But I did.

I stepped right up to him, craning my head back to meet his eyes. He didn't say anything, but he studied me intently, trying to get a read on what was happening.

I rested one hand on the hard expanse of his chest. His skin was warm beneath my touch, his heart thrumming in a steady beat. With my other hand, I reached up and wrapped my fingers around the nape of his neck, all too aware that the only reason I was able to tug his face toward mine was because he let me.

He silently studied me the entire time, but those deep whiskey eyes were broadcasting everything he wasn't saying. Namely, just what in the fuck was I doing?

Great question. Getting Chief Creep off my ass was my main objective. But doing that while also making him think this beast of a man was mine? That Laurel and I would be under his protection? That would be the cherry on top. Because no one in their right mind could look at this guy and think he'd do anything less than irrevocably fuck you up for just looking the wrong way at what was his.

When our mouths were so close I could feel his breath with each exhale, I whispered, "Please play along."

And then I steeled my nerves, closed my eyes, and pressed my lips against this stranger's.

CHAPTER THREE

SUTTON

KISSING a stranger should not feel like coming home.

Except *coming home* wasn't quite right. That was too gentle for what this was. For what stirred inside me when this man banded an arm around my lower back, lifting me flush against him so that only my tiptoes anchored me to the floor. Too gentle for the response that hummed in my body when he parted his lips and brushed his tongue against mine.

And the groan he released straight into my mouth the second our tongues touched? That sure as fuck wasn't gentle.

Jesus, I wanted to climb him like a tree. Was actually gripping the collar of his suit jacket like I might try it right here in the bar. I didn't care that we had an audience. Barely even remembered why I was doing this in the first place. I just wanted to cling on for dear life and allow myself to be taken anywhere—*anywhere*—this man wanted to take me.

The way he cupped his other hand at the base of my skull, his fingers delving into my hair, said he had a lot of ideas about doing just that. Screamed it even louder when he brought his thumb to my chin, guiding me to open myself farther for him, allowing his tongue even deeper. So calm and confident and sure in a situation that was anything but.

My *god*, it'd been a long time since I'd been kissed like this. Actually, I wasn't sure I'd *ever* been kissed like this. Like I was an oasis in the middle of a desert, that first gulp of fresh air after cresting the surface of the sea.

He was *devouring* me. And I was letting him.

His massive body was warm and firm, a steady rock holding me up. And thank god for that, because I had no hope of doing so myself. My nipples were tight points against his chest, and I had very little doubt he could feel them. Because my dumb ass hadn't thought it imperative to pair a bra with my pseudo pajamas. These barely B cups usually didn't need one.

Usually.

Unless, of course, I was dry humping the hottest man I'd ever seen and my pussy was loudly reminding me just how lonely she'd been with only silicone to keep her company.

After too long and yet not nearly long enough, he pulled back, both of us breathing heavily into the scant space between us. "You're trouble, aren't you?"

"More like in trouble. But thank you," I murmured against his lips. Mostly because I was still dangling off the floor, and he didn't seem in a hurry to set me down. "I just really needed—"

"Anything."

"There was this creepy guy, and he—"

"I'll kill him." Storm clouds descended over his features

as he glanced around the room, pinning each man with a glare.

I huffed out a laugh at the sheer gravity of his words. They were spoken with such a deadly calm, I didn't for one second think he wasn't serious. "I'm not sure we need to do all that. I just needed to get away without bringing him back to my room."

He turned his attention back to me, a beat passing. Two. Three. "How about my room, then?"

A slow smile swept across my mouth. I speared my fingers through the short hair at the base of his head, my body lighting up over the possibility of what this man could do to it.

My time here was nothing more than a stopover. In less than twelve hours, I'd be on my way to a new life with my daughter. And I'd never see this sexy beast of a man again. So what did it matter?

What did *any* part of tonight matter?

"That would definitely be easier, considering my teenage daughter is alone in mine."

It took only a moment before realization dawned. His features hardened even more, his jaw ticking as he scanned the bar once again. And I could tell the second he'd spotted Chief Creep. His entire body went stiff, his murderous glare alone enough to send people scurrying.

I looked over my shoulder and confirmed my wannabe suitor did just that, not daring to even spare me a glance. I exhaled a sharp sigh of relief, knowing that even if the guy who wouldn't take no for an answer never saw my knight in brooding glory set foot in Laurel's and my room, he'd assume this man would be there. And that was good enough for me.

"He got the message," my protector rumbled. "But just in case, text your daughter and tell her not to open the door for anyone."

There was absolutely no reason for my stomach to flip over his concern for Laurel when that had been solely my job the entirety of her life. That probably wasn't even the reason for the feeling anyway. The flutters in my stomach were no doubt just the letdown of nerves since I wasn't in fight-or-flight mode anymore.

"She's a mouthy teenager who wouldn't open the door if there was a fire. Believe me, she's fine," I said. "And I'll be up there soon enough. We've been at each other's throats for two days, so I was just giving her some space."

"For how long?"

"What?"

"How long were you giving her space?"

"Oh..." I darted my gaze between his eyes, reading every ounce of desire reflected back at me. "An hour or two."

"So, you've got, what? Forty-five minutes left?" he asked, his gaze dropping to my mouth.

I caught my lower lip with my teeth, loving the way this man looked at me. Who the hell needed a lemon drop when I could get drunk on that alone? "Something like that."

He met my eyes once again, a thousand promises in his stare. "I can do a lot in forty-five minutes."

CHAPTER FOUR

ATLAS

ONE MINUTE, we were standing in the bar, warding off a slimy piece of shit, and the next, we were in the elevator, standing on opposite sides of the car. As if we both knew as soon as we touched—again—it was game over. All bets off.

I'd known she was gorgeous from the second she'd stepped into the elevator earlier and dropped her book at my feet. With her wavy dark-brown hair that fell just past her shoulders, those clear green eyes, and that mouth, there was no denying it.

But watching her now as she stood across from me, her cheeks flushed, lips parted, and eyes bright... *Fuck.* She was looking at me like she wanted to eat me alive, and I was inclined to let her.

The oversized sweatshirt she wore did nothing to accentuate the firm little body I'd had practically wrapped around me, but fuck if it didn't make my cock twitch. Just the thought of her strolling to my bed wearing nothing but that had me hard as fucking granite.

From the way her eyes kept drifting down...how she caught that plump lower lip with her teeth, a look of hunger overcoming her features, I had no doubt she saw my reaction to her. My cock was a little difficult to hide.

It was taking everything in me not to descend on her. Not to close the distance between us in two long strides and crash my mouth against hers once again. I wanted to taste her every-fucking-where.

And I wasn't going to rest until I'd done so.

As soon as the elevator doors opened on my floor, I couldn't hold myself back any longer. Neither, it seemed, could she.

We met in the middle, her body crashing into mine as I cupped her ass and lifted her up. Gripping my face, she wrapped her legs around my waist and brought her lips down on mine.

She still tasted just as sweet as whatever she'd been drinking, and I moaned into her mouth. Her answering whimper as she ground her pussy against me had my cock throbbing, desperate to slide inside her.

With our lips still fused together, I palmed her ass with one hand and fumbled in my pocket for the room key with the other. More desperate than I could ever remember being. *Needing* to get her into my room. To lock us away from prying eyes and ears and spend the entire night worshipping every inch of her.

Except I didn't have all night.

I had less than an hour. But I fully intended to make every second count.

She slid her tongue against mine and rolled her hips over

my cock, a needy little moan leaving her lips. And that single sound nearly did me in.

I groaned, not bothering to keep quiet. "Christ, you're killing me."

She made a sound of protest. "Absolutely not. You're not allowed to die until I get this big guy inside me, big guy."

I huffed out a pained laugh, slapped the room key against the reader, and shoved open the door once it flashed green. Blindly carrying her toward the bedroom, I bumped into various objects along the way—a chair, the desk lamp, a painting on the wall—completely uncaring of the carnage left in our wake.

As soon as my knees hit the side of the bed, I tore myself away from her addictive mouth and tossed her onto the mattress. I watched with satisfaction as her tits bounced beneath her sweatshirt, her hair fanning out around her. And those eyes stared up at me, begging for everything I wanted to give her.

There was so fucking much I wanted to give her.

"Any limits I should know about?"

Her brows twitched, and she allowed her gaze to drift over me from head to toe. "How about I tell you if anything crosses a line? Green, yellow, red."

"Good girl." I removed my suit jacket and tossed it over the chaise at the foot of the bed. "Is that what you're going to be for me tonight?"

A spark of challenge lit in her eyes, and I wanted to meet it head on. "Maybe. But I'm definitely not going to make it easy for you."

My dick jerked at her admission and the realization I had

a brat on my hands. I was going to love seeing just how far I could push her until she finally melted for me.

"Take off your clothes." Jesus Christ. I didn't even recognize my own voice. Low and deep. Almost a plea rather than a demand.

And she fucking knew it.

A smirk ticked up the corner of her mouth. "If you want me naked so bad, do it yourself."

Without a second's hesitation, I reached out, cupped her ankles, and yanked her toward me until her calves hung over the side of the bed. I tossed her shoes and socks behind me before gripping the waistband of her leggings and tugging them off, her panties vanishing right along with them.

The sight of her in that oversized sweatshirt and nothing else was even better than my imagination. Her pretty little pussy peeked out beneath the hem, bare and already glistening. My mouth watered just looking at it.

Unable to wait another second, I dropped to my knees, tossed her legs over my shoulders, and blew a gust of air against her exposed clit. "This okay?"

"*So* okay."

That was the only confirmation I needed before I buried my mouth against her cunt.

"*Oh god*," she breathed, her hands flying to my head as I swiped my tongue through her slit, groaning as soon as her taste hit my senses. "Oh my fuck, I've missed this."

Missed it? That implied her pussy hadn't been feasted on in a while, and I both loved and hated that. Whoever she'd been with who hadn't fallen to their knees every goddamn day to service her cunt with their tongue was a fucking idiot.

But I had no problem making up for their ineptitude. By the time I was done, I wanted her come dripping down my chin. Wanted to be able to smell her on my beard for *days*.

She delved her fingers into my hair as I licked a path through her seam, swirling my tongue around her clit before sucking it between my lips. I allowed her sounds to guide me, tell me what she liked and what she was desperate for more of. Soft moans, a sharp intake of breath, a deep, throaty groan. Or, my personal favorite, a shocked gasp and the tightening of her thighs around my ears, holding me buried against her as if she never wanted me to leave.

Hell, if I had my way, I wasn't sure I would.

She tightened her fingers in my hair, her constant chant of, "*Oh my god, oh my god, oh my fucking god,*" my guidepost. My North Star as I pushed her to come against my tongue.

When she did...when she squeezed her thighs tight around me, her legs shaking as she climaxed with a muffled cry...it was the sweetest fucking sound. The sweetest goddamn taste.

And I wasn't sure I'd ever be satisfied.

After the waves had rolled through her, her body going lax against me, she breathed, "Holy *shit*, you're good at that."

Rather than answer her, I didn't move from the heaven between her thighs. Instead, I lifted my eyes to connect with hers and doubled down on my efforts, this time adding my fingers to the mix. I slipped my middle two inside her, curling them up and stroking her from the inside while I traced unending circles around her clit with my tongue.

"Oh shit. He's going to try to make me come again," she

whispered to herself, disbelief threaded in her tone. Then to me, she said, "You're going to try to make me come again?"

Normally it would've taken an act of God to remove my mouth from her pussy, but I wanted to be very clear about one thing.

I lifted my lips from her and replaced my tongue with my thumb, strumming her clit in a relentless rhythm. "I'm not going to *try*, trouble. I'm just going to. Until you beg me to stop."

She breathed out a laugh, challenge sparking in her eyes. "I can't wait to see that."

And from the smile that swept across her mouth at those words, she knew exactly what she'd done. Thrown down a challenge I had no intention of failing.

She dropped her head back to the mattress as I curled my fingers, incessantly stroking that spot inside her that made her inner thighs quiver. And this time, when I added my mouth, her orgasm was immediate. She cried out a shocked gasp and came apart beneath my tongue for the second time.

I groaned as her taste flooded my mouth, her tangy sweetness intoxicating. But I still didn't let up. Didn't move from my spot between her legs, my mouth affixed to heaven. Wasn't going to until she did exactly what I said she would.

I wouldn't quit until she was begging me to.

CHAPTER FIVE

SUTTON

JESUSFUCK.

That was my only thought as yet *another* orgasm crashed through me. That, and who the hell *was* this guy? He had the body of a Greek god, the mouth of a sailor, the demeanor of a grumpy old man, and the overall air of a book boyfriend.

What alternate reality had I stumbled into?

My previous record for orgasms in a single night had been three, and that had been by my own hand. And this man already had me tied with that number with seemingly little effort. He hadn't even unbuttoned his pants.

I lay sprawled on the bed, my sweatshirt rucked up around my waist, and what I was sure was an expression of pure bliss written on my face.

Finally, he stood from where he'd been kneeling between my spread thighs and towered over me, his massive presence shooting a thrill through me. "Are you ready to get started?"

I breathed out an incredulous laugh. "*Started?* I'm already three in, babe. I'm pretty much finished."

"You think so?" The way he said it, so low and rumbly and *sure*, sent a wave of goose bumps scattering across my skin. The promise in his tone was unmistakable.

"You gonna take me for a ride, big guy?"

"Thought about it."

"And yet you're still standing there, completely dressed."

"What was it you said?" He tipped his head to the side, his gaze challenging. "You want me naked so bad, do it yourself."

Normally, I would have pushed back on a demand like that. But I *did* want him naked. Desperately. Wanted to see every inch of the body I'd been rubbing myself on for half the night. And the clock was ticking by way too fast, so I didn't bother with subtlety.

Quickly and efficiently, I knelt in front of him on the bed and divested him of every stitch of clothing, my breath catching with each inch of skin I revealed.

His body was *insane*. Absolutely fucking insane. Not overly defined, but thick and solid. Strong. He truly was every inch the beast I'd originally clocked him as. A dusting of dark hair covered his broad chest, tapering down to an arrow that pointed straight to his cock. And Jesus Christ.

Jesus fucking Christ.

That thing should have been a registered weapon.

"Fuck me," I whispered.

"That's the idea."

I breathed out a laugh and shook my head, unable to tear my gaze from his cock. "No. I mean, *fuck me*. There is no way that thing is fitting."

His shaft was long and thick, with a vein I wanted to lick

running up the substantial length. I had a four-hour car ride to suffer through in the morning. Stuffing this monster inside me would absolutely not be a smart choice.

But I was so tired of making smart choices. I'd been doing it—or trying to—since I was sixteen. It was time to be a little stupid for once.

"No?" He stepped closer until he loomed over me where I kneeled on the bed. Then he slid his hand up the inside of my thigh and under the hem of my sweatshirt, immediately finding my pussy and sinking two fingers inside. "You think I didn't make sure I got this sweet cunt nice and ready to take me?" he asked, though the question was rhetorical as he pumped in and out. "You think I didn't make you wet enough?"

That, also, was rhetorical. Because I could hear exactly how soaked I was as he fucked his fingers into me, sliding a third inside and stretching me to take him. I sucked in a sharp breath and braced my hands on his broad chest, dropping my forehead to rest against the thudding beat of his heart.

"God, that feels good," I breathed.

"Think I can make you come again with just my fingers?" he asked, though his tone suggested he already knew the answer and he was taunting me with it.

With my forehead pressed against his chest, I rocked my head from side to side—more out of disbelief than denial— even as I rolled my hips against his touch.

"No?" He pumped his fingers into me faster, then brought his thumb up to circle my clit. "Because it feels like your legs are already shaking, and we both know what that means."

It meant—

"Shit," I breathed. "I'm gonna come again." I couldn't keep the disbelief from my tone, too focused on the sensations he was wringing from my body to even hope to hide anything.

He hummed deep in his throat, a self-satisfied sound. "Yeah, you are. All over my fingers. Soak my hand so I can stuff you full of my cock."

Somehow, I was unable to do anything but. Just as a scream tore from my throat, he slammed his mouth down on mine, muffling the sound as he slid his tongue inside. Waves of pleasure rocked through my body as I ventured into uncharted territory with this man.

Four. *Four.*

What in the actual ever-loving fuck?

He hummed low in his throat, pressing his kiss to the corner of my mouth, beneath my jaw, then to the space just below my ear. Against it, he whispered, "There's my good girl."

A shudder ran through me at his words, so simple and innocuous, but loaded with more passion than should have been possible with a man I'd only just met.

Impossible but undeniable.

He slipped his fingers from my pussy, gripped the hem of my sweatshirt, and tugged it over my head in one smooth motion. As soon as my body came into view, he groaned, a deep, throaty sound, his eyes tracking over every bared inch of me.

That noise and the pure appreciation in his gaze immediately quieted any insecurities. I didn't worry about the silver wisps of stretch marks across my lower stomach or the extra pounds on my hips I could never seem to lose. Not when he was staring at me like that.

"No bra?" He ran a hand over his mouth, the soft scrape of his beard against his fingertips sending a delicious shiver down my spine. "You were walking around in a bar with your tits bare, yet you want to be called a good girl tonight?"

"Told you I wouldn't make it easy." I grinned at him, walking my fingers up his bare chest. "But I've already figured out what I have to do to get you to call me one."

"Yeah? What's that?"

"I just need to come. And I bet if I come on that cock, you'll be extra sweet to me."

"You think I'm going to make you come on my cock, trouble?"

"I think you're going to try."

The corner of his mouth twitched in that almost-smile, there for a blink and gone just as fast. "There's that try word again. I'd rather just *do*."

He grabbed a gold-foiled packet, and thank god he was prepared. The only condoms I carried around were for the average Joes, and my big guy was most definitely not average.

With his eyes locked on mine, he tore open the packet and rolled the condom down his length. As much as I wanted to watch his every move, I couldn't tear my gaze away from his. Not with the thousand dirty promises brimming in his eyes. Promises I desperately wanted to cash in on.

"We're going to take this first one nice and slow." He shifted closer, looming over me as he guided me to lie back on the bed. "See how much of me this pretty little pussy can take."

Before I could shove him onto his back, climb up, and show him exactly how much I could take, he spread my legs wide, his palms heavy on my inner thighs, and notched his huge cock at my entrance.

But he didn't push inside right away as I'd anticipated. Instead, he ran his hands up and down my legs, against the creases where my thighs met my body, before slipping over to my mound. Back and forth, again and again. Until, finally, he shifted his hips and pushed his cock inside. Just the tip, though it felt like so much more.

My breath caught in my throat as he let out a low rumble. He studied my face as he slid deeper, gauging my reaction to every inch he was giving me.

And sweet fuck, there were so many damn inches.

He ghosted his thumb across my clit, swept his fingers over my pussy lips. Then he shifted down until he traced the obscene girth of himself as he slid that monster even farther inside me.

"God," I choked out, the single word nearly lost on a moan.

"There you go," he murmured. "Christ, look at you. Look at this pretty cunt. This perfect pussy stretching so tight around me. *Fuck.*"

I couldn't do anything in response except clutch the bedding at my sides, all of my attention focused on where we were joined. On where he was trying to split me in two. Where he was wringing so much pleasure from my body, I couldn't see straight.

Panting, I slammed my head back against the mattress and squeezed my eyes shut. My pussy pulsed around him, as if desperate for more even though I already felt stuffed so full.

And then he brought that rough thumb down on my swollen clit again, rubbing it back and forth quickly. My legs fell open even farther as my orgasm built, that warmth low in my belly blooming. Thrumming. Until it was all I could focus on. All I could strive for.

"There you go. I can feel you," he said. "That good girl pussy is going to come all over me, isn't she? Gonna soak my cock so I can slide even deeper."

The feel of him inside me paired with his words—the low, growly cadence of them proving he was just as affected as I was—was all it took.

Suddenly, I was flying.

This time, his mouth wasn't there to stifle my scream as I shattered into a thousand pieces. I arched my back as my pussy squeezed his cock, all while he did exactly what he told me he would and slid even deeper.

"Oh my god." Panting, I reached down, sliding my fingers next to his and not stopping until I felt where I was stretched wide around his pumping shaft. Then I reached down even farther, feeling how much of him was still left. *Jesus*.

"*Fuck*," he muttered under his breath. "You should see this. See how pretty you look stretched so fucking tight around me. See how much of me you're taking."

Now that he'd put the picture in my mind, I wanted it too. Was suddenly desperate to put an image to this overwhelming feeling of fullness that hadn't abated since the first inch he'd slipped inside. Bracing myself on my elbows, I glanced down between us, whimpering at the sight of him as he pulled his hips back before pushing forward in a slow, deep thrust.

He hummed low in his throat as he split his gaze between my eyes and where he disappeared inside me. He looked wrecked. Like a man on the brink of annihilation. A man standing on the edge of a cliff, just a breeze away from falling into oblivion.

But he was holding back, his restraint clear in every coiled inch of his massive body. And that just wouldn't do. I'd come apart under his mouth and his fingers and his cock.

It was time I made him come apart too.

CHAPTER SIX

ATLAS

FOR SUCH A TINY THING, she sure was strong. My little tornado of trouble reached up, wrapped her hand around my neck, and tugged my face down to hers. The move sent me even deeper, and we groaned into each other's mouths.

I didn't know if it was because it had been so long for me, or because this woman really was trouble with her magic pussy, but I was about three seconds from blowing. And I wanted nothing more than to do it inside her snug little cunt, with no barrier at all.

My cock jerked at the thought, and I had no idea where it had even come from. I'd never gone bare inside a woman. From the second I'd gotten drafted, we were taught to wrap that shit up. Hell, the league had actual seminars about how not to get trapped by a jersey chaser.

But I couldn't deny how badly I wanted to fuck this woman with nothing between us.

Knowing I was seconds from coming, I pulled out of her and maneuvered her to her side, smacking her ass lightly.

"Hands and knees, trouble. And get that ass in the air. Let me see what a mess I've made of your pussy."

She did as I asked, glancing over her shoulder at me with a glint in her eyes that made my dick twitch. "Just to be clear, I'm not doing this because you told me to. I'm doing this because I happen to like this position."

"Whatever you say." I palmed her ass, bringing my hand down in another light smack. "From the looks of your pussy, I'd say you've liked everything."

"Well, you did eat me out for twenty minutes, so that definitely helped."

"I would've done it for twenty more, but I'm on a time crunch here."

"And the clock is still tickin', big guy." She shook her ass at me, tempting me in the most delicious way.

I pressed a hand between her shoulder blades, urging her down. She went readily, presenting her ass to me, that gorgeous pink cunt glistening between her thighs. Unable to stop myself, I leaned forward for another taste.

She shuddered out a moan at the first swipe of my tongue through her slit. And then I was just as gone as she was. My groan was lost in her flesh as I licked and sucked, eating her with abandon. Addicted to her sounds. Drunk on her taste.

"Oh my god, don't stop. Don't stop. *Please* don't stop." She reached back, clutching my head and holding me against her.

As if there were anywhere else in the fucking world I'd rather be.

"Come on, trouble," I murmured against her. "Give me another one, right on my tongue."

"Fuck," she breathed out, her thighs quivering as I feasted on her cunt. "*God*, I'm coming."

I groaned, keeping my rhythm exactly how it had been as she detonated against my mouth. While aftershocks still coursed through her body, I stood, brushed the head of my cock through her slit, and pressed inside, her pussy still spasming around me.

Our groans mingled in the otherwise quiet room, the sound of our panting breaths urging me on. She was too small to shove my cock in deep, especially in this position. So I went slow, pulling out and sinking a little farther inside with each thrust.

Fuck me, she was gorgeous like this. Her ass tipped up, pussy lips spread wide around my cock, and those quivering thighs telling me exactly how close she was to falling again.

And I fully intended to make her. Just to prove I could.

I gripped below her ass, my palms splayed wide, thumbs tracing around where I disappeared inside her. Gathering every bit of that wetness.

She shuddered out a breath when my soaked thumb ghosted over her back entrance. Instead of pulling away, she moaned and pushed against me, fucking my cock without any help from me. She met my gaze in the full-length mirror next to the bed. Her lips were parted, eyes glassy but unwaveringly focused as she stared, her expression daring me.

"What color, trouble?" I asked, circling my thumb there with the barest hint of pressure.

There was a moment's hesitation as her pussy clenched around me. She was no doubt wondering how the hell she'd fit anything else inside her. Then she gave an almost imperceptible nod. "Green."

I pushed my slick thumb inside her, groaning at the onslaught of sensations. How she clenched tight around me. How she whimpered low, reaching back to grip my thigh. How she rolled her hips with every push back against me, taking me a little deeper each time.

"You love this, don't you?" I said, mesmerized by the sight of her. "Love being stuffed so fucking full. Does it feel good?"

"God yes," she panted, her nails digging crescent moons into my thigh and her pussy the sweetest heaven I'd ever sunk inside.

"Show me, then." I brought my other hand down, smacking her ass as I pumped my cock and thumb into her in alternating strokes. "Be a good girl and play with your clit. Make that pussy come one more time."

It was a testament to how far gone she was that she didn't argue or toss back some pithy remark. Not like I'd begun to expect from her. Instead, she shifted, removing her hand from my thigh and snaking it down between her legs. She spread her fingers on either side of my pumping shaft, making us both groan.

"God, you feel so good." She breathed the words almost as if they were meant only for herself, but I couldn't deny how good it felt hearing her praise.

I knew the second her fingers touched her clit, because her pussy rippled around me, tiny quakes signaling her impending release.

"There you go. Make that sweet little cunt squeeze my cock. Come all over me so we can go for round two. I've still got seventeen minutes, trouble. And I intend to use every single one."

She breathed out a laugh that cut off on a gasp, our eyes locked in the mirror. Her entire body went stiff as she sobbed out a moan, her pussy and ass clenching around me. And that was it. I was done for. So fucking lost to this woman I'd only just met.

On a groan, I sank deep, shoving my cock as far into her as I could and spilling myself into the condom. Wishing like hell there was nothing between us.

Long moments later, after she'd collapsed onto the mattress and I'd cleaned up, I joined her on the bed, tugging her exactly where I wanted her. Namely, tucked into my side so we could both catch our breath before diving into the next round.

"Looks like you were prepared for this," she murmured into my chest.

"Hmm?"

She propped herself up on her elbow, jerking a chin toward the box of condoms that sat on the bedside table. "You definitely didn't buy those between when I attacked you in the bar and when we got up here. Ergo, you were prepared."

I huffed out a breath and shook my head. "Joke from some buddies. They find a way to sneak them into my room anytime I travel. Usually, I just toss them."

She raised a brow at me, skepticism written on her face. "But not tonight."

"Not tonight," I agreed, darting my eyes over her face—to those glass-green eyes and those full lips and the dusting of freckles that were, somehow, making my dick hard all over again.

"Well, I'd hate to waste them." She flashed me a smile. "How long did you say we had?"

I glanced at the clock. "Down to twelve."

"How about I add an extra eight? What can you do in twenty?"

"Oh, trouble." I gripped her waist and tugged her to sit astride me, her hands braced on my chest, those perfect little tits just begging for my mouth. And I intended to deliver. "You're going to be sorry you asked that."

CHAPTER SEVEN

ATLAS

EARLY MORNINGS WEREN'T unusual for me. Even if I wasn't waking up to hit the gym before heading to the school, my internal alarm clock went off at five a.m. without fail. The years I'd spent in the league, when my days began before dawn, had trained my system.

Normally, it wasn't a problem. But normally, I hadn't had trouble in the form of a dark-haired vixen in my bed the night before.

She'd stayed true to her word, leaving my room just over an hour after she'd arrived. But even with our brief time together, there was no denying she'd shaken my very foundation. My dreams had been filled with replays of our time together. I'd woken up hard as a fucking rock, humping the goddamn mattress like I was fifteen years old all over again.

Jerking off in the shower wasn't anything new to me—it'd been my standard MO for years—but I did it more out of routine than necessity. That hadn't been the case this morning. When I'd woken up, I could still smell her on my sheets, still taste her on my tongue. And as desperately as I wanted another round with her, this was for the better.

Just a single night of fun that didn't have a hope of reaching me back home.

Getting on the road early meant I made it to Starlight Cove before ten and headed straight for my mom's. I hadn't heard anything more from my brothers, but time—and history —had proven that wasn't always a good thing. In fact, it usually wasn't.

After parking my SUV in her driveway, I strolled to the back door, pressed my thumb against the lock pad so it could read my print, and let myself in. The scent of freshly ground coffee beans greeted me, as did an absolute fucking catastrophe.

Standing at the back door, I braced my hands on my hips as I surveyed the disaster area formerly known as my mom's kitchen. Buckets filled with various levels of water were everywhere, heaps of towels piled on the countertops. The cabinet doors below the sink hung open, the contents scattered on the floor.

I strode over, squatted to get a better look at the pipes, and clenched my jaw at what I found. Duct tape. Fucking *duct tape.*

I pulled my phone out of my back pocket and thumbed a quick text into the group chat.

Group text with Atlas, Xander, Declan, and Lincoln

10:08 a.m.

ATLAS:

Which of you dumbasses had the bright idea to use duct tape to "fix" mom's problem?

LINCOLN:

Don't look at me. I was at the bar.

DECLAN:

Idk wtf you wanted me to do, Atlas. I'm not a fucking plumber.

ATLAS:

Clearly. So when is the plumber coming?

DECLAN:

Whenever you schedule them.

Of course. Because why would anyone else do what needed to be done?

ATLAS:

I'm calling you fuckers when I get done at Mom's and we're going to talk about this.

DECLAN:

Can't wait

After pocketing my phone again, I pressed the heels of my hands against my eyes and groaned. I'd gone away for a single goddamn night, and chaos ensued. Though that wasn't much different from a usual day here. I had no idea why I thought I'd have a reprieve when I left town.

Not when it'd been like this for as long as I could

remember. I'd always been there to pick up the pieces, fix whatever was broken, and make sure my mom and brothers were taken care of.

The constant weight of that had long since settled on my shoulders, as if it were a part of me. But sometimes, I wondered what it would be like to not carry this responsibility. To not be the rock they leaned on. The one who always took care of shit.

But then I would remember why I had to step up in the first place. And how I wasn't sure I'd ever be done atoning for the mistakes I'd made after.

"Atlas!" My mom strolled into the kitchen, coffee cup clutched in her hand and a bright smile on her face. "I thought I heard your groan."

"Which YouTube video told you to use duct tape?"

She strode over, glanced down at me with a twinkle in her eye, and patted my cheek. "Well, good morning to you, too, my little grump."

I pushed up from my squat and stood to my full height, looming over her by nearly a foot and a half.

Rolling her eyes, she patted my chest. "I don't care how big you get, my darling son. You will always be my *little* grump. Need I remind you I went through twenty-seven hours of labor, too many diaper changes to count, and your terrible threes? I've earned the right to call you whatever I want, and I intend to do so. There's nothing you can do to stop me."

Crossing my arms over my chest, I tipped my head to the mess under her sink. "The duct tape, Mom."

"Oh, that." She swatted her hand in the general direction

of her absolutely fucked pipes, as if to dismiss the problem entirely. "They'll be fine for now. Besides, we have more pressing issues to discuss."

"I'd love to know what's more pressing than water leaking all over your kitchen floor."

She stood on her tiptoes, cupped my face in her hands, and turned my head until I had a straight shot into her dining room. And the heaps of packages and letters covering her table. "Been a while since you've picked up your fan mail from the library."

My jaw ticked as I glared at the offending piles. People sending me shit was bad enough. But when some overzealous fans hadn't been able to uncover my address—I paid a shit-ton to keep that under wraps, along with the rest of my family's—they'd found out my mom was Starlight Cove's lead librarian and proceeded to send everything there.

"Throw it all out."

"I will. *After* you go through it and tell me which ones I can share with Mabel and the book club."

I shot her a scowl. "What's the point? Anything I add to the absolutely-not pile are the first ones you share."

"Well, you don't expect me to keep the best ones from everyone, do you?"

"That's the whole point of me going through them," I said with more bite than necessary.

She tsked and shook her head. "I know it's not the book club gossip that has you this worked up. So what is it? The gala wasn't fun?"

"The gala was fine." What came after had been spectacular.

"Well, it must not have been if you're in a state like this."

"It's not the gala that's bothering me." I closed my eyes, pinched the bridge of my nose, and exhaled a heavy sigh. "I hate that they know where you work. I'm just waiting for someone to show up in person."

"I don't think we have to worry about that. They're harmless." She hooked her arm through mine and led us into the dining room. "In fact, I bet there won't even be any panties in this bunch."

That was easy for her to say. She'd never had a stalker show up outside her house or slip into her hotel room or tie themselves to the roof of her car—yes, literally. The league had paid me handsomely for many years. But even with the substantial nest egg I'd accumulated, I wasn't sure it was enough to account for my lack of privacy.

I was just thankful as fuck for every day that went by when a stalker didn't manage to track down my address. It was why I'd settled back in Starlight Cove. Most of the residents didn't care that I'd been the league's top tight end. Their main concern was how I was coaching the high schoolers and whether One Night Stan's was going to bring back two-for-one drinks on Tuesdays.

Despite the fact that this place was too friendly for my liking, it was home. No one harassed me when I went about my business in town or coached my team. At the end of the day, I could escape to my secluded house and not have to worry about a line of jersey chasers blocking my front door.

And that was exactly how I liked it.

CHAPTER EIGHT

SUTTON

EVEN PLYING Laurel with brunch before we'd hit the road hadn't been enough to get myself in her good graces. If there was anything worse than driving hours in a car with a sullen teenager, I hadn't yet found it.

No, that wasn't true.

Driving hours with a sullen teenager with the reminder of my night with Mr. Tall, Dark, and Grumpy anytime I so much as twitched in my seat was definitely worse. There was no denying I'd had fun, but my pussy was an unfortunate casualty of the whole affair.

At least Laurel had finally decided to give me the silent treatment, allowing me to reminisce in peace. It was slightly better than the ranting I'd been subjected to the first hour of the car ride.

I didn't blame her for acting like a complete shit. I was pretty sure I'd acted a lot worse for a lot less when I was her age. Of course, I'd also been dealing with overbearing, ultracontrolling parents—something I'd sworn I'd never be to her.

I preferred to run our two-person household as a democracy. We both got a vote, neither more important than the other. Essentially growing up together had forged a bond between us most people didn't understand.

A bond that this move was testing.

Especially because the move had been the result of my pulling the Mom Card and overriding her up-until-that-point equal vote.

I'd signed a six-month contract to work with Dr. Quinn McKenzie—though I'd known her as Quinn Cartwright in college—at the Starlight Cove Clinic. After that? Who knew what would happen or where Laurel and I would go. But I wasn't about to invite trouble and tell my daughter that.

After almost three years in Atlanta, she'd just started to put down roots, and I'd yanked that away from her. Shoved her to a place that was completely unfamiliar. To both of us. Moving to a town that was basically the size of our old neighborhood? It was going to be an adjustment.

It didn't matter that it was directly along the coast and also bordered a lush forest. Didn't matter that the downtown looked like we'd somehow traveled to a Hallmark movie. Didn't matter that I'd be able to work fewer hours because the cost of living was so much cheaper here.

Laurel hated it on principle. And I couldn't even blame her.

I remembered all too well what it was like to be sixteen, to think your entire life was ruined because of one decision.

To believe with absolute certainty that the friends you had were the only friends you'd *ever* have.

But she'd survive. I knew because I'd survived a hell of a lot steeper challenges—at least she wasn't knocked up by a worthless idiot who'd leave her in the lurch.

I hadn't been so sure at the time, but that worthless idiot was the best thing that had ever happened to me, whether he left or not, because he gave me *her*.

"Hey, Lolo, help me look for 1425 Meadowbrook Lane."

She huffed and rolled her eyes so emphatically I was surprised they didn't fall straight out of her head. "Old age taking your eyesight already?"

"Watch it," I said, though my words lacked heat.

Despite her snark, she set her phone down and lifted her gaze for the first time in three hours. My hope that she'd suddenly spark an interest after taking in her surroundings was definitely nothing more than a pipe dream if the curl of her lip and disgust rolling off her in waves were anything to go by.

"Oh my *god*, Mom. I can't believe you moved us here." She said *here* like I'd driven us straight down into the sewer, and we were bunking next to a family of rats. "There is literally *nothing* to do. No mall, no movie theater. And what the hell is that? Is that a *goat* crossing the road?"

It was, indeed, a goat crossing the road. And a woman running after it, arms flailing.

"Oh, come on. It's not that bad." I glanced around, seeing the town not through the eyes of a teenager but through the eyes of a mom.

As much as Laurel liked living in a bigger city, I didn't like the life I'd had to manufacture in order to make that possible. She was going to be a fully fledged adult in two years, and time was slipping away faster than I wanted to admit. I didn't want to spend her last couple years at home working doubles just so I could pay rent.

"And when was the last time you went to a mall anyway?" I asked dryly.

"At least I had the option!"

"Well, you also have the option not to be a complete brat, but you didn't take that either."

She huffed and sat back in her seat, shooting me a glare. "Do you blame me? I don't get what you thought was going to happen. We lived in Atlanta for almost three years. And then you tell me a week ago we're up and moving to this tiny shithole in Maine. How am I supposed to respond?"

I blew out a long breath, my shoulders sagging even as I tightened my grip on the steering wheel. I wished I could park this freaking car so I could look at her to have this conversation. But we still hadn't found this stupid, fairy-tale-sounding Meadowbrook Lane, and I wasn't going to let this sit any longer.

"Look, I get it. I know you were feeling settled in Atlanta, and it sucks we had to leave. Believe it or not, I don't *want* to make you feel this way. But I didn't have a choice. My contract was up, and there weren't any other positions available in the area. We couldn't have stayed there, even if I wanted to."

What I hadn't shared with her was that being a traveling

nurse had more downfalls than just the constant moving. My last toxic working environment was proof enough of that. For once, I didn't want to worry about what I was walking into. And working with an old friend, whom I'd always clicked with, was about as much of a guarantee as I was going to get. Plus, splitting my time between Quinn's clinic and one day a week at the high school as their nurse meant I'd actually have regular hours for once.

"Yeah, but what about the position in Boston? At least there, I'd have something more to do than tipping cows or whatever the hell they do here."

I blew out an exasperated sigh. "Like I've told you eleventy billion times, I didn't get that job. I got *this* job." I glanced over at her, her jaw set, brow furrowed. My beautiful, stubborn girl. "I love this fire in you, and I never want to stifle it. But I'm doing my best here, Lolo. I know you don't think so right now, but Starlight Cove is a good option for us. I'll be able to work less, so we can hang out more. Plus, I have a friend here, and I haven't been able to spend much time with Quinn since college."

"Yeah, well, I have zero friends here."

"That's not true. Your best friend is here." I reached over and jostled her shoulder repeatedly. The move earned me another eye roll but not before I saw a tiny quirk of her mouth.

"After this move, you're *definitely* not my best friend anymore."

"No? Well, maybe I'll earn back the title after I bribe you with pizza, ice cream, and a scary movie tonight."

"Don't be so sure," Laurel grumbled.

After what felt like years, Meadowbrook Lane finally appeared around a bend, and I turned down the scarcely populated street. It held a handful of homes, all of them set back far enough from the road on plushly landscaped lawns that I couldn't even *see* the houses. A rich-person neighborhood if I'd ever seen one.

"Finally," I grumbled under my breath, turning down the driveway of 1425.

Thank god we'd gotten here early enough that it was still light outside. If I'd had to navigate this in the dark, I wasn't sure I'd want to travel down this incredibly secluded driveway. That was how horror movies started.

Finding a rental in a town that had basically zero available at any given moment had been a feat I hadn't been expecting when I'd accepted the job. Luckily, a friend of a friend of Quinn's had a place they weren't using but also hadn't gotten around to renting out. Even better, it was a third of the cost my rent in Atlanta had been.

As we drove down the long, winding path, I glanced over to find Laurel's face a replica of mine—pinched brow, pursed lips...an eternal skeptic.

"Where the hell are we?" she mumbled. "Getting murdered our first night here will only prove my point, you know."

"We're not going to be murdered." Probably. "Don't be so dramatic."

"I'm sixteen, Mom, it's pretty much a prereq—holy *shit*."

"What?" I asked, whipping my head around to where she was staring.

And then I saw it.

"Holy fuck is more like it," I murmured.

A house the size of the governor's mansion loomed ahead, just through a copse of trees. When Quinn had told me this rental was a guest cottage, I'd been expecting a large main house. I hadn't been expecting *this*.

A winding, brick-lined path led to a huge, two-story Craftsman. It looked both modern and rustic, with its dark gray siding and stone facade surrounding the front door. A covered porch housing a pair of Adirondack chairs was framed by timber supports matching the exposed beams in the peaks of the roof.

Our quaint little cottage—a miniature replica of the main house, complete with its own front porch—sat tucked into the back corner of the lot, the ocean as its backdrop.

"At least the house is cute. And look—it's right on the beach," I said.

She rolled her eyes, but it wasn't the overdramatic gesture of just a few minutes before. Which meant I was making progress. I'd take any small step I could get.

"Why don't you make sure the door is unlocked?" I told her. "I'll start cleaning up and then we can unload."

With attitude dripping from her pores, she slunk out of the car and headed for the cottage's front door while I began picking up the disaster that was the inside of our car.

A minute later, she opened the passenger door, sank into her seat, and pulled out her phone, not saying a word.

"Um...hello? What's up?"

She lifted a single shoulder in a shrug. "It's locked."

I blew out a sigh. "Of course it is."

Quinn had set all this up for us—something I was eternally grateful for—and this was the first snag we'd hit. I didn't want to spend time running around looking for this key. I just wanted to move in as much as possible before it got dark, get some pizza and that ice cream I'd promised Laurel, and relax after three days of driving.

"All right, I'll go to the mansion and see if anyone's home to give us our key." I stepped out of the car and headed toward the main house, hoping Quinn had squared everything away and my new landlord knew we were arriving today.

I climbed the porch steps, rang the doorbell, and waited. And waited. Annnnd waited. Just my freaking luck—an empty house, which meant nowhere for Laurel and me to go. We could explore town, but we were both exhausted.

Giving it a final try, I rang the bell once again just as a man grumbled from inside, "Jesus, I'm coming."

The door swung open, and I came face-to-chest with an absolute beast filling up nearly the entire width of the doorway. I slid my gaze up and up...and up...to a tense jaw covered in a short, thick beard, a pair of full lips, and a stern brow drawn down over whiskey eyes.

Whiskey eyes I was *very* familiar with.

The last time I'd seen them had been when I'd kissed him, thanked him for the whopping *eight* orgasms, and headed back to my room and my daughter. What I hadn't done was wake up next to them, despite how much I'd wanted to.

But we'd both known what our time together was and

what it wasn't. Just a single night of fun, nothing more, nothing less. And I hadn't realized exactly how much I'd needed it.

Thanks to my most recent dating disaster, I'd practically sworn off men. But if I was going to do a round two—or three, as it were—Mr. Tall, Dark, and Grumpy wouldn't be the worst choice.

Except...*fuck*.

"I'll call you back," he said into a phone I hadn't even realized he'd been holding. Probably because I'd been too stunned. Not anymore, though.

The reality of the situation was slamming into me, pieces my brain was too slow to pick up on finally clicking into place.

My savior from the hotel bar was nowhere to be found. In his place was this man who was somehow scowling even harder than he'd been last night, and I hadn't thought that was possible.

Worse, he was standing in the main house on the property my daughter and I were renting.

Fuck me. I'd had a one-night stand with my landlord.

Because of course my first foray into the land of book-worthy sex would be with someone I shouldn't have slept with.

But it didn't have to be a big deal. Maybe it *wouldn't* be a big deal. We were both adults. And there'd been no false pretenses of what our time together had been. Maybe he'd shrug it off. Maybe we could laugh about the coincidence of it all. Maybe—

"Are you stalking me?" he snapped, his voice whip-sharp,

eyes even sharper. His words were so unexpected, it took a moment for them to register.

When they finally did, I could only huff out an incredulous laugh as I stared up at him. "Excuse me?"

His jaw ticked as he shot a glance behind me, before sweeping his gaze over me from head to toe. Except this time, there was only derision behind those eyes. Nothing like the heated looks he'd given me last night. Nothing like the gazes that had set my soul on fire.

"How do you know where I live?" he demanded. "Did you go through my wallet when I was in the bathroom? Do you even *have* a daughter, or was that a line?"

"Okay, *wow*," I said, dragging out the word.

I was used to people making snap judgments of me and my life, but this was a first. A *stalker*? Like, what, I just hung out in hotels, waiting for unsuspecting men to fuck me into a stupor and then followed them home because I had nothing better to do?

"Look, buddy, I hate to apparently be the first one to break this to you, but your dick isn't that good."

Lie. It was *absolutely* that good, and the vaginal orgasms he'd given me were proof enough of that. But he wasn't getting that info from me.

"How arrogant do you have to be to think a woman would drive 250 miles just to get another ride? I'm not sure if you know this, but you're not the only dick in town. I could replace you with a single stroll down Main Street. Hell, I have a battery-operated friend that'll get me there just as easily as you did last night. So, in case it wasn't perfectly clear, I'm not here for another orgasm."

His brow pinched even more, his scowl somehow deepening. "Then what the hell are you here for?"

"My key." I flashed him my teeth in what absolutely would not pass for a smile. "Looks like things might be a little awkward at the backyard barbecue, *neighbor*."

CHAPTER NINE

ATLAS

WHAT. The actual. *Fuck.*

When I'd called this woman trouble last night, I hadn't realized exactly how fitting it would be.

Last night had been one of the best nights I'd had in recent or even distant memory. I'd let my guard down for the first time in forever because I'd figured, what could it hurt? A single mom who wasn't from my hometown? She hadn't wanted to spend more than an hour in my hotel room, so it was safe to assume she wouldn't be a clinger. It had felt like a no-brainer to me.

And look where that had gotten me. My one-night stand was now my new tenant, living in my backyard for the next six months.

When my mom had told me someone needed a favor since I wasn't using my guesthouse anyway, I'd been an idiot and agreed. If there was something I wouldn't do for my mom, I hadn't yet found it. Besides, I'd figured there was enough space between the two houses that I wouldn't even know they were there.

Now, I wasn't sure even ten miles between the residences would've been enough.

Since moving back home to Starlight Cove, I'd made very deliberate decisions not to shit where I ate. I didn't fuck around with the women in town because I didn't want them to fuck around with me. That was a flat-out rule. One I hadn't broken—or even been tempted to—in five years.

And then in waltzed this tornado of a woman, gorgeous and charming...trouble with a capital T. Ruining the very foundation I'd so carefully laid.

Because, while we hadn't fucked in Starlight Cove, I had no doubt her being not just here in my town, but *here*, in my backyard, was absolutely going to fuck me.

"*You're* the one who called *us*. Are you even listening, jackass?" Lincoln asked from the other line.

Declan snorted. "He hasn't yelled in a full minute, so I'm going with no."

"'Course I am," I grumbled into the phone.

And then went right on ignoring everything the two of them were saying about our mom's wrecked pipes in favor of glaring out the window at my new tenant. Same as I'd been doing for the past thirty minutes.

In all that time, she hadn't once glanced my way. Probably because she was too busy being a one-person moving company. She hauled the shit out of the little trailer, a younger version of herself following behind and matching her every effort.

So, the whole daughter thing *hadn't* been a line. Which

meant she probably hadn't been lying about anything else either. Which also meant I'd shoved my whole damn foot in my mouth when I'd accused her of stalking me.

Probably one of the worst conclusions I could've jumped to. But I'd been on edge after going through the fan mail at my mom's—there *had* been panties in the bunch, not to mention a voodoo doll and a lock of hair—so this timing was just plain old bad fucking luck.

Watching her now was a wholly different experience from last night. The woman I'd had beneath me had been flirty and playful. Now, she was nothing but determination and grit. And, if I wasn't mistaken, a whole lot of pissed-off energy. All thanks to me.

That energy was serving her well, though. I hadn't seen her so much as pause in the act of unloading boxes and moving various pieces of furniture into the cottage.

I'd had to stop myself more than once from storming out there to help. It wasn't my place. And I definitely didn't need to interact with her more than the bare minimum. That would be best for everyone.

But that plan was shot to hell when she rested one end of an overstuffed chair on the seat of a rolling chair, hefted the other side, and began pushing it toward the front door of her cottage. *Alone.*

"Jesus fucking Christ," I muttered.

"Oh, *now* you're listening?" Linc said.

"Gotta call you back."

"For fuck's sake, not again. Let's just—"

I ended the call with my brothers and tossed my phone

onto the kitchen counter before storming out the back door, glaring the entire way.

As soon as I was close enough to her, I barked, "What the hell are you doing?"

It was the same tone I used out on the field. The one that snapped my players into shape when needed. The one that said I wasn't here to fuck around.

But this little cyclone of mayhem didn't even spare me a glance.

She continued on her way, guiding her moving partner—aka the rolling chair—toward the cottage's front door. "Don't worry about it."

"You aren't giving me a choice. If you hurt yourself on my property because of your own stupidity, I'm the one who's going to get sued," I snapped.

"Oh my *god*. You're ridiculous. I'm not going to *sue* you. Get over yourself."

"Why didn't you just ask me for help?"

She barked out an incredulous laugh. "Oh, because our last interaction went *so* well? I didn't want the guy I'm *stalking* to call the police."

"And in a town this small, it'd probably be the sheriff who showed up," Trouble's sullen-looking doppelgänger said. She eyed me suspiciously, giving me a once-over and dismissing me just as quickly.

"That's my daughter, not another stalker," Trouble said. "Just want to make that clear."

Groaning internally, I clenched my jaw. I'd fucked up, and I needed to own that. "Look, it was an—"

She held up a hand, stopping me. "Save it. I'm not

interested in whatever excuse you're going to give. You were an asshole, plain and simple. The only interaction I want to have with you is once a month when I pay rent."

With that, she pushed forward, rolling the piece of furniture straight over the threshold and into her new home.

Trouble's daughter strode past me toward the trailer. "Damn. I haven't seen her that mad since I borrowed her favorite pair of jeans without asking and ruined them. If I were you, I'd run for my life."

That was exactly what I should be doing. Running as fast and as far away from this woman as I could. Problem was, I couldn't stop thinking about her or how good our hour together had been. How it had been the first time I'd actually *wanted* a woman to stay the night.

I'd watched her walk out of my hotel room with an ache in my chest that absolutely did not belong there. And that scared the hell out of me.

This woman was trouble, and I didn't *do* trouble. There was no space in my life for it.

So I planned to do exactly what she wanted and stay away.

CHAPTER TEN

SUTTON

I'D TAKEN a chance renting this place sight unseen, trusting that Quinn wouldn't steer me wrong. And I'd been right. More than a decade had passed since we'd been close, but she still knew me. Proof of that was in how well she'd nailed this.

With its bright yellow kitchen, two decent-sized bedrooms, and a quaint living space, the cottage was perfect. Well, other than the fact that it was mere yards from an infuriating asshole.

Infuriating because said asshole had given me the best orgasms of my life, only to turn out to be a shitbag. The latter, apparently, was now required for any man I met, considering I was o for 3 in as many months.

Those women-only communes full of tiny houses weren't looking so bad right about now.

After my run-in with the asshole, Laurel and I had spent the rest of the day getting settled in. While unpacking was never fun, I loved the process of setting up a new place. It'd been a while since we'd done that, and I'd missed the ritual of it.

Thankfully, the cottage had come mostly furnished, nearly all of which I actually liked. There was a feminine touch I appreciated, and I couldn't help but wonder exactly whose feminine touch had helped with the design.

Before the sudden and completely unwelcome twinge of what absolutely was *not* jealousy could derail my thoughts, a knock sounded at the door.

"Thank god, I'm starving," Laurel mumbled from where she sprawled on the couch, making no move to get up.

"No, no, you sit. I've got it." Rolling my eyes, I abandoned my kitchen organization project and headed to the door, opening it to Quinn's smiling face.

She stood on the front porch, her shoulder-length blond hair haloed by the setting sun, a pizza box in one hand and a bag in the other. "I have no problem delivering on the pizza, wine, and ice cream, but you two are on your own for the horror movie."

"Hey." I grabbed the pizza and handed it off to Laurel before wrapping Quinn in a hug. "It's so good to see you."

"You too," she said, squeezing me back. "Two years is too long."

We'd managed a quick visit a couple years ago when she'd been in Atlanta for a conference, but before that, it had been even longer since we'd seen each other. I couldn't deny how nice it was going to be to have a friend so close. Being a traveling nurse didn't allot me many of those.

"Thankfully, we don't have to worry about that for a

while." I stepped back and ushered her inside, closing the door behind her. "You remember Laurel?"

Quinn smiled at my daughter. "Of course. You're looking more and more like your mom when we first met."

"That's what people tell me." Laurel set the pizza box on the coffee table before loading a plate with two slices, swiping a pint of Ben & Jerry's from the bag Quinn had set down, and heading to her bedroom. "Thanks for these."

After the door snicked shut, Quinn turned to me with a raised brow. "I remember her being a lot friendlier. Both when she was little *and* a couple years ago."

"Yeah, that's my fault." I made a quick detour to grab the corkscrew and wineglasses I'd just unpacked before sinking down onto the couch with a sigh. "I'm pretty much *the worst parent in existence* because I *ruined her life* by moving here."

Quinn sat on the cushion next to mine, handing me the bottle of wine she'd brought. "Right, of course. The whole trying to give your child a better life bullshit. Seriously, would you think of someone other than yourself?"

"I know, right?" I poured a healthy amount of wine for both of us before passing her a glass. "I was wondering when Laurel and I were going to get to the whole hating-my-existence portion of our relationship. Things had been going too smoothly for too long."

Quinn laughed, but she still shot me a worried glance over the rim of her wineglass. "This job isn't going to cause an issue with you two, is it?"

Settling into the corner of the couch, I shook my head. "We'll be fine. She just needs a few days to get over things."

"I hope so. Otherwise, I'll feel like an ass for being so

grateful this timing worked out. Seriously, I can't tell you how much I need you at the clinic and to take over the weekly shift at the high school. Ford's been begging me to hire someone for months and finally threatened to do it himself if I didn't get on with it."

"And you couldn't have that," I said on a laugh. I knew her well enough to realize she wouldn't cede control of her business to anyone, even her husband.

"Absolutely not. He'd probably hire Mabel, and then my clinic would be overrun by sex toys."

"Wow. So much to unpack in that sentence. Let's start with, who's Mabel?"

"The town's surrogate grandma, among other things. You'll meet her soon."

"I better, considering the sex toys part."

"Don't worry, she won't let you get through your first meeting without hawking her goods."

I snorted. "You make her sound like a sex toy dealer."

"That's *exactly* what she is. She sells them at any and every town market. She even has a she shed in her backyard called the Pleasure Palace where she hosts parties. I lived with her and her husband for a while when I first moved back, and it was an *experience*."

"Well, she sounds like an absolute queen."

"She'll probably swing by soon, and you can see for yourself." Quinn grabbed a slice of pizza and settled back on the couch. "Speaking of, how do you like the place?"

"It's amazing. The cottage is going to be perfect for us." As long as I didn't have to run into the owner often. Or ever. "Seriously, thank you for finding it."

"I didn't *find it* so much as worked some serious magic to make it available for you and Laurel. The owner isn't exactly social, but I can't blame him. If I had his history, I'd protect my privacy too."

I froze with my wineglass halfway to my mouth. "What do you mean, his history?"

"He's been in the public eye basically his whole life. His dad used to be some big-time rock star. And then, Atlas played in the league for...I don't know...ten, fifteen years?"

Atlas. His name didn't ring a bell, though that wasn't a surprise, given how little I watched sports. It fit him, though. As did the profession. If I'd been thinking clearly, I would've connected all the dots before now, considering how we met, how he looked, and the mansion he called home. But apparently my brain wasn't firing on all cylinders where he was concerned.

"So, what, he's some big football legend?"

Quinn shrugged. "He *was.* They called him the Mountain."

"Of course they did."

A smile twitched at the corner of her mouth. "Ah, so you've met?"

Twice in twenty-four hours, actually. Memories of our brief hour together at the hotel flashed in my mind, recalling details better left forgotten. Like how he'd stared up at me from between my legs, his mouth wet from my pussy. Or how he'd whispered the filthiest things against my ear every time he sank inside. Or how he'd fucked me from behind, gripping my hair and holding my head so I couldn't do anything but watch in the mirror as he absolutely ruined me for other men.

I wasn't exactly closed-lipped around friends when it came to my sex life. Had never been. But for some reason, I didn't share any of that with her.

Probably because I wanted to keep what had happened totally separate from my current life. Better to pretend it took place in an alternate universe. If for nothing else than to be able to use memories of the hotel room as fap fodder without also recalling how the jerk had answered his front door.

"Unfortunately," I said.

Quinn laughed. "I think he gets that a lot."

"I'm not surprised. He's an ass, and I'd be happy never seeing him again." Okay, that was a lie. He was extremely enjoyable to look at. As long as he didn't open his stupid mouth.

"How do you think that'll work out for you?"

"Fine." I shrugged. "I might be living in his backyard, but I never ran into my neighbors in Atlanta."

Quinn raised a brow, amusement written on her face. "Starlight Cove isn't Atlanta. Besides that, it's going to be a little difficult to avoid him."

I eyed her warily, something in her tone raising my hackles. "Why?"

"Because Atlas Steele is the high school football coach, and your weekly shift at the school starts on Thursday."

CHAPTER ELEVEN

ATLAS

JUST LIKE EVERY other night since Trouble had arrived, I'd slept like shit, my dreams absolutely consumed by the one woman I shouldn't be thinking about.

After finally accepting I wasn't going to get any more sleep, I'd climbed into the shower and attempted to jerk off to a faceless woman. Same as I did every other morning.

But *she* kept infiltrating my thoughts.

Rather than give in and replay every second of our time together, I scrubbed myself down while glaring at my hard and ever-persistent cock. I'd shut off the water without finding any relief, and only then had I noticed I'd forgotten my goddamn towel.

It was a shitty start to what would no doubt be a shitty day.

That was proven as I yanked open my kitchen cabinet, reached for the bag of coffee beans, and came up empty. In all the chaos of this week, I'd forgotten to pick some up at the store.

Out of habit, I glanced out the window into my backyard...and straight toward the now-occupied cottage. Except I saw no signs of life there, her car nowhere to be found.

I had no fucking idea why the fact that she was gone made me clench my jaw and glare at absolutely nothing. And *that* only pissed me off more.

By the time I got to my mom's for breakfast, I was in a shit mood with no hope of hiding it. And it was only made worse by the state of the kitchen. It was still an absolute fucking disaster because of the pipes. The plumber had been booked all week and wasn't able to come over until tomorrow.

It didn't seem to bother anyone else, though. Mom, Declan, and Lincoln sat around the dining room table, the pile of my fan mail still scattered across the surface.

I jerked my chin toward the mess and scowled. "I thought I told you to get rid of all that."

"I will..." Mom shot me a smile over the rim of her coffee cup. "Eventually."

Lincoln grinned as he shoved half a muffin into his mouth. "We paid her fifty bucks to let us poke through the pile first."

I split a gaze between my brothers. "You're assholes."

Declan shrugged. "Never claimed otherwise."

"Don't you two have more important shit to deal with than my fan mail?"

"No," Declan said, at the same time Lincoln said, "It can all wait."

"I'm not so sure about that."

"You're probably right." Lincoln nodded. "I should take care of the fridge sooner rather than later."

"What fridge?" I glanced over my shoulder at my mom's, eyeing it top to bottom. It would just figure something was wrong with it, considering everything else going on here.

"The one at the bar," Lincoln said. "That fucker's as dead as a zombie."

"*Dead?* When the hell did that happen?"

"Last night."

"And you're just telling me *now?*"

He raised a brow at me. "Yeah, I wanted to avoid this for as long as possible."

I blew out a heavy sigh and gripped the back of a chair, the wood creaking under my hands. "Did you get it cleaned up?"

"What's there to clean up?"

I clenched my teeth, my jaw ticking as I stared at my youngest brother. "Jesus, Linc. There's going to be water every-fucking-where. And you just *left* it?"

He leaned back in his chair, the picture of indifference, and shook his head. "God*damn*, you're grumpier than usual this morning. Don't worry about it."

"One of us has to, and it's clearly not you. Now I've gotta go to the bar and deal with that instead of heading to school for my actual job."

"Maybe I can help," Mom said, sitting up a little straighter. "Someone can cover my shift at the library. There are all kinds of different help videos on YouTube. I bet I can find something—"

"No," Declan, Lincoln, and I all said at the same time.

"*I'll* go to the bar. I'll even text you updates, you control freak." Lincoln kicked the chair next to him, sliding it toward me. "Now, sit down and have breakfast with us."

"With *us*? No. *You're* going to clean up the bar like you just told me you would. And I want an update before I finish my first cup of coffee." I stalked over to the coffee station, pulled a mug down from the cabinet, and grabbed the pot. Only to find it empty. *Empty.*

Because of fucking course it was.

I shot a glare toward the dining room. Who the fuck left an empty pot without starting another this early in the morning? Lincoln and Mom were talking, but Declan winked at me, holding his coffee cup up in a salute.

"Little fucker," I muttered under my breath as I readied the machine to make another pot...only to find the bag of coffee grounds empty. I braced my hands on the counter, closed my eyes, and blew out an exhausted sigh, ready for this entire day to be over.

On the plus side, there was no way it could get any worse.

TURNED OUT, I was wrong. My day could *absolutely* get worse.

First, I'd gotten halfway to work before realizing I'd left my playbook on my kitchen counter and had to turn around. Then, the ancient water fountain outside my office finally kicked it, creating a fucking water park in the hallway—and on my pants. And now *this*.

How the hell did people expect me to coach this team to

the playoffs if so many of my goddamn players were missing during practice?

I stormed into the school office, the door ricocheting off the wall in my wake, and took in the mess in front of me. Half a dozen of my players filled the space, some lounging on the mismatched chairs, all of them acting as if they didn't have a game to prep for. "What the fuck are you doing? Is no one interested in playing some goddamn football today?"

Jackson glanced over with a shrug. "Sorry, Coach, we had our orders."

"Whose orders?" I barked. Because whoever they were, we were going to have words.

"Nurse Sutton."

"Nurse Sut—" I darted my gaze around, looking for whoever the fuck this person was and cranking myself up to give them a piece of my mind. You didn't just *steal* football players in the middle of practice. There were protocols to follow. Proper channels, clear communication... Some basic fucking courtesies. And this *nurse* thought she could just—

All the air was sucked out of the room, my internal tirade coming to a screeching halt when my eyes landed on trouble. My Trouble.

No, not *my* anything.

Someone was playing a cosmic fucking joke on me. They had to be. Because Trouble—Sutton, apparently—stood with a clipboard in hand, one brow raised in my direction. Her lips were pursed as she regarded me, eyes challenging, before dismissing me just as quickly.

But I remembered when those same eyes had been blissed out after her sixth orgasm. Remembered her throaty little moans falling from those plush lips every time I sank deep. Recalled exactly how she—

"Coach Steele," she said, and I ignored the way my muscles tensed at hearing my name from her lips. "I see you're an equal opportunity asshole."

"You—" I glowered at her, trying to get a read on just what the fuck was happening here. But I had no idea because she'd thrown me off my game. I was *never* off my game. "You can't say 'asshole' in front of the kids."

The kid standing closest to me snorted—no doubt because I'd just stormed in here, throwing around far more colorful language—and I shot him a glare that shut him up real quick.

Not her, though.

This infuriating woman just shrugged. "I call 'em like I see 'em. If you don't want me to call you an asshole in front of the kids, stop acting like an asshole."

I crossed my arms and clenched my jaw, refusing to allow her to get under my skin. Well...any more than she already was. But that ended right here, right now. I didn't care if she was my tenant, and I didn't care if we had to, apparently, work together. I had no room in my life for anything else. Certainly not a mess like this.

"We're in the middle of practice," I snapped. "This game against Central isn't going to win itself. Whatever you need can wait."

Instead of rising to my bait, she just gave me her back as she focused on some paperwork in front of her. "If you want these guys on the field this weekend, they're going to stay here until I'm done with them. These incomplete physical forms say they can't do *anything* until I sign off, let alone participate in an away game. So, do you want them to play or not, Coach?"

"Yeah, Coach, you want us to play or not?" Jackson echoed.

"Was anyone talking to you? Drop and give me thirty."

He grinned, shooting a glance at his buddies. "You're joking, right?"

I pinned him with a glare. "Does it look like I'm joking?"

"Damn, Coach," he muttered, but he dropped as instructed and began his push-ups. "Who pissed in your Cheerios this morning?"

I flicked a brief glance at Sutton before turning my glower back on him. "Make it fifty."

———

LATER THAT NIGHT, I wasn't in any better of a mood by the time I left the school and stalked to my car in the pouring rain. This day had gone from shitty to shittier, and I wanted a hard reset on the entire fucking thing.

I turned onto my driveway, my headlights bouncing over the terrain, the shapes distorted thanks to the rain. But not distorted enough that I didn't see a pile of something in the middle of the path. I slowed to get a better look and stopped entirely when it moved.

"What the hell?" Throwing my SUV into park, I opened the door and got out, the rain dousing me in seconds. I stalked over to investigate, squatted down, and found a pile of... kitten?

It gave a pitiful mewl, the tiny thing shivering and soaked to the bone. A gust of wind kicked up, nearly toppling it over.

"You've got to be fucking kidding me."

How the hell did this get all the way out here? I lived too far off the beaten path for it to be someone's pet, besides the fact that it didn't have a collar.

I scooped up the pile of pitifulness and held it out in front of me. The entire drenched ball of fur fit in the palm of my hand. I might be an asshole, but I wasn't so much of an asshole that I'd leave this thing out here to figure shit out on its own.

With another muttered curse, I unzipped my jacket, tucked the kitten inside, and headed back toward my SUV. Certain I'd pissed off karma at some point, based on my week so far.

I *hated* cats. What, with all the ways they were constantly plotting your murder and all. Worse, I had no fucking idea what to do with one.

As usual, I'd stayed late at the school, which meant the vet clinic was closed for the evening. My brothers would only make matters worse if I asked for help. And my mom was at her weekly book club and wouldn't be home for a couple hours. Which meant I was up shit creek without a paddle.

As soon as I pulled around the side of my house toward the garage, the lights from the guest cottage caught my attention, an idea taking shape. A bad fucking idea, especially when I'd just decided to stay as far away from the woman as possible.

But I didn't have much of a choice, now did I?

It was either ask the little demon nurse for help or watch

this pitiful creature waste away, all because it was unlucky enough to find itself in my driveway.

Glancing down at the nearly drowned animal tucked in my coat, I clenched my jaw, blew out a heavy sigh, and accepted that this was my only option.

Without allowing myself a moment to second-guess my decision, I stalked over to the cottage, pissed off every step of the way, thanks to the rain pelting my face and this damn animal I didn't want tucked in my jacket.

What appeared to be every light in the cottage was on, and the front window was open despite the downpour, the covered porch granting it shelter.

I rang the doorbell and waited. And waited. And waited some more. Stepping to the side, I ducked down and glanced in the front window.

Sutton's mini-me sat on the couch, her feet propped up on the coffee table while she scrolled on her phone. Completely fucking ignoring everything else, me included.

"Hello?" I knocked on the window, but she didn't even spare me a glance. I knocked again, harder this time. "I can see you, you know."

"Maybe you shouldn't be a weirdo who stares in windows, then."

"I wouldn't have to if you'd answer the door. Didn't you hear me knock?"

"You mean the pounding that rattled the floors? Yeah, I heard it. So what?"

"So, why didn't you answer the door?"

"Who answers the door when they're home by

themselves except a woman who wants to get murdered in a horror movie? Not on my watch, buddy."

"I'm not here to murder you."

"I don't know. That's probably what every murderer in the history of the world has ever said."

"We've met. I'm the landlord. And the football coach. I've seen you at school this week. Laurel, right?"

"Knowing my name isn't helping your case, weirdo."

"Will you *please* open the door?" I said through clenched teeth. "I've got a serious situation here."

Her entire body sagged with a heavy sigh. But she dropped her feet off the coffee table and stood before stalking over to the front door and swinging it open for me. "Didn't learn your lesson the other day, huh? Well, whatever. Doesn't matter. My mom's not home."

Eight o'clock, and Sutton wasn't home? There wasn't a whole hell of a lot to do in Starlight Cove this late. And the thought that she could be out on a date sparked something low in my gut that I refused to examine.

"I'm not here about your mom," I barked, as much for her as for myself.

Laurel just raised her brow at me, a move so eerily similar to her mother, I nearly staggered back. "Then what are you here for?"

I reached into my zipped-up jacket and pulled out the still-soaked ball of fur.

Her other brow followed the first as she split a glance between me and the animal. "You came to show us your kitten?"

"I came to see if you had a kitten or a cat or...I don't know. Anything at all to take care of this...thing."

"That *thing?* Shouldn't you have gotten all that before you picked up your new cat?"

Jesusfuck. Why did teenagers have a way of making you feel so fucking stupid with every word that came out of their mouths?

"I didn't plan for this. I found it in the middle of my driveway. Should I have left it there for your mom to run over whenever she happens to show up?" I snapped my mouth shut, shoving down whatever misplaced irritation I had when it came to that woman. "Look, I just need some help. Do you or don't you have any cats?"

"We do not."

"I don't suppose you *want* one?"

"Why are you trying to get rid of your new pet?"

"It's not my pet! I don't even want it." I scrubbed a hand over my brow and tucked the kitten back inside my coat.

She shrugged, projecting that teenage air of indifference. "Doesn't matter. You were chosen by the Kitten Distribution System."

"By the fucking what?"

"You know, kittens just get delivered randomly." She gestured toward where the tiny creature was curled up in my jacket. "Clearly."

"Why the hell did the system pick me? I hate cats."

She shrugged again. "I've heard that happens sometimes."

"Well, we're both fucked. I don't know what the hell to do with this thing. Can you help me or not?"

"I can't." She shrugged, shot a glance over my shoulder, and said, "But maybe she can."

CHAPTER TWELVE

SUTTON

LAUREL and I had been in Starlight Cove for less than a week, and we were still finding our footing. Thankfully, she'd started to thaw slightly, even filling me in on some small-town gossip she'd caught at school. And she hadn't stormed straight to her room for a couple days, so I was calling that progress.

Still, when my girl had a craving for sushi, I didn't care if I had to drive thirty minutes to get it. I was damn well going to.

The fact that it was raining and that I didn't know this area well yet meant the whole ordeal took longer than I'd planned. It was dark by the time I got home. And I'd been right—this long, winding driveway *was* creepy as fuck when there was only enough light from my headlights to cast eerie shadows along my way.

I drove down the path, studiously ignoring the mansion and its asshole occupant as usual. Once I parked in my spot, I glanced toward the glowing lights of the cottage out of habit, my gaze jerking to a stop at the large man standing on my porch.

My heart leapt into my throat for half a second, a million scenarios flitting through my head, each worse than the last, until I realized I *recognized* that hulking form. And I was very accustomed to the scowl Atlas shot me over his shoulder, made all the harsher by the porch light casting deep shadows across his features.

I'd done so well avoiding him this week. At least until this afternoon at the school. I'd known running into him there had been inevitable. I'd just been grateful Quinn had given me a heads-up so I hadn't been blindsided like Atlas clearly had been.

That, at least, had been fun.

With a sigh, I grabbed my purse and the bag of sushi, tugged up my hood, and ran toward the front porch, dodging puddles as I went. Once under the shelter of the overhang, I shucked my hood and cast a glance at my daughter, who stood by the open front door, completely occupied with her phone. And completely uninterested in the six-and-a-half-foot beast blocking the entire width of the doorway.

I eyed Atlas head to toe. "Are you stalking me now?"

His brows slammed down. "What? No, I—"

"Don't appreciate being accused of stalking people?" I tipped my head to the side. "Weird. I thought most people loved it."

He scrubbed a hand over his mouth, releasing a sigh so weary, it sounded like it could fill an entire hot air balloon. Then he plucked something out of his jacket and stuck his huge palm out toward me, a tiny furball cradled in it. "I found this in the driveway. I fucking hate cats, and I don't know what to do with them." Then, softer, as if it pained him to say, he added, "I was hoping you did."

My brows inched farther up my forehead as I split my gaze between the tiny, drenched kitten and Atlas's glowering face. "Well, you might hate them, but you were the chosen one. So..." I trailed off with a shrug in a *what are you gonna do* gesture.

"You both keep saying that." He split a glare between Laurel and me. "What the hell does that even mean? Kitten distribution whatever the fuck..."

My daughter just rolled her eyes. "It's not my problem. I'm going back to ignoring strange men who come to our home."

"We already covered this," Atlas said, his words terse. "Football coach? Landlord? Any of this ringing a bell? I'm not some creep lurking around."

"I don't know," Laurel said as she dropped down on the couch. "A guy showing up at my house, peering into my windows, and trying to get me to help him with a kitten? Sounds like a creep to me."

"You peered in our windows?" I asked, more confused than angry. Because *what?*

His spine went ramrod straight, and he shot me a glower. "Only because she wasn't answering the door, and I knew she was in there. I needed help."

"And you didn't think to take the kitten to, I don't know, a vet?"

He huffed out an impatient breath, as if this entire conversation was exhausting him. That made two of us. "This is Starlight Cove. We have one vet, and the clinic has been closed for hours."

When I didn't respond, he stared at me for a beat, his jaw clenching. Then he gave a sharp nod before tucking the sleeping ball of fur back in his jacket. "Whatever. I'll figure it out."

Before he could stalk off, glower and all, I reached out and brushed my fingers along his arm. And pointedly ignored the zing of awareness that shot through my body at the brief contact.

There was going to be absolutely *none* of that.

"Don't stomp off in a huff. I get enough of that from my teenager. Just give me a second." I stepped around him, tossed my purse and Laurel's goodies inside, and told her, "I'll be right back. I'm going to help the creeper with his cat."

"It's not *my* cat," Atlas grumbled.

I pointedly glanced at the animal tucked in his jacket. "The Kitten Distribution System says otherwise."

"Stay sexy and don't get murdered," Laurel said, not even glancing up from her phone.

"What the fuck does that mean?" Atlas said. "Jesus, we've been over this. I'm *not* a murderer."

"Relax. It's not specific to you. It's from a podcast." I tugged my hood back up in deference to the rain and gestured in front of me to the yard cloaked in darkness. "Lead the way."

He hesitated for half a second, his gaze darting over my face as if he were searching for something. Finally, he gave a short nod and headed in the direction of his house.

Not gonna lie, when I'd dreamed about some pussy-tending by the big guy last night, this wasn't what I had in mind. Though it was undoubtedly much safer. The only way *my* pussy was being taken care of around here was going to be by my own hand.

Once we made it to his back door, he pressed his thumb to the top of the keypad and opened the door when it flashed green. He gestured for me to enter in front of him, that stony expression ever-present on his face.

I tentatively stepped inside, my gaze cataloging everything in sight. A tidy mudroom with more giant men's sneakers than a Foot Locker led directly to a kitchen straight off my dream board. It was huge but somehow cozy, with soft gray cabinetry and granite countertops. An eat-in island anchored the space, but that wasn't what captivated me.

No, that was all thanks to the floor-to-ceiling wall of windows along the back that I somehow just knew would face the ocean. Though it was too dark to see anything right now, I had no doubt it was a multimillion-dollar view. And with Atlas's pro footballer money, that turn of phrase was probably literal.

A huge, plush sectional sat in front of the windows, a might-as-well-be-a-movie-theater-sized TV mounted above the stone fireplace in the corner. The whole space was warm and inviting...the exact opposite of the man who lived here.

I tore my gaze away and found Atlas staring at me, his brow furrowed, mouth set in a hard line. Like he was suffering through every second he had to spend in my presence. As if I needed any more proof after the stalker comment that he clearly and adamantly regretted the night we'd spent together.

And wasn't that a shocker? Another asshole disguised as a normal man. I had a list of those a mile long.

"What?" I asked, a bit sharper than necessary.

He shook his head, darting his gaze away. "Nothing. What do we do now?"

Right. Back to the task at hand so I could get the hell out of here.

"I know there's no DoorDash—Laurel's loving that, by the way. But is there *any* sort of delivery system in town? A back-alley exchange sort of thing to get you by for the night?"

He scratched his jaw, the rough scrape of his nails against his beard sending a frisson of awareness skating down my spine. "Kind of. There's a town bulletin I could post on for some supplies."

"Then do that. Because you can't give this kitten whatever random shit you happen to have in the house, unless you want cat diarrhea everywhere."

He made a face, lifted the kitten out of his jacket, and looked it over, as if eyeing how much damage such a tiny thing could do. Then he glanced at me with a raised brow.

I held up my hands and shook my head. "Whatever, it's your funeral. And I am *not* helping you clean up."

"Fine." He gripped the animal in one hand and pulled out his phone with the other, his thumb flying over the screen faster than I would have expected. After a few moments, he tucked the device back into his pocket and pinned me with another stare. "Done. Now what?"

This man was so utterly clueless, it might have been endearing if I hadn't forced myself to hate him on principle.

I heaved a deep sigh and glanced at the animal curled up

in his giant man-paw. It wasn't their fault the KDS had fucked up. I took off my coat and hung it on the back of one of the stools at the island, then held my hands out to him. "You give me sleeping beauty and go find a towel or a blanket."

He passed me the kitten, and it was like holding on to air. It couldn't have been older than a couple weeks, barely weighed more than a pound, and probably wouldn't have survived if Atlas hadn't grabbed it.

Dammit. I didn't want to give him points for that, but I had to.

Cradling the kitten on its back, I did a quick scan, confirming there was one missing body part. The KDS gifted a girl kitten to an overgrown man-child. That was going to be fun.

I glanced up to find Atlas still standing there. Still glowering at me. I rolled my eyes. "Don't worry, I'll take good care of your pussy."

He inhaled sharply before devolving into a coughing fit. "What?" he managed through a rough throat.

"Your cat." I held her up between us. "I've got her. Go get what we need."

"Her?"

"Yep. Congrats, it's a girl." I strode around him and headed toward the absolute dream of a couch.

I'd expected it to be comfortable, but I did not expect it to feel like I was sinking into a cloud when I sat down. I had to hold in my sigh of contentment as I sank into the feather-soft cushions, the kitten held against my chest. With the rain soaking her fur, it was hard to tell if she was white or gray, but I just knew she was going to be cute either way.

It was only a few minutes before Atlas came storming back into the room, glower in place. He'd shed his coat at some point and now stood there in a black T-shirt, his biceps the size of freaking cantaloupes on full display as he held enough blankets and towels for a fort as big as this entire room.

"Gee, I really hope that'll be enough," I said dryly.

A crease formed between his brows. "You think we need more? I can get more."

Watching this man fumble, staring at this tiny kitten like it was the very mystery of life, was kind of hilarious. It was as if he'd never been around an animal before.

I breathed out a laugh. "I'm joking. Have you seen her? She could nap in one of your shoes."

"Would she like that?" he asked with such sincerity, I couldn't bring myself to make fun of him.

"I think one of those will be fine. Towel first, so we can get her dry." I accepted the towel he passed over, gathered up the kitten, and dried her off. All while he watched on as if the entire process was completely alien to him. "Haven't you ever had a pet before?"

He shot his gaze to mine, something flashing briefly in his eyes before he shuttered them, blocking off any emotion from leaking through. "No," he snapped. "No pets."

"Okay," I drew out the word. "Didn't know that was such a touchy subject. Well, Kitten 101 is to keep them safe, warm, and fed. You've got two down, and you're working on the third with your town bulletin."

He didn't say anything, but I felt his stare on me, nonetheless. Just like I'd been able to that night in the hotel. Just like I had every other time I'd been in his presence.

"Swap you," I said, handing him the damp towel and gesturing for one of the fleece blankets in his hands. I made a tiny nest on my lap and placed the sleeping kitten in the center. "And don't feed her, like, tuna straight from a can or cow's milk. You're going to want to stick with kitten formula or wet kitten food for now. Unless you want to deal with the aforementioned diarrhea situation."

"The one you won't help me with."

"Glad we're on the same page." I raised a brow at him as he stood over me, hovering with his arms still full, as if he was unsure what to do. "You can sit, you know. And maybe hold her."

He hesitated for a moment before dropping the pile of blankets and towels on the floor next to the couch and sitting down, warily eyeing the kitten.

After several moments of silence, he cleared his throat. "Did you have any pets when you were young?"

The question sounded like it was torn straight from his soul, and I wasn't sure if that was because he was trying to hold it back or trying to force it out.

I breathed out a laugh and shook my head. "God, no. There were absolutely no pets allowed in our pristine home. My mother had a coronary if I didn't change clothes immediately after visiting a friend whose house was full of dogs."

"Why would you need to change?"

"Heaven forbid anything less than perfect show up in the Sinclair estate, even dog hair on a sweater."

That was far more information than I'd intended to give. Far more information than I *usually* gave, even after months of knowing someone. As a rule, I didn't talk about my childhood. Or my parents. Especially when I'd worked so hard to cut them out of my life. To rid Laurel and myself of their toxic, overbearing presence.

And I had absolutely no idea why I'd done so with *him*.

Maybe it was the week I'd had, fumbling my way through a new town and a new routine. Maybe it was because it was late and I was tired. Maybe it was just because I wasn't on my game like usual. Maybe it was because I couldn't remember the last time someone had asked me questions about myself and waited for the answer. *Wanting* the answer.

"How about Laurel?" he asked. "Did she ever want a pet?"

A pang settled low in my gut at the question. He'd pushed on a bruise he hadn't even realized was there.

She used to beg me for a kitten or a puppy—she wasn't picky. She'd fold her little hands under her chin and hit me with those green eyes that were mirrors of my own. Starting on her sixth birthday, she'd begged me every day for a year.

It was just one of many things I hadn't been able to give her.

"She did, but we never had one. It was challenging being a traveling nurse and not knowing where we'd be going next or if the rental would allow pets. Never mind that I was only twenty-two and just hanging on. A baby raising a baby. There was no way I could add a pet in the mix. We were barely surviving, just the two of us."

"Your parents?" he asked.

I barked out a humorless laugh, keeping my focus on the purring ball of fur curled up in my lap. "My mother freaked out about the possibility of a pet. What do you think she did when she found a pregnancy test in the garbage when I was barely sixteen?"

He stared at me with those weighted eyes. The same ones he'd pinned me with that night in the hotel. Making me feel something I had no right to be feeling, especially with him.

"Was that hard?" he finally asked, his voice gruffer than usual.

"Which part? The constant moving or becoming a mom at sixteen?"

"Both."

I could've lied. Could've kept up the act that nothing kept me down and that I could handle anything, just like I'd been doing my whole life. But instead, I said, "Yeah, it was."

The weight of his stare sank into me, and an awareness zinged between us. Reminding me exactly how good it had been when we'd been together in his hotel room.

Before I could do something stupid like lean into him and reacquaint myself with how his lips felt contrasted against the rough scrape of his beard, there was a knock at the back door, and someone called out, "I've got the kitten supplies for you, Atlas!"

The tension between us snapped like a twig, the interruption effectively breaking us both out of this weird trance we absolutely did not belong in.

CHAPTER THIRTEEN

SUTTON

"WHY DO we even have to go to this?" Laurel asked with as much teenage attitude as she could muster.

"Because it'll be nice to see what this town is all about. And because Quinn invited me."

"So, how about you just go with Quinn? I'll stay here and continue marinating in the existential dread that is my life."

"Have you thought about looking into drama classes?" I said before tossing over her favorite hoodie—which happened to be *my* favorite hoodie.

"We never did shit like this in Atlanta."

"That's funny. I don't ever recall Atlanta having an adult-book-fair-slash-ice-cream-social. Must have missed the memo."

She heaved a sigh and rolled her eyes. "Whatever, this is dumb."

"Noted. Now, get your ass in the car." I tugged on a sweater before grabbing my purse. "And next time, be a little bit more grateful that I gave you *my* favorite hoodie instead of taking it for myself."

"*Your* hoodie?" she asked incredulously. "Um, excuse you, this is mine. *You* always steal it."

"Okay, you're clearly suffering from delusions. And what better way to fix that than a change of scenery?" I opened the front door and gestured her out.

She hesitated only a moment before rolling her eyes with a huff. Still, she tugged on the hoodie before heading to the car, and I counted that as a win.

I drove us toward the quaint downtown I'd only seen in passing. Surprisingly, the pictures didn't do it justice. Not only did it feel like we'd stepped into Stars Hollow, but it also felt like the culmination of every small-town Hallmark movie ever created.

Various shops and businesses ran along Main Street, their brick facades and flower boxes at every window only adding to the charm. Vintage-style streetlights lit the way, along with the twinkle lights woven into each tree along the sidewalks.

After I found a parking space, Laurel and I headed in the direction of the festivities, following the crowd.

"Tell me how your first week has been." I bumped my shoulder into hers. "Have you made any friends?"

"Tons," she deadpannned. "That's why I'm on the couch every night scrolling on my phone."

Laurel's favorite defense mechanism was sarcasm—something she came by honestly—so I knew this was hard for her. I'd known it would be. I remembered what it was like to be sixteen. Although our circumstances were vastly different, the core story was still true. She was trying to figure out who she wanted to be in the world, and friends were a big part of that journey. I hated that I'd had to sever the bonds she'd been developing, but it was unavoidable.

"Okay...well, are there any boyfriends or girlfriends on the horizon?"

"Pretty hard to do when this entire school is less than half the size of my old class."

I blew out a heavy sigh. "Lolo, I get this is difficult, and I'm sorry. But whether you like it or not, we're here for at least six months. So you can either sulk and be a brat about it the entire time, or you can make the most of it. Maybe make some lifelong friendships and hopefully have a good time while you do it."

She rolled her eyes, her standard response to absolutely anything I said.

"This isn't easy for me either, you know. I left good friends, same as you."

"And don't forget the boyfriend."

This time, it was my turn to roll my eyes. "*Ex*-boyfriend. And I'm not at all sad about leaving Doug behind."

"You never told me what happened with him."

Maybe because he'd turned into a controlling creep who'd somehow been tracking—without my permission—not just my location, but hers. Or the fact that one of his colleagues hit on my sixteen-year-old daughter, and he brushed it off like it was no big deal.

But she had enough shit in her life to worry about—this move included—so I didn't want to pile more on her. Especially when we didn't have to worry about him anymore.

"My red-flag detector was faulty."

She hummed in acknowledgment.

"Besides"—I hooked my arm through hers and tugged her into my side—"I kind of like it when it's just you and me."

"That's because you have an abysmal history with men." Though her words were sharp, she lessened their potency by leaning her head against mine.

"You should be grateful about that. I'm doing all this for you, you know. So you can learn from my mistakes and not have to make them yourself. You're welcome."

She snorted, and I knew that was as close to a laugh as I was going to get. "So, what are we supposed to do here? Just wander around?"

"I guess? Quinn said there was a book fair, free personal pizzas with a completed book map, and ice cream. And I guess a few of the local businesses have stands set up."

"Is this something we have to look forward to by living in a small town? Any excuse for a stupid social event?"

"From what Quinn said, yeah, pretty much."

"God, please don't tell me you're going to make me come to all—"

"Laurel! Hey!" A cute girl with warm brown skin and black hair done up in space buns waved and made her way over to us.

"Friend or foe?" I whispered out of the corner of my mouth.

"Friend, I guess," Laurel said to me before turning her attention to her friend. "Hey, Cami."

Cami grinned, seeming genuinely happy to see my daughter. "I didn't know you were going to be here."

"Me neither." Laurel slid a glance toward me. "My mom dragged me without consent."

I waved, smiling brightly. "Hi, I'm Sutton, the mean mom."

Cami was shocked for half a second, a look I'd been seeing the entirety of my daughter's life, before she shot me a smile. "Hi! My mom's around here somewhere too." She glanced down the street before turning back to us with a shrug. "I think they mostly just hang out at One Night Stan's, reliving their childhood book-fair days." Then to Laurel, she said, "It's *so* boring. You should come hang out with us."

I squeezed Laurel's arm twice, our silent signal asking if she needed my help. She didn't squeeze back, so I took that as a good sign. I turned to her with raised brows. "Yeah, I wouldn't want you bored out of your mind any more than you already are."

"Yeah, okay," Laurel said, stepping toward Cami. "I guess I can hang out for a while."

"Keep your phone on," I said. "Text me when you're ready to go."

"'Kay. Stay sexy and don't get murdered."

Cami's eyes lit up with recognition. She gripped Laurel's elbow and shook it as they headed in the opposite direction. "Oh my god, are you a Murderino?"

A grin curved up the corners of my mouth as I watched them walk away, grateful for this tiny bit of normalcy in my daughter's life. She'd been tight-lipped on the details of school life, but it made me feel better to know she had at least one friend her age in this town.

But now that my date had abandoned me, I needed to find something to do while she enjoyed herself for a bit.

I walked down the street, strolling past various storefronts, some of which had tables set up out front with their wares. Candles, body products, cooking supplies, and—

I did a double take at the table set up under a tent, a bright-pink glittery sign hanging at the back and sex toys spread out on the table like a buffet. Holy shit, Quinn hadn't been joking. This *had* to be Mabel.

With my brows raised, I stepped over and said, "So, you really *do* sell sex toys at any town event."

"Hush, now," she hissed at me. She was an older white woman, anywhere between sixty and eighty. Her gray hair was curled tightly and cropped close, and she wore a shirt that read *I still like to play with toys. They're just for grown-ups now.*

"These are *personal massagers*," she said loudly enough for any passersby to hear. Then she braced a hand on the table and leaned closer to me, lowering her voice so it stayed between just the two of us. "The personal massagers bit is to appease the fuddy-duddies on the town council. But yes, they are sex toys, and I'm happy to help you with whatever you need! I'm Mabel, by the way. And you must be Sutton."

The shock I felt at having her know who I was must've been written across my face, because she shot me a grin.

"There aren't many secrets in Starlight Cove. I'm in book club with Atlas's mom. Plus, I had my annual physical yesterday and saw you in passing. I didn't get a chance to introduce myself because I had to get home to George. Our

Liberator chair arrived, and I needed to tell him where to put it."

Holy shit, I wanted to be her when I grew up. "Good for you. Anything that makes positions a bit easier, am I right?"

She grinned broadly before resting a hand on my arm. "I wanted to tell you I'm sorry we couldn't host you in our home like we did for Quinn when she moved back into town. But George and I decided we wanted to have a bit more *fun* with the space."

With the way she said "fun," I had no doubt she was talking about sexy-time fun. And honestly, good for her. I loved seeing an older queen getting hers. Between these toys and her new Liberator, her house was going to be rocking, and I, for one, didn't want to get in the way.

"I hope that cottage of Atlas's is treating you right," she said with a wink. "Though I'm sure he's taken care of you nicely."

I narrowed my eyes at the unmistakable sexual undercurrent in her tone. Something I wanted to clear up real quick—never mind that it was true. As far as I was concerned, that had happened in a different lifetime. Both of us had hit the restart button when we'd walked away from that hotel room.

And the last thing I needed was rumors about the new single mom in town climbing the brick wall.

"Not gonna lie, Mabel, he's been challenging." I eyed her collection spread out in between us. "And I think a new toy for a new town is exactly what I need. Tell me, which is your favorite?"

FIFTEEN MINUTES LATER, I left Mabel and strolled off with a brand-new *Pussy Destroyer*—a clit-slash-G-spot-penetrator combo—clutched in my not-at-all-discreet hot-pink bag. That woman had a story about everyone. She should've been wearing a crown emblazoned with "Gossip Queen" for all the tea she'd served. My brain was full of information, and I could definitely say it had been time well spent.

Not only had I found out that there was a website dedicated solely to fanfic written about Starlight Cove's sheriff, Brady McKenzie, but I also got an invitation to her infamous book club. While it sounded like fun, I wasn't sure it was such a good idea for me to be in a book club with the mother of the man whose dick I'd ridden with abandon just last week.

An outdoor area was set up in front of One Night Stan's, the local bar Mabel had directed me to. And she'd been right—this seemed like the place to be, with not an open stool in sight. Fortunately, someone was just leaving as I walked by, so I snagged their spot and settled at the bar.

A guy about my age stood behind it as he served waiting patrons, a dazzling smile on his face the entire time. I'd worked enough bartending gigs to make ends meet that I had no doubt he was raking in the tips. With that laugh and those dimples? Yeah, he was definitely killing it.

"Hey there." He gave me a quick once-over, one side of his mouth ticking up. "You're new."

I raised my brows. "How long do I have to be in Starlight Cove before I'm no longer new? It's been a week already."

He braced his arms on the bar top and leaned toward me, his eyes sparkling and that dimple popping. And...damn it all to hell, he did absolutely nothing for me. There was nary a flutter in my stomach, not a single wisp of interest for this objectively hot man.

That was just fucking great. Not only had Atlas ruined me for all other mortal men in the dick department, but apparently, I couldn't even enjoy flirting anymore.

"In this town?" he asked. "At least a year or two. We don't get a ton of newcomers other than during tourist season, so it's going to take a while before the novelty wears off."

"Great. I love being under the spotlight."

"Can I get you a drink to dull the beam a bit? First one's on the house. You know, for being the new girl in town." He flashed a smile. "I'm Lincoln, by the way."

"Sutton."

"Nice to meet you, Sutton. What brings you to our fine town?"

Before I could respond, Lincoln was yanked back, and in his place was a looming bear of a man—brick wall, indeed.

Atlas glared down at my new friend, irritation written in every coiled inch of his body. "I thought I told you to quit flirting with the customers."

"No, you absolutely didn't. And even if you did, I would've ignored it. Flirting's the best part of my job." Lincoln shot me a wink, and I couldn't hope to hide my snort. This guy was a charmer with a capital C.

"Then go flirt inside," Atlas bit out, crossing his arms over his chest, those biceps I hated to love showcased clearly even through his hoodie.

"Can't." Lincoln shrugged, then spread his arms wide to encompass the outdoor bar. "This is my domain tonight."

"Not anymore. I've got it."

Lincoln raised his brows, his gaze darting between Atlas and me. "You've got it? Since when?"

"Since right now."

"What are you even doing here? You hate this shit. Told me this morning there was—what was it you said?—no amount of money or favors in the world that would get your ass here tonight."

Atlas's jaw ticked, irritation rolling off him in waves. And for once, that irritation wasn't directed at me. "Your point?"

"Just wondering what changed, is all." Lincoln slid his glance toward me, that dimple popping as he offered me a smile before he focused back on Atlas. "I have a few guesses..."

"Keep them to yourself," Atlas snapped. "No one cares."

"I don't know... It seems like Sutton might care. Maybe we should ask her."

"Maybe you should fuck off."

"Is there, like, an asshole Olympics or something you're training for?" I asked.

Lincoln barked out a laugh and clapped Atlas on the shoulder. "See, that's why I'm in charge out here. You scare all the customers away." He leaned toward me with a conspiratorial whisper. "My brother hates all things social. Or, actually, all things, period."

"Your *brother*?" My brows lifted as I split my gaze between them, cataloguing their similarities.

They were both tall, though Atlas was taller. Broader, too. But they had the same dark hair, the same piercing eyes. That was where the similarities ended, though. Atlas's demeanor screamed *fuck off*, while Lincoln's did nothing but invite you in.

"One of 'em." Lincoln eyed Atlas, something that looked an awful lot like amusement flashing across his face. "So, believe me when I say he doesn't usually—"

Atlas shoved a tray into Lincoln's stomach, effectively cutting off whatever his brother was about to say. That only made Lincoln laugh, which, in turn, made Atlas's scowl deepen. "Go inside. I'll handle the bullshit out here."

Lincoln tilted his head to the side, as if trying to get a read on his brother. Then he shrugged. "Sure thing, boss." He walked backward toward the building's entrance, shooting me a quick smile as he went. "I'll let you *handle* it."

As soon as Lincoln was inside the bar, I narrowed my eyes at the pain-in-the-ass man in front of me. "Just to be clear, am *I* the bullshit in this scenario?"

When Atlas's only response was a tic of his jaw, I huffed out a laugh and shook my head. "Right...of course I am. Look, I know you hate that I'm here. But I'm not going anywhere. So, if you could cool it on being a grumpy asshole all the time, that'd be great."

His nostrils flared, no doubt in response to the confirmation that I was sticking around for the foreseeable future. Then he braced his hands on the bar top, the move making his muscles bunch and coil and reminding me what a pretty package this jackass was wrapped up in. "Are you going to order a drink or just waste more of my time?"

Unbelievable.

This motherfucker had some nerve. I didn't understand how my initial assumption of him at the hotel could have been so utterly wrong.

"Your brother's a nice guy." I grabbed my purse and shopping bag before sliding off my barstool. I didn't make it a habit to stay somewhere I wasn't wanted. "Too bad it doesn't run in the family."

CHAPTER FOURTEEN

SUTTON

THERE WAS something so refreshing about coming home after work and not being exhausted down to my very bones. While my days at the clinic were busy, it was nothing like the filled-to-bursting schedule I'd come to expect in a day. On top of that, I felt a connection to my patients that I hadn't in... well, ever.

I wasn't used to being able to spend twenty minutes with a new mom, listening to her fears while encouraging her she was doing great. What I had been used to was the inordinately high number of people who came into the ER with a random object stuck in their butt, claiming they had no idea how it had gotten there.

That, I definitely didn't miss.

It had been a couple weeks since Laurel and I had moved to Starlight Cove, and while I actually sort of liked this too-cute-to-be-real town and the people within it, my daughter still wasn't completely sold.

She was making more friends, though, and spending time

with them outside of school. She and Cami were hanging out tonight, which meant I had the cottage to myself for a bit.

After changing out of my scrubs into leggings and a T-shirt, I grabbed my current book and settled on the couch, ready for these characters to stop dancing around one another and bang already.

I shot off a quick text to Laurel, reminding her to let me know when she was ready to come home. Then I tossed my phone onto the couch next to me and cracked open my book just as a notification sounded.

Expecting it to be my daughter's reply, it took me half a second to register who this message was actually from. But as soon as I did, my spine went rigid, my hackles rising.

"Motherfucker," I muttered under my breath.

It wasn't the first—or even the fifteenth—time my ex had texted me since I'd broken things off. And the messages had only gotten more insistent since Laurel and I had moved—something I'd mentioned in my singular response to him, hoping it would be the final nail in the coffin.

Unfortunately, that hadn't deterred Doug.

DOUG:

Don't forget you left your favorite pillow at my house. Let's plan a weekend so I can get it back to you.

He followed it up with a picture of said pillow, just to prove his point. And yeah, that was definitely my favorite pillow. But it could have cost me ten grand, and it wouldn't have been worth it to set up a meeting with this guy.

As if he hadn't been giving off enough red flags before—

hello? Stalking my daughter's and my locations without my permission? Talk about over-stepping. But his continued contact even after I'd shut him down shoved those flags straight into blood-red territory.

Of course, the nice, unassuming guy I'd met at a coffee shop would turn out to be the biggest creep I'd dated in five years. And that was saying something. Laurel's assessment of my dating history wasn't wrong. My normally sharp instincts seemed to abandon me when it came to men.

Rather than tell Doug exactly where he could shove my pillow, I ignored the text and blocked the number. Why I hadn't done that sooner would forever remain a mystery. Usually, I liked to see my enemies coming. But what could this guy do now that Laurel and I were nearly a dozen states away?

Needing a change of scenery, I tugged on a hoodie and grabbed my book before slipping out the front door. The yard shared between our cottage and Atlas's oversized—yet incredibly tasteful and warm, dammit—mansion was straight out of a home design and landscape magazine.

Large pots filled with greenery lined a concrete patio, a circle of chairs surrounded a fire pit, and an outdoor kitchen anchored the space. String lights hung from trees, crisscrossing the area above and illuminating the yard. And then there was the freakin' pool. The shape was organic, as if it had always been there, with edges that blended into the surroundings, a cascading stone waterfall, and...an Atlas?

Fuck.

He swam laps, his huge body gliding effortlessly through the water. The glow of the string lights bounced off his toned shoulders, back, and arms, highlighting every bunch and coil of his muscles as he moved.

I bit back a groan as I pressed my lips together, not wanting to let him know how much his presence affected me. That would give him way too much power over me. And who the hell knew what a guy like that would do with a power trip?

I didn't know anything about him, other than the fact that he could make me come as easily as snapping his fingers and what I'd gathered around town. The consensus was, he really *was* an asshole to everyone, grumpy and aloof. People called him the big, mean one, and I wasn't inclined to disagree.

Add to that the fact that he was the son of a former rock star *and* he'd been a professional athlete—a group who, in my opinion, tended to think they could get away with anything— and it was a recipe for disaster.

I'd just gotten through dealing with a man whose self-importance wouldn't allow him to back down and leave me alone. And Doug had been a peon compared to the mountain-sized man currently pulling himself from the pool.

Sweet fucking Jesus.

I'd already seen everything before—every significant inch of him—and I was irritated as fuck to realize my memories had forgotten some of the best details. Like the overwhelming width of his shoulders. Or the bulk of his chest covered in dark hair. Or the size of those thighs encased in his swim trunks. Wet, tight swim trunks that left nothing to the imagination.

Holy hell, how was he still *that* big after swimming in this cool night air?

I wondered if he even realized he had an audience. I was tucked away on the porch, and though it was fairly close to the pool, I could still get away with hiding. In fact, maybe I could slink back inside and not have to talk to him at all.

Making up my mind, I shifted with the intention to stand, but his voice stopped me cold.

"Enjoying the show, trouble?"

***

ATLAS

I NORMALLY DIDN'T GIVE A FLYING fuck what people thought of me and hadn't for a very long time. It would have been difficult as hell to get through my life as the son of a rebel rock star, and then as a professional athlete, if I did. I wore that disinterest like armor, allowing everyone else's thoughts and opinions to bounce off me. They didn't matter. I didn't *care*.

So then, why the fuck had my last conversation with Sutton been playing on repeat in my mind?

The thing was, I *was* that grumpy asshole. All the time, to everyone. Hadn't given two thoughts about it before. It just came naturally. I'd faced enough loss and disappointment in my life that I no longer wanted to deal with the bullshit. So I treated all encounters as though they just weren't worth my time.

But with Sutton, I couldn't do that. She'd snared me, somehow, her very presence pissing me the hell off. Mostly because I still wanted her with the fierceness that had gripped me that night in Portland and refused to let go for even a second since.

That she was under the impression my reaction to her was because I hated her being here shouldn't bother me. Especially when that was the infinitely easier explanation. It kept things simple. Helped reinforce that wall between us.

Because I sure as hell didn't have room for complications in my life. Definitely not in the form of a tenant. And abso-fucking-lutely not in the form of Sutton Sinclair.

It may have taken her a while to notice me in the pool, but from the second she'd stepped out her door with the book she'd been reading this week, my attention had been locked on her. That was how it always seemed to be whenever she was around. She was like a homing beacon, constantly drawing my attention.

And I fucking hated it.

What I hated even more was how easily I seemed to be able to read her. Her pinched brow and pursed lips said she was irritated about something—unsettled, even. Worse was the fact that I wanted to know exactly what had caused her to feel that way so I could fix it.

"Seriously?" she said, exasperation heavy in her tone. "I can't even go outside without running into you?"

"Oh, I'm sorry," I said flatly. "Am I bothering you by swimming in my own pool at the house I own?"

She huffed out a breath as I grabbed a towel to dry off. The cool air against my wet skin barely registered because I was so focused on the way her eyes tracked my every movement as I ran the towel across my chest and down my stomach.

"You're just...*everywhere*," she said. "No matter where I go, no matter what time, you're there. Taking up all this... this...*space*."

The way she spat the last word, I wasn't sure if she meant that I was physically taking up space—which, yeah, I wasn't exactly a small guy—or something else. Either way, it didn't matter.

"I'm not going to apologize for taking up space."

She threw up her hands, muttering to herself just loud enough for me to hear. "No, of course not. Why would he apologize for *anything*?"

Something was clearly bothering her...more than just me existing. And I didn't particularly like that. Liked even less the fact that I cared in the first place. Why the hell should it bother me if this little tornado of trouble who tore into my life completely uninvited was upset?

Still, I couldn't stop myself from asking, "What's wrong?"

"I'm trying to read, and you're annoying me." She very pointedly looked down at the open book in her lap, not meeting my eyes. "That's what's wrong."

It definitely wasn't. She'd stormed out here like she was on a mission to forget something, and it wasn't that book. But if this was how she wanted to play it, I'd let her.

"What's got you frustrated?" I asked.

"It's none of your business."

"Is it that book?"

She didn't even spare me a glance. "I *said* it's none of your business."

I eyed the paperback, doing a quick estimation of where she was in the story. "Where are you, chapter fifteen?"

Dropping her head back on her shoulders, she heaved a deep sigh toward the sky as if this conversation were draining every ounce of her will to live. "Twenty-two. And it's *none of your business.*"

My lips twitched, knowing damn well that while this wasn't what had sent her out here in the first place, she definitely *was* frustrated about it. "Keep reading. Chapter twenty-five is what you want."

"*You—*" She caught herself—no doubt on the way to reaming me a new asshole—and narrowed her eyes at me. "You're only saying this to irritate me, and it's not going to work."

"Whatever you need to tell yourself, trouble."

"Where's your kitten?" she asked. "Petting her is the only benefit to having you in my space."

"I think you mean *my* space. This is my home, you know."

"Believe me, you've made it very difficult to forget that I live in your backyard, Atlas."

I wrapped the towel around my waist and sat on a lounge chair. Mostly to hide the fact that my cock twitched in my too-thin swim trunks, all thanks to the way my name sounded falling from her lips.

Why the hell did she affect me so damn much? And why couldn't I stop it from happening?

"The kitten is inside. She drank herself into a sleep coma after all the milk I gave her."

Sutton's reaction was exactly as I'd expected. She widened her eyes briefly before narrowing them at me and pressed those gorgeous, full lips into a flat line. "It's your funeral. But don't come crying to me when you want help cleaning up cat shit on your twenty-thousand-dollar couch."

"What if it's on my bedroom rug? Would you help clean it up then?"

"No! I'm not going to help—" Her words cut off as she snapped her mouth shut and shook her head. "Since you don't play football anymore, is this how you've chosen to spend your time? Goading people by being an asshole?"

"Not people...just you."

"And what makes me so lucky?"

I leaned forward, bracing my elbows on my knees, and met her gaze. "When I piss you off, your eyes look exactly like they did when I made you come."

Her mouth dropped open, portraying the same shock I felt that I let something so revealing slip. What in the ever-loving *fuck* was I doing? Those thoughts were relegated to the shower and the brief five minutes a day I'd finally allowed myself to think of her.

"I cannot believe you just said that to me." Her tone was heavy with disbelief, but there was no denying the interest threaded through as well. "I came out here to—"

"You came out here to get your mind off something," I said, daring her to deny it because we both knew it wasn't the damn book. "And judging by how much you've engaged in our argument, I'd say mission accomplished."

She huffed out a breath, her gaze scrutinizing as she regarded me. "You actually *are* an asshole, aren't you?"

I didn't know why her thinking of me as nothing more than that rankled. But I could handle that. Especially since I'd accomplished what I'd set out to.

"Maybe so." I darted my gaze over her face, taking in her expression. The concern and unease that had been written over every inch of her when she'd first walked out had been replaced by irritation at my hand. "But it got you to stop thinking about whatever made you come out here looking like that in the first place."

The hard stare she'd been pinning me with softened, confusion and what looked a hell of a lot like gratitude sweeping over her features. *Fuck.* What I needed to be doing was reinforcing these walls between us, not tearing them down.

But I couldn't seem to keep my head where Sutton was concerned.

She eviscerated every ounce of my best intentions, crushing them like dust under her shoe. And if I didn't get my head in the game fast, I was going to have a fucking problem.

CHAPTER FIFTEEN

ATLAS

SEVERAL PATRONS WERE SCATTERED around One Night Stan's when I strode inside later that week. The custom refrigerator I'd ordered had been delivered earlier, and I wanted to make sure everything was good.

Lincoln stood behind the bar, filling a mug from the tap, and lifted his chin in greeting. "Was wondering how long you could stay away."

I grunted in response and walked around the bar, checking out the appliance that had cost a small fortune. "Fridge working okay?"

He slid the mug of beer down to a patron before facing me. "Well, it hasn't pissed all over the floor like the last one, so I'd say that's a win."

"Good. And it doesn't look like there's any damage to the floors from that mess. Next time things go tits up in here, I don't want to find out the next day."

"Yes, sir," Lincoln said, saluting like a jackass. "I'll call you right away, boss."

"Don't be a dick."

He just raised his brows at me, silently asking, *you think I'm the one being a dick?* "You've been more of an asshole lately than usual. What's up?"

I pressed my lips in a thin line, refusing to give him even an inch, because the little shit would take that and run for miles. But it turned out I didn't have to say a goddamn word.

He studied me for a minute before his brows flew up, and pure fucking glee swept across his features. "Oh, I don't believe this. It's the hot girl from the other night, isn't it? *Sutton*. She got under your skin."

"She's not the 'hot girl from the other night,'" I said through clenched teeth. "She's my tenant."

"Oh shit, she *lives* with you?"

"She doesn't *live with me*." I crossed my arms and glared at him. I didn't need the fucking thought of her in my bed permeating my brain during waking hours. Because god knew it was there enough while I slept. "She's renting the guest cottage."

"Still, she's on your property, which means you can't escape her. Goddamn, I fucking *love* this. Wait till Dec hears about it."

"Wait till Dec hears about what?" our brother asked, setting his motorcycle helmet on the bar top before settling on a stool.

Of course. The fucker was never around when we needed him, but the second I didn't want him to show, there he was.

The smile on Lincoln's face was evil. "Atlas has himself a little complication in the form of his hot new tenant."

Declan turned to me, his brow furrowed. "Since when do you have a hot tenant? How the hell did you get talked into that?"

"Mabel," was all I said. All I *needed* to say.

Declan hummed, tapping his fingers on the bar top. "So, you've got a hot tenant living in your backyard?"

"Stop calling her hot," I snapped, unable to keep the growl from my voice. "And it's not just her. She has a daughter too."

"Shit, you've got a little kid staying with you?"

"For the last fucking time, they're not staying with me. They're renting the guest cottage. Secondly, her daughter's not little. She's—I don't know—maybe sixteen."

Lincoln's brows flew up. "No shit? Damn. Sutton doesn't look old enough to have a teenager. How old is she?"

I threw up my hands. "I don't fucking know. I don't know anything about her."

Except all the things that had been thrust upon me without my permission since she'd upended my life. Like how she had a dance party with her daughter every night when she got home, which I only knew because she blasted the music loud enough to rattle my windows. Or how she apparently treated the kids at school like adults rather than children, which I was made aware of because my players couldn't stop going on and fucking on about how great she was. Or how she'd taken it upon herself to be my kitten's guardian angel, which became apparent when I'd tripped over yet *another* package for the furball this morning.

I shouldn't know anything at all about her. But I couldn't avoid it.

"Enough bullshit. Let's get back to the promise that you two shitheads are going to fill me in if things go sideways in here."

"Don't drag me into that," Declan said. "I wasn't even around when the fridge shit the bed."

"I *did* fill you in." Lincoln crossed his arms over his chest and raised a brow. "If I hadn't, you wouldn't have anything to bitch about right now."

Declan leaned one elbow on the bar and glanced at me. "He's got you there."

I scrubbed a hand down my face, exhausted to my fucking core, thanks to trying to hold everything together. My family, this bar... Myself. "What the fuck are you even doing here, Dec?"

"Came to tell you I can't work next week, so you'll have to take my shifts."

"I can't take your shifts because I have other shit to do," I said. "Like lead my team toward the playoffs."

"Well, someone other than me needs to work them," Lincoln said. "I already basically live here. I'm not going to work seven, twelve-hour shifts in a week just so Dec can go off and do whatever the fuck."

"I don't know what to tell you." Declan shrugged. "I've got somewhere else to be, so work it out."

"Right, yeah. I'll work it out." Lincoln tossed a rag under the counter, the force knocking over a mug. "Can't count on you for shit anyway. I don't know why I thought next week would be any different."

"Don't get pissed at me," Declan shot back. "I'm not the

one who saddled us with this place. Dad is. You want someone to be pissed at, direct it at him."

"A little hard to do when—"

"All right, assholes, keep it down." I glanced around the bar, noticing a few curious heads turned in our direction. We hadn't kept our family's shit locked up tight for years just for these two to ruin it. "I'll get next week handled. But Dec, you know goddamn well this was a shitty move. Even for you."

That last bit wasn't necessary, but it also wasn't wrong. And from the way Declan's jaw clenched as he stared at me, he knew it. Which was why he didn't argue or snap back. He just pushed off from the bar top, grabbed his helmet, and strode straight out the front door without a backward glance. Not caring what kind of a mess he left in his wake.

Lincoln braced his hands on the bar top and blew out a heavy breath. "We can't keep doing this, Atlas. I'm busting my ass here, but you can't always pick up the slack. And fuck knows Dec isn't going to. Maybe it's time for Xander to come home."

"You know it's not that easy."

"Well, make it that fucking easy. I'm drowning over here, man. And you're the only one of our brothers who even bothers to toss me a lifeline."

The problem was, I knew what Xander would say if I called him. The same thing Declan did at least once a week. That we should just sell the bar. Split the proceeds and move on. Stop allowing a man who'd been gone for years to dictate our lives.

But one brother had already fled this town without

looking back. If we didn't have this bar anchoring us here, I was certain Lincoln and Declan would both follow suit.

And I hadn't worked this hard for this long to keep my family together, only for it all to go to hell in the end.

CHAPTER SIXTEEN

SUTTON

SOMETIMES I MISSED the anonymity of a big city. There was something to be said for being able to swing by the grocery store at 2 a.m. for some emergency ice cream without running into a soul. I couldn't do that in Starlight Cove—only partially because the grocery store wasn't even open past eight. But also because I couldn't walk anywhere without someone calling out a hello.

I'd only been here for a short time, and the residents already knew me by name. Case in point, the four people who'd stopped me between my car and One Night Stan's just to say hi.

So, when my name was called for a fifth time, I didn't think twice before turning around. Since I'd been expecting to be greeted by a patient from earlier in the week or one of Mabel's friends, it took me a moment to register what I was actually seeing.

Doug—as in, weird ex-boyfriend Doug who lived more

than a thousand miles away—strolling toward me with that smile that always seemed a bit too calculated.

What in the actual fuck?

I glanced around at the handful of people milling about on the sidewalk, grateful now for this nosy small town because at least there'd be witnesses if I needed them. While I wanted to believe I didn't have anything to worry about from this guy—he was just a harmless accountant—that still didn't stop my hackles from rising.

"Sutton, hi." He rested a hand on my hip and leaned down to kiss my cheek.

I stiffened at the contact and stepped out of his reach. "What are you doing here, Doug? And how the hell did you know where I moved?"

He was still smiling, as if this behavior was totally normal and nothing at all to be alarmed about. "Susan told me."

Of fucking course my former landlady and all-around busybody would spill that info to my ex.

"That still doesn't explain how you knew I'd be *here*, right now."

This "chance encounter" was so reminiscent of the dozen other times the exact thing had happened that I started to second-guess myself if I'd actually deleted the tracking app he'd used.

He shrugged, either unbothered by or indifferent to my tone. "Pure luck. I just figured if you were going to be out anywhere on a Saturday night, it would be on Main Street. Looks like I was right."

I inhaled deeply and clutched my purse tighter, my fight-

or-flight instinct getting a workout. "Why exactly are you here?"

He finally seemed to read the sharpness in my tone, and a small crack formed in his facade. "Your pillow. I told you, I have it."

"And I told you I didn't want it."

"But it's your favorite. I didn't want you to be without it."

"Are you joking?" I breathed out an incredulous laugh and shook my head. "This is crossing so many lines, it's unreal."

"What lines? I'm just being nice. I know how much you love that thing, so I wanted to give it back."

"You know what I love even more? My privacy. And for people to respect my boundaries. I thought my not responding to your texts was a pretty clear sign to stop contacting me. It sure as hell wasn't an invitation to follow me here."

"But—"

"No." I held up my hand and shook my head, taking another step away from him. "Keep the pillow. Or don't. Throw it away for all I care. We aren't a couple anymore, and this behavior is not okay."

"C'mon, Sutton. We were good together, weren't we? I thought we could give the long-distance thing a try. I miss you."

"It's not going to happen." When he opened his mouth, no doubt to argue, I said, "And I'm involved with someone." Never mind that that someone was called the *Pussy Destroyer*, and I'd purchased it from the town's sex toy dealer.

Doug did not need to know the details. "Now, it's time for you to leave."

Without waiting for him to respond, I turned around and strode into One Night Stan's, exhaling a sigh of relief when the door shut behind me. It was loud and busy inside the bar, but I spotted Quinn almost immediately as she waved me over to a booth in the back.

I tossed my purse into the seat before sliding in across from her. "Sorry I'm late. It's been a hell of a night, and it's only gotten started."

"Good thing I already ordered you a lemon drop, then, isn't it?" she said, sliding the drink closer to me.

"I love you so much. Have I told you that today?"

She laughed and took a sip of her drink. "So, why's it been a hell of a night?"

I really didn't want to get into my abysmal dating history, but I also didn't have anyone else to talk to about it. Laurel didn't need to concern herself with this. Plus, I could use a friend's outlook.

"My ex is turning out to be more of a creep than I gave him credit for."

She raised her brows. "Did he mail you a package filled with doll heads or something?"

"I'd actually welcome that. Unfortunately, he brought me something himself. He just cornered me outside."

Quinn's smile dropped, and she glanced toward the front door before returning her attention to me. "He followed you here? From *Atlanta*?"

"See?" I leaned toward her over the table. "That's weird, right?"

"Yes, that's weird! What reason did he give you?"

"He wanted to return my pillow."

"Your *what?*"

"You heard me."

"I've heard of a lot of excuses, but that is—*oh my god...*" Quinn's wide eyes were caught on something behind me, but I knew better than to spin around in my seat right away.

"Is this a look or don't-look situation?" I asked.

"This is a, *I think your creepy ex just walked into the bar because this rando is carrying a pillow* situation."

"What?" I spun around, and sure enough, there he was, standing at the front and obviously looking for someone. Looking for *me*.

Despite my direct rejection and clear instructions that I didn't want further contact, Doug had ignored all that. Just like he'd ignored every other boundary I'd set. Jesus, what the hell would it take to make this guy get my rejection through his thick skull?

"I need to take care of this," I said to Quinn before sliding from the booth and walking toward where he stood by the bar. Enough was enough.

I should've gotten mean outside. Should've told him to fuck off and that if I ever saw him again, I was calling the police and filing a restraining order. Because now, I had to do all that in Starlight Cove's hot spot on a Saturday night with three dozen residents as my witnesses.

"There you are," he said as soon as his eyes landed on me, and there wasn't an ounce of hesitation in his tone.

"Have I been unclear, Doug?" My voice was loud and firm enough to be noticed, and I could feel the sudden attention focused on us. "I didn't think so, considering how many times I've told you we're done. But apparently you need this spelled out for you in black-and-white. We are not together. We will never be together again. I don't ever want to see you again. Which is exactly what I told you after I removed the tracking app you installed on Laurel's and my phones."

Gasps and murmurs sounded around us, but those had nothing on the searing heat I suddenly felt against my back. Even without turning around, I knew who was there. Could sense Atlas behind me even though his body didn't touch mine.

"What the fuck do you mean, he used an app to track you?" Atlas's voice was low and deadly serious.

I glanced back at Atlas, and though his words were directed to me, his attention was focused solely on Doug. If I'd thought the big guy had been glaring at me this whole time, it had absolutely nothing on the death stare my ex was on the receiving end of now.

Reaching back, I tugged Atlas's head down toward mine until my lips were next to his ear. I didn't want my ex to overhear what I was going to say, but I also didn't want his murder on my conscience, so I needed to calm things down.

"It was harmless, so you can turn off the beast mode," I whispered. "He did it so he could *accidentally* run into us while we were out because he was too chicken to ask me to hang out."

He turned his head, the soft brush of his lips against the shell of my ear sending a shiver rolling through me. "Guys like that don't ask you to hang out, trouble. They wear your skin as a suit."

Before I could respond, he stood back to his full height. His previous stormy expression paled in comparison to the anger rolling off him in waves now.

Apparently cluelessness was a general affliction for my ex and not something reserved for only me. He either didn't care or didn't notice that the only thing standing between a six-and-a-half-foot angry beast and his scrawny ass was me, because he said, "Who are you?"

"It doesn't matter who the fuck I am," Atlas said, stepping even closer until I felt him along every inch of my back. "All you need to know is she's *mine*."

I didn't know if it was the words or the way he said them —all low and deep and growly—but my stomach flipped, and I needed to stop that shit immediately.

Forgetting for a moment that this played perfectly into what I'd told Doug outside, I spun around, resting my hand on Atlas's chest. I stared up at him, brows raised, my silent *I'm what, now?* clear.

Instead of responding to my unspoken question, he brought one of his hands down to cup my ass, hauled me up against him, and lifted me straight off the floor. Against my lips, he murmured, "Now it's time for *you* to play along, trouble."

He gave me a second to catch on to what he'd said. Another second after that before he pressed his mouth against mine.

And then it was game over.

Fireworks burst behind my closed eyes, a potent

reminder of exactly how explosive our brief hour together had been. A moan I had no hope of holding in escaped as I melted against him.

I wrapped my arms around his neck and returned every ounce of his hunger, meeting his tongue stroke for stroke. Forgetting for a moment that we were doing this for one reason and one reason only—to get my ex to back off. Forgetting, too, that there was a bar full of people around us. Forgetting that this was all fake, nothing more than a ruse to get Doug to finally leave me alone.

This most *definitely* wasn't going to lead to another night in either one of our beds.

By the time Atlas pulled back, both of us were panting, and there was no denying the bat-sized bulge trapped between us. Before I could string together a coherent thought, he set me down, guided me behind him, and stepped toward my ex.

Clueless as ever, Doug still stood right where he'd been, having had a front-row seat to the ruse. Instead of leaving like he should have, he was motionless, jaw tense as he stared at me.

At least until Atlas blocked his view. "Don't look at her. Don't even *think* about her." He pointed a single finger toward the door. "And get the fuck out."

"Look, man, I—"

Atlas took another menacing step toward Doug, the move only emphasizing their massive size difference. "I *said*, get the fuck out. And don't come back."

This time, my ex didn't try to argue. He shot another look in my direction, quickly averting his eyes at Atlas's responding growl, before finally slinking out of the bar, my pillow in tow.

I exhaled a heavy sigh, relief overcoming me as cheers erupted at the tables surrounding us. At least until Atlas turned his intense gaze on me.

"You and I need to talk. Now."

CHAPTER SEVENTEEN

ATLAS

ADRENALINE PULSED THROUGH ME, something I usually only felt this intensely on the field. But my body was buzzing, half of it coiled and ready for a fight, the other half desperate to pin Sutton to the nearest surface and fuck this out of my system.

Though I was faintly aware of other things around me—the buzz of conversation in the bar, the sounds of glasses clinking together, the feel of my brother's eyes on me—the only thing I could seem to focus on was a single thought.

Protect her.

It was a thrum in my veins, overriding everything else and not allowing me even an inch to breathe.

I turned to Lincoln, who was watching me with raised brows. "Come get me if that piece of shit sets foot back in this bar."

Then, without waiting for a response, I grabbed Sutton's hand and tugged her toward the back office. Furious as hell she'd been in this position in the first place—that her ex had *put* her in this position.

Her nervousness that night at the hotel suddenly made a lot more sense. And I had to physically restrain myself from going after that bastard and seeing just how much he liked being harassed.

After storming into the office, I slammed the door and turned to face Sutton. I ran my gaze over every inch of her, reassuring myself that she was here and safe and unharmed. He hadn't done anything to her—physically, anyway. And now he was gone. If it took me scaring him to finally get him to back the fuck off, so be it.

I leaned back, bracing my ass against the desk, and wrapped my fingers around the edge until the wood creaked under the pressure.

Several long moments of silence stretched between us until she finally asked, "You okay?"

I shot her a scowl. "I'm supposed to ask you that. Jesus Christ, trouble, your ex-boyfriend just stalked you halfway across the country, and you're asking me if *I'm* okay?"

She huffed out a breath and rolled her eyes. "He didn't *stalk* me."

"What he did is the literal definition of the word."

She pursed her lips to the side, as if she wanted to argue but was holding back. Then she blew out a breath and flicked a gaze down to my hands. "I asked because you look like you're about to rip that desk in half with your bare hands."

I didn't doubt that was true. I usually kept a better handle on my emotions than this, but it seemed all bets were off when it came to her. I wanted to fuck or fight, a desperate need for either clawing up my throat, and I had no idea which option would be worse.

"That's because I'm holding myself back from either going after him and ending up in jail tonight, or doing something we might both regret."

I knew she understood my meaning immediately because her gaze dropped to the front of my jeans, where I was still hard, thanks to that kiss and this adrenaline pulsing through my system. It didn't help that I'd closed us off in this tiny room, and her goddamn shampoo or body wash or perfume or whatever the fuck permeated the space, causing me to drag in lungfuls with every inhale. It was soft and floral, far too sweet for this demon who'd clearly been sent to earth solely to torture me.

She took a step toward me and raised a brow. "I'm a nurse, Atlas. So I definitely can't condone the first option."

I tracked her slow advance, my gaze cataloging every inch of her. From her loose, wavy hair kissing the tops of her shoulders to those full, pouty lips to that deep V of her sweater showcasing just a shadow of her tits.

Meeting her eyes again, I asked, "And the second?"

She stepped between my legs, so close her hips brushed the insides of my thighs, and rested her hand against my chest. "With how I'm feeling right now, I'm not so sure I'd regret it."

She might as well have waved a red cape in front of a bull, because nothing short of the world ending could have held me back after her admission. I didn't stop to think, didn't second-guess this compulsion beating like a living, breathing being inside me. I just pushed off from the desk and cupped a handful of her ass, lifting her up and guiding her legs around my waist. And then my mouth was on hers, my tongue sliding between her lips and reminding us both exactly how combustible we were together.

"Do you think this is a good idea?" she asked between kisses, my face gripped in her hands and the roll of her hips driving me damn near out of my mind.

I was so fucking desperate for it. For *her*.

"No, it's not a good fucking idea." I nipped her jaw and trailed kisses down her neck, scraping my teeth against her collarbone. "But that doesn't mean I'm going to stop."

"Oh god," she moaned, tipping her head to allow me more access, pressing her pussy against me even harder. "I meant because you told Lincoln to get you if my ex showed up."

"Then you better hope that piece of shit has more than two brain cells to rub together and does what I told him." I laid her down on the paper-strewn desk, her legs still wrapped tight around my hips as if she couldn't bear to lose the pressure against her clit. "Now, let's see how fast I can make you come."

Proving she was just as lost as I was, she reached down without hesitation and tugged off her sweater, presenting me with an unencumbered view of her perfect little tits.

I growled low in my throat and captured one tight peak between my teeth, tugging hard enough to draw a gasp from her. "Stop walking around with your tits bare under your shirt."

"Stop telling me what to do," she shot back. "I'll walk down Main Street naked if I want to."

Obstinate little shit. Her antagonism, while pissing me off, only made me hotter. Harder. I never thought I'd say this, but I liked the fight. And I especially liked it with her.

I sucked one of her nipples into my mouth before pulling back to blow a gust of air over it, grinding my cock against her clothed pussy. "I'm not so sure you don't do it just to piss me off."

"Seriously," she said on panting breaths, arching her back toward me, "your ego is out of control. Not all of my decisions revolve around you."

"You're going to prove exactly how well-founded my ego is by how fast I can make you come."

"You can't just—" Her objection was cut off when I undid the fly of her jeans and tugged them off before dropping to my knees.

I didn't wait before diving in. Didn't tease or torment her. I was on a mission to make her come again as soon as possible. So, I tossed her legs over my shoulders and got to work.

The first taste of her against my tongue tore a rough groan from my throat. *Jesus fucking Christ.* I thought I'd inflated my memory of her. Thought there was no way I accurately remembered just how sweet she tasted. But as I laved her pussy with my tongue, circling her clit in a relentless rhythm, her arousal that flooded my mouth proved otherwise.

I wanted to tell her how much I loved her sounds. Loved the feel of her beneath my hands. Wanted to tell her how fucking good she tasted. How she could serve me her pussy daily, and I'd gladly sit down to dine for every single meal. But I couldn't drag myself away from her cunt for even a second. Not when her legs were already shaking, her thighs clamped around my head like earmuffs, her fingers in my hair, tugging me closer.

And then there was the never-ending stream of *oh my god, oh my fucking god, yes, please, yes* that did me in.

"You better cover that mouth, trouble," I said against her pussy. "I don't want anyone to hear my girl come but me."

Without hesitation, she did as I told her to, her eyes bright and wild as she stared down at me. Pressing my forearm across her hips, I held her in place because she couldn't seem to decide whether she wanted to get closer or farther away. I sucked her clit between my lips, flicking it with my tongue before lightly scraping my teeth over it. That was all it took.

She choked out my name on a moan, trapping the sound behind her palm, but that didn't dilute its effect on me. Especially not when her hips rolled restlessly beneath my forearm as she came and every bit of her pleasure dripped from my lips, soaking into my beard.

While her body still quaked with aftershocks, I stood, undid my fly, and wrapped my hand around my cock. So fucking hard for her. I stroked once down my length and groaned. Precome already leaked from the tip, my dick just as desperate as I was to be inside the heaven that was her pussy.

"Condom," Sutton managed between panting breaths.

Right. Protection. That was normally my line, but the thought hadn't even been a flicker in my mind. And if I weren't already so far gone, that would've worried me. But right now, all I could focus on was sheathing myself in her tight cunt.

I didn't carry condoms. There wasn't a need. I'd never

once fucked someone in Starlight Cove, but I couldn't bring myself to care that I was going to break that rule tonight. Thankfully, my brothers didn't hold any such reservations, keeping this place stocked.

I reached over and yanked open the desk drawer, fumbling around inside but only coming up with an empty box.

"Fuck," I growled, tossing the useless package aside. The one goddamn time I needed a condom, and suddenly there were none to be found. "I don't have one. You?"

She gave a slight shake of her head, her chest still heaving, thanks to how hard she'd just come on my face. "I left my purse in the booth." She bit her lip and eyed me for a moment before saying, "I just got tested, and I have an IUD."

Fucking *Christ*.

My cock jerked at her words, more precome spilling over the crown. I was immediately reminded of just how much I'd wanted to be bare the first time we'd fucked. How I'd thought about filling her with my come. Thought about watching it leak out of her before shoving it right back in and fucking her all over again.

I had no idea why that got me so hard. Not when I'd spent my entire adult life *avoiding* exactly that. But, as with everything else that involved Sutton, it didn't make sense.

"You want me inside you bare, trouble?"

"I just want you inside me." She hooked her leg around my waist, pressing her foot against my ass and tugging me closer. "As long as you're clear, I'm not particular about the details."

She was laid out in front of me, completely naked, her

dark hair fanned across the paperwork scattered on the desk. And I hadn't even taken off my shirt. Had done little else but shove down the front of my boxer briefs just enough to free my cock. I couldn't even wait the thirty seconds it would take to rid me of my clothes. Couldn't wait to feel her surrounding me again.

"It's been a while since I've been tested, but there hasn't been anyone. Until you." I gripped my shaft, sliding it through her slit, coating my length with her arousal.

She shuddered out a moan when I focused my attention on her clit, flicking the head of my cock against it. God*damn*, she was so fucking tempting, the heat of her pussy beckoning me inside.

I knew as soon as I sank deep, I'd want to spend all fucking night there. Would want to see how many times I could make her come. How many times I could fill her up.

But once again, time wasn't on our side.

Sounds from the bar filtered into the office continuously, reminding me anyone could walk in at a moment's notice. And I had no intention of allowing them to see Sutton spread out, completely naked, taking every inch of my cock. That was for my eyes and my eyes only.

"Let's see if I remember what you like."

The statement was a joke. Of course I remembered. I couldn't fucking forget. Our single hour together played on a loop in my mind every night when I closed my eyes, no matter how desperately I'd tried to stop it.

I notched myself against her entrance and locked my eyes with hers as I pushed inside, groaning over the tight fist of her cunt. "I think your pussy was sent here to destroy me."

She wrapped her fingers around my forearm, her nails digging crescents into my skin. "You say the sweetest things."

"And you shouldn't be saying anything at all." I pressed my thumb against her clit, rubbing it in fast, tight circles. "We both know I remember exactly what you like. Now, hurry up and come on my cock before someone walks in."

"Don't tell me what to—" She broke off on a moan when I tilted my hips and drove into her in fast, shallow thrusts. The head of my cock brushed her G-spot with every stroke, and I didn't relent.

I pressed down on her stomach with one hand, rubbing her clit with the other. All the while squeezing my ass cheeks in an effort not to blow before she came. She felt fucking incredible, all wet and tight and warm, her pussy pulsing around me as I pushed her exactly where she needed to go.

"C'mon, trouble. Show me how much you've missed my cock so I can slide so fucking deep and fill you up."

Her eyes heated at my words, and when I flicked my finger against her clit faster, she let out a long, low moan. As soon as I felt that first rhythmic pulse on my cock, I stopped holding myself back.

"There's my good girl. Such a good fucking girl for me, making me come so hard." I settled myself deep, my hips pressed against the soft flesh of her thighs, and spilled inside her as she came around me.

For long moments, all I could do was brace myself over her, my forehead pressed between her tits, my heartbeat pounding loudly in my ears. By degrees, everything came back to me—the fact that I was in the office of my family's bar, that I'd fucked Sutton on the desk, and that I'd done so without a fucking condom. Then the reason we were back here in the first place slammed into me like a ton of bricks.

While an orgasm courtesy of Sutton's demon pussy helped to calm the raging beast inside, the need for retribution still overwhelmed me. I forced myself to pull out of her, only allowing myself the briefest glimpse of my come spilling out of her before I grabbed a tissue and cleaned her up.

"Where's Laurel?" I asked, sharper than I'd intended, but I was pissed at myself that I hadn't thought of her until now.

Sutton shot me a look as she tugged on her sweater. "You just had your dick inside me, and you're asking about my daughter?"

"I don't know where your ex went, and I want to make sure she's safe, trouble. Is she at the cottage?"

At my words, the crease between her brows melted away, and she shook her head. "She's staying over at a friend's house tonight."

I nodded once, relief I wasn't ready to examine swamping me. "Good."

"What do you mean, good?"

Without answering her, I reached into my back pocket and pulled out my phone. "Add your numbers so I have them." At her cocked brow, I added a gruff, "Please."

She exhaled a heavy sigh but did as I asked before handing my phone back. "What are you going to do now?"

"Take you home. And then I'm going to make sure your ex got the message."

CHAPTER EIGHTEEN

SUTTON

THANK god Laurel was staying at Cami's tonight, because I had no idea how I would've explained my...*everything*... otherwise. It'd been hours since One Night Stan's, and I was still reeling from the events of the night.

I didn't know if it was a good or bad thing that Quinn had been gone when Atlas and I had emerged from the office. She'd left my purse with Lincoln, along with a message that she'd had to make an emergency house call. It meant there'd been no questions when Atlas and I had left together, though there had been plenty of curious looks tossed our way. Something I had no doubt I was going to have to contend with at some point.

The grumpy beast had followed me home, going as far as walking me to the cottage. He'd glared at the cheap lock on the doorknob as if it had personally offended him before ordering me to stay inside and then storming back to his black SUV.

Let the record show that the only reason I did as he'd

instructed was because it was late, I was tired, and those two orgasms he'd given me made me want to curl up and slip into a much-earned sleep.

Lying on the couch with the hum of the TV lulling me, I was on my way to doing just that when a sharp knock startled a yelp out of me.

It was only Atlas's gruff, "It's me," that allowed my racing heart to settle back into a normal pace.

Or as normal as it could manage when the beast himself was in my general vicinity. My entire body seemed to malfunction whenever he was around. Most of all, my common sense.

Case in point, when I'd let him strip me down and fuck me on a desk in his family's bar. As if I needed a reminder of exactly how combustible we were together.

Shoving those thoughts into the furthest recesses of my mind where they belonged, I glanced out the front window to verify it was him—as if I couldn't recognize him from that low growl alone—and opened the door. He did a quick sweep of me from head to toe before storming inside, filling up far too much of the cottage as his gaze darted around the space.

"Please, come in," I said dryly, closing the door behind him.

"Pack a bag. We can move the rest of your stuff over tomorrow."

I could only blink at him for long moments, my thoughts whirring a thousand miles an hour. Because...what the *fuck*?

"Did you hit your head?" I asked. "Run into a telephone pole while you were gone? Maybe slip on some leaves and crack your forehead on the pavement?"

He scowled at me. "I'm not in the mood for games, trouble."

"Good. Neither am I. So this game you're playing where you think I'm going to do whatever you tell me to can end right now."

"I'm not playing a game," he bit out.

"And I'm not moving in with you." I huffed out a laugh and shook my head. "Do you hear yourself? You don't even *like* me."

"That's the second time you've said that, and it's starting to piss me off."

"Why? It's the truth."

Rather than refute me, he snapped his mouth shut, his jaw ticking as he stared down at me.

"Excellent rebuttal." I heaved out a sigh and sat on the couch. "What happened? He said he wasn't going to leave?"

Atlas crossed his arms over his chest and glared out the window. "I couldn't find him."

"That's not a bad thing. It probably just means he left already."

"What it means is he could be anywhere, and he already knew how to find you in Starlight Cove. It's not a stretch that he could figure out you live *here*. And all you have to keep him out is that flimsy fucking excuse for a lock."

"I think you're overreacting."

"And I don't think you're reacting enough."

"I thought Starlight Cove was supposed to be safe?"

"That was before Pillow Humper came to town."

I huffed out a laugh, unable to tamp it down. "You're being ridiculous. Pillow Humper? Really?"

"Don't tell me the thought didn't cross your mind."

I wasn't going to tell him that, because it absolutely had. Who knew what my ex had done with my pillow in the months since I'd called things off. "I'm not moving in to your house, Atlas. And I'm not going to worry about what Doug may or may not do."

"Who the fuck is Doug?"

"Pillow Humper, as you like to call him." I stood, gripped Atlas's elbow, and tugged him toward the door. "I'm tired. I'm going to go to bed and wake up to news that Pillow Humper is gone. And you're going to go back to your house and cuddle your kitten, or whatever it is big, grouchy men do to fall asleep. I'll see you later."

Without waiting for a response, I pushed him outside and shut the door in his face.

He stood there silently for several long moments before snapping, "Check all the windows. And lock this goddamn door." Then he stormed off, leaving me alone once again.

And with all these conflicting feelings I didn't know what to do with.

Part of me was irritated that he had the gall to think he could tell me anything at all. I was an adult who'd been handling her shit for a long damn time, and I didn't need his help.

But another, smaller part of me—the one who hadn't been able to count on anyone else her whole life—was preening under his protection.

CHAPTER NINETEEN

ATLAS

Group text with Mom, Atlas, Xander, Declan, and Lincoln:

5:28 p.m.

MOM:

Atlas, why aren't you answering your phone? What's this I hear about you chasing some guy down Main Street with a chainsaw?

LINCOLN:

It was for a good cause. His girlfriend was being harassed.

MOM:

GIRLFRIEND?!?! Why is this the first I'm hearing about a girlfriend????

DECLAN:

I wish I wasn't hearing about it at all.

LINCOLN:

Don't worry, Mom, you're not far behind the rest of town. Atlas and his new lady friend made their declaration at the bar on Saturday. Word spread like wildfire.

MOM:

And the chainsaw?

XANDER:

What have we told you about not believing everything Mabel says?

MOM:

How do you know it was Mabel?

XANDER:

I don't have to be in town to know that.

MOM:

So Atlas having a girlfriend isn't true?

LINCOLN:

No, it is. The chainsaw thing is a little over the top, though. Even for him.

MOM:

How serious is this?? How long have they been dating?? And why hasn't he brought her over to meet me??????

DECLAN:

An excellent question. Atlas?

LINCOLN:

He's probably busy with his new girlfriend doing coupley things. But he told me he'd bring her by this week for family dinner.

MOM:

Perfect! I can't wait!!!

DECLAN:

Neither can I.

MOM:

Does she have any allergies, Atlas? What's her favorite food? I want to make a good impression!

Group text with Atlas, Xander, Declan, and Lincoln:

5:42 p.m.

ATLAS:

I'm going to kill you.

DECLAN:

Which one of us are you talking to?

ATLAS:

Yes.

CHAPTER TWENTY

SUTTON

QUINN:

Don't think I didn't notice how you ran out
of the clinic like your pants were on fire. You
can't avoid me forever.

SUTTON:

I have no idea what you're talking about.

QUINN:

Sure you don't. Just know my interest only
grows the longer you put off this
conversation. And the more rumors I hear.

IT WASN'T that I was *avoiding* Quinn exactly. More just...
artfully dodging any one-on-one interactions with her ever
since the night at One Night Stan's. Because the truth was, I
didn't know what to tell her.

Mostly because I didn't know myself.

Other than Atlas driving me home—and then showing up on my porch the following morning with a toolbox in one hand and a new dead bolt in the other—he'd been scarce.

And that was fine with me. *Totally* fine. For the best, actually.

Because between him goading me just to take my mind off a shitty day, to claiming me where anyone could see, to his almost innate sense to protect me, things were only getting more confusing. And I definitely didn't need that.

Something I'd learned time and time again was that people's views of teenage single moms weren't very flattering. Adding fuel to that fire by spending more time with Atlas would only fuck me over in the long run. And I was not interested in being fucked over in a town this small. Especially when my daughter and I had to make our life here for the foreseeable future.

This was my first time being on the receiving end of small-town gossip, and I could officially say I didn't love it. I'd heard a dozen speculations today from various patients, each person more desperate than the last to find out what was really going on between Atlas and me.

Hoping I could smother the rumors if I didn't give them oxygen, I'd neither confirmed nor denied any of them, even the more outlandish ones. Who in their right mind thought our fling was actually part of a reality show and Starlight Cove was about to become famous? As much as I'd been desperate to squash all talk of Atlas and me, I figured that would only stretch this out longer than necessary.

Needless to say, I'd been exhausted by the end of the day and hadn't been able to leave fast enough.

After I swung by the library to pick up Laurel from a study group, we headed back to the cottage. We didn't even make it two steps inside before she asked, "What's for dinner?"

The age-old question I'd never been able to escape, even during the times she was mad at me.

"Tacos," I said. "Sound good?"

"As long as we can have guac with them." Laurel tossed her backpack on the kitchen counter.

"Great, you can be in charge of that," I said.

She groaned with the force that only a sixteen-year-old could muster. "I never agreed to that."

"Yeah, well, I never agreed to come up with three meals a day, every day, for the rest of my life. Yet here we are."

"And you say *I'm* dramatic."

"Go change and get comfy. We can binge that new murder documentary tonight."

"Fine," she grumbled, but I spotted unmistakable interest in her eyes before she headed to her bedroom.

Once again, I was thankful my daughter liked hanging out with me most of the time. Okay, a solid 70% of the time, but I'd still take it.

I grabbed her backpack, intent on hanging it on the hook by the door rather than the any-fucking-where she usually dropped it, when a bright-pink flyer fell out of the front pocket and floated to the floor. I reached down and picked it up, the bold font at the top catching my eye and proclaiming, CLASS TRIP TO PARIS.

I quickly scanned the paper, my attention pinging to the important details. *Fuck me.* A week for my daughter in the

City of Love would cost more than I'd paid for my first car. My heart dropped, a boulder taking up residence in my stomach.

Laurel desperately wanted to see the world, and Paris was her number one bucket list location. But this was a lot of fucking money, and being a single mom didn't exactly allow for the cultivation of a nest egg.

Her bedroom door opened, and I shoved the flyer back into the pocket before hanging up her backpack. I knew she'd talk to me about it when she was ready. And the truth was, I needed a little time to figure out some kind of plan where I could make this a possibility for her.

After a quick detour to my bedroom to change, I pulled out the taco fixings and started dicing a tomato. "Are things better at school?"

Laurel pulled out another cutting board and grabbed three avocados from the counter. "Define better."

"Are you still actively plotting my demise every day when I drop you off? Or have we graduated past that to just sullen resignation?"

"Maybe somewhere in the middle."

"That's progress. You and Cami are hanging out more. Things are clicking?"

Laurel shrugged. "She's cool. I just miss my old friends."

I glanced over, taking in the slump of her shoulders, and blew out a long sigh. "I know you do. But you'll make those same connections here. And maybe we can plan a trip there in the summer."

She glanced up at me, her eyes bright. "Really?"

Fuck. Why had I said that? If I had any hope of sending her to Paris, I sure as hell couldn't afford a random trip to Georgia this summer.

Before I could respond, a knock sounded at the front door. I glanced over at her with a raised brow. "You expecting someone?"

"No. My one friend is busy tonight. Maybe it's the guy you made out with at the bar over the weekend."

My mouth dropped open, a shocked breath leaving me. "Excuse me?"

She rolled her eyes. "Please, Mom, we live in a town of, like, twelve people. Did you think I wasn't going to hear about it?"

"Well, I-I...guess I didn't think that through exactly. Look, it was just a—"

"Oh my god, please stop. I *promise* you don't need to have this conversation with me. Make out with whoever you want. One of us might as well be having some fun."

The knock came again, louder this time. I wiped my hands on a towel before heading to the door and glancing out the front window. My brows shot up the second I spotted who stood on my porch.

Less than two days was definitely not enough time for me to get my shit together following the kiss and subsequent fuck that had rocked my entire world. Especially not when I had all these confusing emotions swirling inside me. But it looked like I didn't have much of a choice.

I opened the door to a looming Atlas, his hands braced on the doorframe, the overwhelming bulk of his body blocking out anything beyond his shoulders. Rather than imposing, his stance only served to remind me exactly how safe and protected I always felt in the shadow of his presence.

He gave me a quick once-over like he always did, that barest hint of attention lighting me up in ways that should have been illegal. Then, without so much as a hello, he stormed into the cottage. "We have a problem."

"We have a what?"

"A *problem*." He glanced around, offering a grunt at Laurel that I assumed was supposed to be a greeting.

"Well, this seems like something I don't care about." She wiped her hands on a towel, the guacamole forgotten as she headed toward her bedroom. "Call me when dinner's ready."

As soon as her door shut, Atlas turned back to me, arms crossed. "We need to fake date."

My brows hit my hairline as I stared up at him, not quite able to believe what I was hearing. "We need to what now?"

"*Fake date*," he enunciated, as if that was the issue I was having. "I know you're familiar with the concept. It was in that book from—"

"I *am* familiar with it. What I am unfamiliar with is why *we* need to do that."

His attention snagged on my lips for the briefest moment, but I still felt it...*everywhere*. "Our activities at the bar didn't exactly go unnoticed."

If the rumors I'd been fed all day were anything to go by, that was the biggest understatement of the century.

"It was just a kiss," I said, my voice sounding unsteady, even to my own ears.

Ha. The lie was laughable. It wasn't *just* anything, and neither was what had come after. From the look he shot me and the heat in his eyes, he knew it too.

"It's never *just* anything in Starlight Cove," he grumbled. "People are also hung up on my...investigation...yesterday."

"What investigation?"

"I did some asking around."

"About?"

"Pillow Humper."

"So?"

"They're drawing the conclusion that we're together."

My stomach flipped...for no other reason than because I was clearly drunk. Except I hadn't had so much as a drop of alcohol tonight. Which meant it was the casual way he'd said *we're together* that had caused this chaos inside me.

I cleared my throat, shoving those feelings aside. "Why would they be doing that?"

He flattened his mouth into a hard line, his brows bunched, jaw ticking. As if he didn't want to tell me. Finally, he said, "I was on a time crunch. The fastest way I could get people to talk was to tell a few...white lies."

I narrowed my eyes at him. "What kinds of white lies?"

He stared at me for a long moment, that impenetrable gaze locked on me. I had no doubt he'd made far tougher people than me cower with that look alone. Too bad I seemed to be immune to it.

When it was clear I wasn't going to take his scowl as an answer, he heaved a sigh. "That Pillow Humper stalked you across state lines, and I needed to find out where the hell he was because I didn't want my—" he cleared his throat before rubbing a hand over his mouth "—girlfriend being harassed."

There was that goddamn stomach flip again.

"Your *what?*"

"I just rolled with what I already said at the bar," he snapped. "And it worked. I found out he left town. But details still got back to my mom. And my shit-stirrer of a brother confirmed it."

"Okayyy..." I said, drawing out the word.

"She's expecting us at dinner this week. She's already asking about your food preferences."

Mouth agape, I could only stare at him in a stunned stupor. I had no idea why I hadn't anticipated this becoming so much larger than just Atlas and me. Sure, our night in Portland had stayed between us. But that possibility had been removed the second Atlas had stepped up behind me at One Night Stan's.

"I know this is...inconvenient." He blew out a heavy sigh. "But I'm willing to offer an incentive."

"It better be one hell of an incentive." I wasn't so sure he could offer anything that would get me to agree to this. Not when this would end up being the exact opposite of what I needed— namely, to stay far, far away from the man who turned my brain to mush and zapped every one of my instincts into silence.

The less time I spent around Atlas Steele, the better.

He studied me for long moments, as if hoping to get a read on what could lure me to his side. Then he blew all my best intentions out of the water with a few choice words. "I'll waive your rent for the rest of your lease."

Holy fucking fucknuggets. Six months of free rent? My *god.* That was probably a tiny drop in a very large bucket to a former pro football player. But on my end? That amount of money would be life-changing, offering me a hell of a cushion.

A cushion I could use to send my daughter to Europe.

While I'd always been able to provide the necessities for Laurel, there'd been so many things in her life she'd *wanted* that I hadn't been able to give her. It had been hard as hell getting a GED and putting myself through nursing school, all while scrounging to make ends meet.

We'd been given a bit more breathing room as I racked up years of experience, but I still had an ungodly amount of student loans that didn't exactly allow for a ton of discretionary spending.

That could all change with this agreement.

I tried to get a read on him, see if he was as conflicted as I was, but he'd shut down his emotions tighter than Fort Knox. "I'm not lying to my daughter."

He studied me for a moment, then lifted one massive shoulder. "Laurel can be in on it."

Her timing was as impeccable as ever, because she chose that moment to come strolling out of her bedroom. "What am I in on?"

He raised a brow, clearly deferring to me on what, if anything, I wanted to tell her. So I did. I gave a brief rundown of the situation we found ourselves in and Atlas's proposed solution.

It was a testament to how many romances she read

because she didn't even blink. She just split a gaze between us before settling it on me. "What's in it for you?"

"He's cutting us a deal on rent."

She lifted a single brow, then turned her attention to Atlas. "Okay, what's in it for *me*?"

I nearly huffed out a laugh but somehow managed to tamp it down. I should have expected that was coming from her.

If Atlas was thrown by her question, he didn't show it. Instead, he asked, "What do you want, kid?"

She paused for all of three seconds before she walked over and pulled out the bright-pink flyer I'd stuffed into her backpack earlier. She smacked it against his chest. "This."

Atlas grabbed the paper, quickly scanning the details. Then, without hesitation, he nodded. "If your mom says you can go on the trip, done."

I couldn't stop the surprise from showing at his immediate agreement, despite the fact that the deal on rent and this trip for Laurel were going to cost more than my first *four* cars. At least.

I had a feeling this was going to be a very, *very* bad idea. I was already intimately aware of just how charged things were between Atlas and me—and I wasn't even talking about when we were naked. It hummed in the space between us even now.

The last thing I needed was to suddenly be his girlfriend and have to spend more time in his presence.

But I could handle myself. I could *control* myself. Especially when, on the other side of this, my daughter would get something she desperately wanted.

"Can you give us a minute, Lolo? We have some things to discuss."

"Fine. I don't need to know your sex schedule anyway."

"*Laurel.*" My mouth dropped open in shock, though I really shouldn't have been surprised. She came by her lack of filter naturally.

With a shrug, she walked past us and headed out the front door. "I'm going down to the beach to make sure I don't hear any part of it."

Once the door shut behind her, Atlas turned his attention back to me. "Is that a yes?"

"It's a yes, with stipulations. Rule number one, no kissing in private."

His eyes heated as his gaze dropped to my mouth, and I felt the brand of his stare against my skin. It didn't take a genius to guess he was recalling what we'd done in the bar a couple nights ago. How he'd kissed me like I was his to claim... Taken me like he couldn't help himself.

Worse, I was recalling how much I'd loved every minute of it.

"We'll need to in public," he said, his voice just a low rumble.

And we both knew exactly how heated those public kisses could get. But he was right. We'd already participated in some PDA, so it would look strange if we suddenly stopped once officially becoming a couple.

"Fine," I said. "If we go out, you're paying."

He pinned me with a look that said he was offended I had even suggested otherwise. "Obviously."

"What about events?"

Blowing out a sigh, he ran a hand over his beard. "My mom's going to expect us at weekly dinners. Probably need to make an appearance at the Harvest Festival. And homecoming. There are some...traditions before the game."

"What kinds of traditions?"

"A kiss."

Ignoring the low flare of jealousy that had sparked in my belly, I raised my brows. "And who do you usually do that with?"

"No one."

"Never?"

"Never," he said without hesitation, and I absolutely was not going to examine why that settled me so much. "It's just for people on the team who have partners. It'll be suspicious if we don't join."

"Fine."

"Anything else?"

"Yeah. When this all ends, you have to promise that whatever happens between us won't affect my work with the team. I like being their nurse."

His gaze softened the slightest bit, and he dipped his chin in a nod. "It won't. They'd stage a revolt if you left."

Now, it was my turn to soften. While I'd worked with kids here and there, I'd never had so many of my hours devoted to them. And I found I loved it. Loved my job here, period. Working at the clinic was more relaxed than I was used to, but it was still interesting enough to keep me on my toes each day.

I wasn't sure I'd be ready to leave when my contract was up.

"Do we have a deal?" he asked.

I had a sudden, overwhelming feeling that I was about to make either the best decision or worst mistake of my life. But considering Laurel would get her dream trip at the end of this, and my last worst mistake had just stalked me across the country, I was hoping for the best.

"We have a deal, *boyfriend*."

CHAPTER TWENTY-ONE

SUTTON

LAUREL:

We have a swimming pool in our house

SUTTON:

What?

LAUREL:

There's water everywhere

Like literally everywhere

Shoes are floating around

SUTTON:

Is this a joke? Because it's not funny. I'm at work, and we're swamped.

LAUREL:

SO IS OUR HOUSE ::sends image::

SUTTON:

Is that my favorite hoodie floating next to the couch?

LAUREL:

MY favorite hoodie and yes

SUTTON:

Fuck

LAUREL:

The fuckiest

WELL, that was just fucking fabulous. Between the multiple pukers, the asshole who'd called our clinic incompetent because it was 100% female-run, and the delivery mix-up that left us without coffee, it had already been a day from hell. And now this.

The clinic was booked for the rest of the day with back-to-back patients, and we were already short-staffed because the flu was going around. I didn't want to leave Quinn in the lurch, which meant there was no way I could duck out, even for something like this. So, instead, I slipped into the back room and called Atlas.

It barely rang once before he answered. "What's wrong?"

For some unknown reason, his gruff voice brought a smile to my face. "Nice to know you're grumpy even over the phone."

"Trouble..." he said, his tone making it clear his minimal patience was gone altogether.

I blew out a heavy sigh. "The cottage is flooded."

"What do you mean flooded? Is there a burst pipe?"

"No, I mean *flooded*. The entire house. Our clothes and shoes are floating around."

"You're at the cottage? I thought you were at work."

"I am. Laurel just got home from school and let me know. We're absolutely buried here, and I can't—"

"I'll take care of it," he said without hesitation, even as shouts and the distant sound of a whistle carried over the line.

"But you have practice—"

"I said I'll handle it," he cut in, his tone brooking no argument. "Take care of your patients. I'll take care of Laurel and find out what's going on."

"Are you sure? I can—"

"See you at home."

The line went dead before I could respond. Though, with what, I had no idea. Thankfully, there was enough activity in the clinic to keep me busy. Because I definitely didn't need to analyze the hum of contentment that had settled over me at those handful of gruff words coming from him.

IT WAS our late night at the clinic, which meant I didn't pull into the driveway until almost seven thirty. The cottage was dark, not even the porch light shining, but the first floor of Atlas's home glowed brightly.

I didn't know how long it took to drain an entire house, but I didn't think the zero activity coming from the cottage was a good sign. I grabbed my bag and climbed out of my car, intent on heading toward the cottage, when Atlas's voice stopped me in my tracks.

"Trouble." He stood at his back door, the light from inside illuminating his intimidating silhouette. His features were cloaked in shadow, but somehow I knew he was tracing his gaze over me from head to toe, that quick check of me he always seemed to do. "Laurel's in here."

That didn't bode well. If Laurel was at Atlas's, that probably meant the cottage was uninhabitable. Though I could have guessed as much from that single picture Laurel had sent me. But I'd spent the past several hours hoping beyond hope that she was overexaggerating things. That the camera angle had made it seem worse than it was or she was leaning into that drama she loved so much.

Blowing out a sigh, I changed direction and headed toward him. "How bad is it?"

Instead of answering, he asked, "Have you eaten?"

"What? No, I— Atlas, how bad is it?"

He grabbed my bag as soon as I was close enough and tipped his head toward the kitchen. "Eat first. I ordered pizza. I thought your daughter was fucking with me when she said I needed to order three."

That startled a laugh out of me, my shoulders relaxing for the first time in hours. "She has a hollow leg when it comes to pizza."

"More like a hollow body. She ate more than I did. Called me a lightweight."

"You *are* a lightweight," Laurel said from the couch in the family room.

"No one's ever dared to call me that in my life."

"Everyone else was probably just scared to tell you the truth, but I'm immune to your scowls," she shot back.

Either I was delirious from exhaustion and seeing things, or…had the corner of his mouth actually twitched?

He turned to me, lowering his voice. "Is she always like this?"

"Pretty much."

"Quit pretending you don't like it," she said. "Also, how about Cleo?"

"No," Atlas said without sparing my daughter a glance.

I raised a brow at him in question. "What's that all about?"

"She thinks the kitten needs a name."

"The kitten *does* need a name," Laurel said, the *you fucking idiot* silent.

"I mean, I agree with her," I said. "Now, someone fill me in on what's going on."

"That's all you, Daddy Grump," Laurel called.

I snorted a laugh as Atlas shot her a scowl, but he didn't put any heat behind it.

He blew out a sigh as he turned back to me. "The company I usually use to winterize the pool had some issues, so I had to hire someone else."

"And?"

"*And* they're incompetent fucks, because while they were draining the pool, they managed to flood the entire cottage. It ruined the floors, the drywall, the furniture. Everything needs to be replaced."

"Great. So, what you're saying is, we're fucked."

"My conclusion exactly," Laurel said.

"What about our stuff?" I asked Atlas. We weren't pack

rats by any means and always traveled light. But that just meant the items we did keep were important to us.

"Laurel packed a bag, and I grabbed some things for you. We can go back and see what's salvageable after it's been drained."

This was a whole fucking lot to take in, and I had no doubt I was still in the shock phase. But my mind was spinning, trying to figure out a solution for Laurel and me.

"Okay. How long before it's livable again?"

He rubbed a hand along his jaw and eyed me. "Depends on supply chains, work schedules, and how much money I throw at the contractors to get it done."

I leaned against the counter, crossing my arms over my chest. "How long, Atlas?"

"Best-case scenario? A few weeks. The more likely scenario? A couple months."

Breathing out a laugh, I shook my head as every contingency plan I'd come up with vanished. "Great. What the hell are we supposed to do until then? There are literally zero rentals in Starlight Cove. Where are Laurel and I—"

"You two can move in with me."

His words hit me just as hard as they had last week when he'd demanded the same thing.

I narrowed my eyes at him, my gaze pinging across his stony expression. "You *made* them do this."

He glanced down at me, his brow raised. "I made them flood my own guesthouse so I could shell out tens of thousands of dollars to have it redone, just to have you move in with me?"

Well, when he said it like that, it *did* sound over-the-top ridiculous.

"It doesn't have to be a big deal, trouble."

Was that true? Maybe sharing a home with the one man I couldn't seem to get out of my thoughts—the very same man who made my knees literally weak—wouldn't be a big deal.

And maybe if I just continued to repeat that to myself, it would eventually be true.

I glanced around Atlas toward Laurel. She lounged on the couch, the kitten curled up on her chest and a soft smile on my daughter's face I hadn't seen in far too long. "What do you think, Lolo?"

She shrugged. "My room has an en suite bathroom, and it's downstairs, all the way on the other side of the house from your bedrooms. Which means I'll be saved from any sex noises bleeding through the walls."

I met Atlas's gaze and swallowed thickly, my mind immediately conjuring memories of when we'd slept together. Both times. How he'd worked my body in ways I hadn't even been sure were possible.

His eyes blazed as he stared back at me, jaw tense. Like he was recalling everything the same as I was and forcibly holding himself back from tossing me over his shoulder and running me upstairs for a repeat.

Good, because that couldn't happen again. Now that Laurel and I were stuck here with nowhere else to go, it was even more imperative that I didn't give in to this attraction sizzling between us.

No matter how much I wanted to.

CHAPTER TWENTY-TWO

ATLAS

I THOUGHT it would be easier to sleep now that Sutton and Laurel were staying in my house, as safe as I could make them besides the steps I'd already taken to make it so.

Turned out, I was a fucking idiot. In more ways than one.

Exhibit A: moving Sutton and Laurel in with me under the assumption I could handle it.

Exhibit B: the fact that I'd built this house so that the nicest guest room shared a wall with mine. For as much as I'd paid for this place, shouldn't these walls be a little fucking thicker?

I shouldn't have been able to hear Sutton getting ready for bed, but I definitely could. And, apparently, even the rustle of fabric got my dick hard now. When I'd heard the shower turn on? *Fucking hell.* I'd had to shove a pillow over my head in the hopes of drowning it out.

Except all that had done was conjure up images of each time I'd been inside her. Her throaty little moans, those crescent-shaped marks she left on my thighs, the sound of her begging for more. And the image that had played on a near-constant loop in my mind since I'd fucked her on the desk—the sight of her cunt with my come spilling out of it.

So yeah, I hadn't gotten a whole lot of sleep last night.

Which was why I was out before dawn, trying to force those memories out of my head with a grueling run. Problem was, running left a whole lot of time for me to think, and thinking was the absolute last thing I needed to be doing right now.

I needed a distraction, but the streets were empty, everyone still asleep in their beds. A before-dawn wake-up call for Lincoln or Declan would throw me straight into a retaliation war with either or both of them. So, instead, I popped in an earbud and called Xander who I knew would be heading to the gym.

It rang three times before he picked up. "You don't usually call this early. What's up?"

"Wanted to check in. How're things going down there?"

"Same shit, different day," he said, the hum of road noise and the persistent click of a blinker coming through the line. "Been working too many fucking hours every week. I don't even remember what my bed looks like."

"City life will do that to you."

He grunted in response. "Did you get the Mom Situation handled?"

"Which one?" There seemed to be a different issue every time I blinked. I didn't know how, but our mom was a conduit of chaos. If she didn't go looking for it, it found her anyway.

This week, she'd attempted to replace a light switch and managed to cut power to the entire block instead.

"The pipe thing while you were at that event a few weeks ago."

The same night I'd met Sutton. Jesus, had that really only been weeks ago? It felt like an entire fucking lifetime.

"Yeah," I said. "I took care of it."

Just like everything else. No one else needed to worry about it. I could handle it.

Lincoln's plea came back to me then. This would be a perfect opportunity to tell Xander we were drowning. And that maybe now was a good time to come home. With his credentials, he'd have no problem securing a job here. And Xander sure as hell wouldn't have to work sixty- or seventy-hour weeks in Starlight Cove.

It was on the tip of my tongue to tell him as much when he cut in. "Shit, hey, I got a situation here. Gotta run."

"All right, talk to you—" But the line was dead before I could get the words out.

I blew out a heavy sigh and focused again on my run, blocking out everything but the thud of my shoes against the pavement. By the time I made it back home, the house was dark, everything still and silent as I shut and locked the door behind me.

I hadn't even made it two steps into the kitchen when a sharp meow cut through the air, and a creature attacked my leg.

"Jesus fucking Christ," I hissed, my heart thumping wildly, and not from the run.

The kitten's arms were wrapped around my calf, its beady black eyes staring up at me with murderous intent.

I glared down at her. "Nice try. Your heart attack kill plan failed." I reached down and plucked her from my leg, cringing at the scrape of her claws against my calf.

Cupping her in one palm, I held her up in front of me, just a white ball of fluff. "I'm not putting you in my will, so it doesn't matter if you off me. You're not getting anything."

The kitten meowed in response.

"No, I'm not going to change my mind. It's already been allocated to my mom and brothers."

Another meow as I placed her on my shoulder and grabbed a protein shake from the fridge.

"Just be grateful you don't have any siblings. They're a pain in the ass. Always having to look out for them. Making sure they're handling their shit. But does anyone do the same for you? Nope. Not even a 'Hey, how are things going?' Well, I'm glad you asked. I think I really fucked up, and I don't—*ow*, Jesus! All right, I'll get you your breakfast. God*damn*."

I plucked the kitten off my shoulder and set her on the floor before readying her food. "Evil, murderous little shit. If Laurel suggests Jack the Ripper, I'm saying yes."

Wednesday

ATLAS:

Early meeting. I made coffee. Creamer is in the fridge, sugar in the cabinet to the right of the sink.

SUTTON:

It's a little weird that you know how I like my coffee. You even got the flavor of creamer I love.

ATLAS:

Lucky guess

Thursday

ATLAS:

Picking Laurel up at the library and bringing her to Cami's.

SUTTON:

I was supposed to get her after work. Why are you playing Daddy Grump taxi?

ATLAS:

Because she asked me to.

Friday

SUTTON:

Any idea how my car's gas tank got refilled when it was on E after I got home last night?

ATLAS:

I had an early morning errand, and your car was blocking mine.

SUTTON:

Your driveway is three cars wide.

ATLAS:

So?

SUTTON:

So, that's clearly a lie.

ATLAS:

Gotta go. Practice.

CHAPTER TWENTY-THREE

SUTTON

TURNED out I didn't have to worry about living under the same roof as Atlas and putting my willpower to the test, because he was never home. Always gone before I woke up and never returned until after I was in bed.

But even without him being present, he was still *present*. Sending lunch to the clinic on the days I'd been too slammed to grab anything, setting up profiles for Laurel and me on all his streaming services, even leaving a stack of romance books from the library on the counter for me.

Honestly, I was getting whiplash from it all. Worse was that I didn't *like* not seeing him for the week. Yeah, he drove me up a wall most of the time, but I'd grown accustomed to our interactions. And now that they were gone, I actually missed them.

I was gathering my things after our last patient had cleared out of the clinic when Quinn cornered me in the back room.

"Not so fast," she said. "I let last week slide when you

avoided me like the plague. Even allowed you this entire week to give me every excuse in the book. But two weeks without answers? I'm not letting you dodge me anymore."

Fuck.

"Dodge you about what?" I grabbed my bag, doing my best to pretend I had no idea what she was talking about. None at all. Certainly not about the beast of a man who was suddenly my pretend-but-real-to-everyone-else boyfriend I'd moved in with.

"Don't even try it." Quinn crossed her arms and stared down her nose at me, her unwavering attention making me shift on my feet. "Time to fill me in on whatever the hell is going on between you and Atlas."

Double fuck.

"I want to fill you in. I do. But Alicia needs to leave, so maybe now isn't a good—"

"Alicia wants to hear this as much as I do."

Our receptionist came strolling in, securing her locs back with a hair tie, and smirked at me. "Oh, I *absolutely* do."

"Well, Laurel's waiting out front, so maybe we could rain-check this?"

"Oh, please." Quinn rolled her eyes. "She's got her earbuds in, completely oblivious to the world around her."

"She didn't even notice when I told her I was coming back here," Alicia confirmed with a nod.

"See?" Quinn said. "No more dodging. It's time to spill. You and Atlas are a fully fledged couple now? How did that happen?"

That was a great question—one Atlas and I hadn't yet

discussed. So, I figured it was best to stick to the facts as closely as possible.

"Things just kind of spiraled after that kiss in One Night Stan's."

Her brows inched up. "I'm not surprised. It was one hell of a kiss. Reminded me a bit of the first kiss I shared with Ford, actually, right there at that bar."

"Really?" I asked.

"Yep. Well, except that we were tucked away in an alcove so no one would see, and yours was right there out in the open for *everyone* to see. And talk about."

"Mhmm," Alicia said with a nod. "Been hearing about it nonstop around here."

I cringed. "Yeah, that maybe wasn't my best idea."

"I don't know." Quinn shot me a grin. "It seems like it's turned out okay so far. Your new grumpy boyfriend scared your weird, overzealous ex out of town, at least."

"That was definitely a perk."

"If I were you, it would've scared the hell out of me to have him suddenly show up after breaking things off."

"It...wasn't my favorite."

"Well, thank god you've got Atlas," Quinn said.

"And he's not messing around." Alicia shrugged into her coat before grabbing her bag. "After that whole thing went down, I heard he was storming all over town with his rage face on."

I breathed out a laugh. I'd seen that rage face a time or twenty. "He's a bit like Laurel in his overdramatics."

A soft smile tugged up the corner of Quinn's lips. "Bet that makes your house pretty entertaining."

"That's one way to put it," I mumbled, following Quinn and Alicia as they headed toward the waiting room.

"What's all this about, by the way?" Quinn gestured to me, flicking her finger up and down. "You never change before you go home."

I cleared my throat. "That's because I'm not going home. I'm meeting Atlas at the Harvest Festival."

"There's *another* festival?" Laurel groaned from her perch on the couch, a textbook spread out in her lap. "How many freaking festivals does one town need?"

"I don't think we've found the limit yet," Alicia said, flipping off the lights.

"It's true." Quinn shrugged. "I wouldn't be surprised if they decided to do a lobster costume festival next."

"So stupid," Laurel mumbled, shaking her head.

"It might be stupid, but you're stuck going to it," I said.

Her mouth dropped open as she stared at me. "Seriously, Mom? I have so freaking much homework to do. I have an AP test on Monday I need to study for, a paper due in English, and flashcards I have to make for Spanish."

I glanced down at my watch. I had ten minutes before I was supposed to meet my fake boyfriend to sell this to the town. The house was a fifteen-minute drive from here, which meant I'd be really fucking late. But forcing Laurel to attend this wouldn't win me any points. And it definitely wouldn't win Starlight Cove any points.

I blew out a long breath. "All right, I'll take you home, but let me text Atlas and tell him I'll be late."

"I can take her," Quinn said.

"I thought you were picking up Ford at the firehouse?"

"I can do both." She shrugged. "Besides, maybe Laurel would like to enjoy some eye candy before she closes herself off to study. They usually wash the trucks at five on Fridays. If we hurry, we might be able to catch a show."

"Sounds good to me." Laurel slammed her textbook closed and shoved it into her backpack. "Let's go."

Alicia laughed, hooking an arm through my daughter's and heading to the front door. "You better hurry. It's a *good* show."

"Are you sure this is okay?" I asked Quinn as we followed them. "This won't mess up your plans for the night?"

She waved a hand through the air, dismissing my concerns. "Nah, it's fine. Besides, making my husband wait tends to have fantastic results for me."

I breathed out a laugh. "If you're sure."

"I am. You just go enjoy your date with your new man. And good luck."

"What are you wishing me luck for?"

She shot me a grin as the four of us strode out the front door. "You and Atlas are hard launching in front of the whole town. You're going to need all the luck you can get."

"Great." I blew out a sigh, not loving that we'd apparently be the center of attention tonight. "How big are these festivals anyway? I have no idea where to meet him."

Alicia cleared her throat. "I don't think that's going to be a problem."

"Yeah, I figured it wasn't big enough that I'd get lost."

"No, I'm pretty sure she means because your *boyfriend* is here," Laurel said.

"My wh—" My words cut off as I turned toward her, my

gaze snagging on Mr. Tall, Dark, and Grumpy leaning against his SUV.

And damn, he looked good in his worn jeans, a white T-shirt that clung to his broad chest, and an open flannel. Looking every bit of that grouchy lumberjack I'd first pegged him as.

Had he somehow gotten *hotter* since I'd last seen him?

"Atlas. What are you doing here?"

He swept his gaze over me in a slow, unhurried path, the move sending shivers down my spine. Once he was apparently satisfied I was in one piece, he lifted his gaze to mine and pushed off the side of his SUV. He strode toward me with purposeful steps. And with his focused gaze directed solely on me, it was hard to remember this wasn't real.

Definitely not the way he was looking at me, as if I was his to take care of. His to protect.

"This is our first public date," he said. "Did you think I was going to let you meet me there?"

"Um...yeah?"

"Doesn't seem like he's real interested in that idea, Mom."

Atlas peeled his gaze away from me for the first time and glanced to my right, finally noticing Quinn, Alicia, and Laurel hanging on our every word. Okay, it was mostly Quinn and Alicia. My daughter looked like she wanted to be anywhere but here.

Atlas grunted out what was probably supposed to pass as a greeting. "You coming with, kid?"

"Not even if you paid me." Then Laurel got a calculating

look in her eye and raised a brow at Atlas. "*Would* you pay me?"

"Don't be a brat," I said before he could answer, because knowing him, he'd probably agree. "You can come with us out of the kindness of your heart, or Quinn can take you home. Those are your options."

"See ya," she said without hesitation. "Hope the hard launch goes *great*."

"I want to say ditto, but it sounded a lot more sarcastic coming from her, and I actually mean it." Quinn reached out and squeezed my arm. "Let me know how it goes."

"I expect a full report on Monday!" Alicia said with a wave.

Quinn and Laurel walked to Quinn's car while Alicia headed to hers, leaving me behind with this behemoth of a man and enough chemistry between us to power a small country. Yeah, so time away *definitely* did not help. If anything, it only seemed to make this thing between us more potent.

"You ready?" he asked, his voice gruff.

It was like jumper cables had been attached to my nipples. They perked up immediately at the sound.

"Not even a little." I crossed my arms over my chest in an effort to hide my reaction to him. "Let's go."

CHAPTER TWENTY-FOUR

ATLAS

I DIDN'T DO FESTIVALS. Besides the fact that Starlight Cove had three thousand of them a year, there was also all the shit you had to do at these fucking things. Face painting. Bobbing for apples. Corn mazes, eating contests, hayrides. I'd decided to just swear off them entirely and save myself the irritation.

But the football team was hosting a fundraiser this year, which meant I didn't have the option to skip it. And, by extension, Sutton didn't either.

I'd spent the week assuming my fuckup had been inviting her to move in with me, so I'd been putting as much space between us as possible. It turned out my *actual* fuckup had been thinking that time away from her would somehow help. Hopefully dull this attraction between us.

Well, I'd fucked myself, because being away from her had only accomplished the opposite. My body somehow craved her even more now, as if it was making up for lost time. I kept sneaking glances at her, which only pissed me off further. Especially when I couldn't seem to help myself.

"You look like you're on your way to your own funeral." Sutton gave me a brief once-over. "It's not instilling a lot of confidence in me that I'm going to enjoy myself tonight. You do remember attending was your stipulation, right?"

Better she think my foul mood was solely because of this festival and not because of how she turned me inside out simply by existing.

"Not by choice," I grumbled.

"Well, I have the perfect idea to get that stick out of your ass."

"I don't have a stick up my ass."

"No? Then you're going to *love* a hayride." She tugged me to a stop and gestured toward the trailer filled with hay bales, a huge grin on her face.

"Not happening," I said, planting my feet and crossing my arms over my chest.

She tipped her head to the side. "And here I thought you didn't have a stick up your ass."

"I don't. I just don't want to—"

"Have any fun?"

"She's right, Coach," Mabel called from her perch in the back. Her husband, George, sat in the driver's seat of the tractor, looking for the entire world like he'd rather be anywhere else. "And at a perfect time too. You get the whole trailer to yourselves!" She leaned toward us, cupping a hand around her mouth and whisper-shouted, "I won't even charge you!"

"You hear that, big guy? Not just a hayride, a *free* hayride. How can you say no to that?"

I didn't know if it was the sparkle in Sutton's eyes, that sexy-as-fuck teasing smirk she shot my way, or how her hand felt in mine as she tugged me along, but I didn't put up a fight.

"Let's show the kids you can have some fun and that their moniker of Coach Asshole doesn't quite fit," she said.

I snapped my head toward her, blindly following wherever she led me. "They call me Coach *what?*"

Her low, sultry laugh made my dick twitch, a memory from that night in the hotel room slamming into me. Her on her hands and knees, crawling toward me on the bed, her laugh sweeping over me as she tugged open the fly of my—

"Off we go, Georgie." Mabel's words tugged me out of my memory, and I glanced around, realizing that while I'd been trapped in sexual Nirvana, Sutton had somehow managed to guide me on to the worst activity at the festival, bar none.

I hated these goddamn things. Because A, they were fucking stupid. B, I wasn't a ten-year-old child. And C, I was too goddamn big for something like this. I took up three-quarters of the bale without even trying, which left Sutton plastered to my side just so she wouldn't fall off—something I didn't mind but definitely shouldn't be enjoying as much as I was.

"This is such a treat!" Mabel said with a clap of her hands. "I don't believe I've ever seen you at a festival, Atlas. What was it you called them? 'A waste of time and city dollars'?"

I crossed my arms and shot her a scowl. "I never said that."

"I don't know, it sure sounds like you." Sutton bumped her shoulder into my arm, shooting me a smirk.

Mabel hummed in agreement. "Oh, honey, the things I've heard this young man complain about would keep us talking for *hours*."

"Is that your way of telling me he's always been a grump?"

"Since he was just a boy," Mabel confirmed with a nod. "Some might think you two aren't a good match because of that, but there's no denying your chemistry. That kiss—*whew!*" She fanned herself and winked. "I don't think a soul alive could deny the attraction between you two lovebirds."

Sutton shifted against me, no doubt recalling the kiss Mabel was referring to. Not to mention everything that had happened after. How Sutton had come against my tongue, then again on my cock, all before I'd settled as deep as I could and filled her up.

Fucking Christ.

I needed to stop that train of thought immediately. My cock was already at half-mast, and the last thing I needed right now was to be sporting full wood while trapped on this godforsaken ride with Mabel as witness.

George took us throughout downtown. And he drove this tractor about as well as he drove his car, which wasn't saying much. He steered us directly over a giant pothole, causing the entire back end to lurch and sending Sutton scrambling.

She yelped, her hands flying out as she tried to gain purchase and not fall off the tiny portion of the hay bale she occupied. On reflex, I wrapped my arm around her, palming her hip as I tugged her into my side.

"Aww," Mabel cooed, her eyes alight as she watched Sutton and me. "I just *knew* you were a big teddy bear, Atlas."

Sutton blew out a long sigh. "All right. I'll tell the kids at school they can't call you Coach Asshole anymore." She rested her hand on my stomach, low enough that my troublemaker dick perked up even more at her touch. "At least, not *all* the time. But I'll be honest, sometimes you really do deserve it."

Mabel cackled. "Right you are, Sutton. I was just tickled pink when I found out you two were an item! I was a little surprised at first, what with Atlas being the big mean one in town, and you being, well, not. But I can see it now. Very Brady and Luna. Have you met the sheriff and his wife?"

Sutton shook her head. "Not yet."

"I think you'd really get along with Luna. And the sheriff? Well, he's kind of like this one." Mabel hooked a thumb toward me. "Grumpy and growly on the outside but protective and sweet when it comes to his woman."

"Oh, I'm not—" She snapped her mouth shut when I squeezed her hip in warning, having no doubt she was about to slip and say she wasn't mine.

And I had no fucking idea why the hell a true statement had uneasiness churning in my gut, but I shoved the feeling aside. Bottled it up like every other confusing emotion I felt around this woman, which was turning out to be a whole fucking lot.

A gust of wind shook the trees as the leaves rattled,

raining down around us, and Sutton shuddered beneath my arm.

I stared down at her with a frown, already shrugging out of my flannel. "Where's your coat?"

"In my car."

"Why didn't you grab it?"

She lifted a brow. "Someone kidnapped me before I had the chance."

"Put this on," I said, already wrapping my shirt around her shoulders. Hating how much I loved how she looked in my clothes.

"Well, isn't that sweet? I bet he's a doll behind closed doors, isn't he?" Mabel asked.

"Oh, definitely," Sutton said with a heavy dose of sarcasm Mabel didn't seem to pick up.

"I just knew it! Tell me, what's the most surprising thing he's done?"

As soon as Sutton glanced up at me, a mischievous glint in her eye, I knew I was fucked.

"Well," she said, leaning toward Mabel as if she was about to spill the juiciest gossip. "Before I agreed to move in with him, he showed up outside my bedroom window, holding his phone over his head while it blasted 'Pony' by Ginuwine."

"No!" Mabel gasped, her eyes wide and full of interest.

"Yes," Sutton confirmed with a nod.

I shot her a scowl. "I don't think that's quite—"

She pressed her finger against my lips, silencing me, her eyes sparkling. "It was, pookie. There's no reason to be embarrassed. I was the only one who saw your Magic Mike impression." Turning back to Mabel, she said, "It was a little over the top, but I overlooked it. How could I not? When he rolls those hips like that..." Sutton fanned herself like the troublemaking instigator she was. "You won't tell anyone that, will you?"

"I would never," Mabel promised, a hand to her chest. "Well, no more than just my dear, closest friends anyway."

Yeah, her dear, closest friends who had a subscription to the *Starlight Cove Gazette* and who subscribed to her social media channels to get alerts anytime she went live. Not to mention everyone in the book club, including my mom. If small-town gossip were a sport, Mabel would take gold every fucking time.

"Well, we're all friends in a small town, right?" Sutton shot me another evil grin, living up to every bit of her nickname. "There was also the time he—"

I squeezed her hip hard, stealing her words as I leaned down to whisper in her ear, "Careful, trouble. Or I'll have to find another way to stop you from running that mouth of yours."

I didn't mean for my words to sound suggestive, but from the look she gave me as she rested her hand on my chest, there was no doubt they did. Unable to help myself, I dropped my gaze to her lips, remembering how soft they were. How she'd teased me, her teeth grazing my bottom lip, her tongue sliding against mine. That tiny little moan she always breathed straight into my mouth when we kissed.

And fuck me, but I wanted that again. Wanted to taste her. Wanted to—

"My *goodness*, things are sure heating up in here! I hope

you two are finding some privacy even with Laurel around." Mabel leaned forward, dropping her voice to a conspiratorial whisper. "And that you're getting use of your purchase, Sutton. Toys are always more fun when played with together!"

I snapped my head toward Sutton, who was working awfully hard to avoid my gaze. That alone told me everything I needed to know. At some point since she'd moved to town, she'd purchased a little something from Starlight Cove's sex toy dealer.

And I desperately wanted to know what it was.

CHAPTER TWENTY-FIVE

SUTTON

I DIDN'T KNOW how sitting on a hay bale in a trailer being pulled by a tractor could manage to turn me on, but there was no denying it had.

Or, maybe, *possibly*, my body's reaction had been thanks to the mountain of a man sitting next to me, enough heat pouring off him to power the whole town. But that hadn't been what lit me up from the inside out. Nope.

Instead, that honor had gone to the way he'd looked at me, as if he was fighting this pull too. And those words he'd whispered, the soft brush of his beard against my ear, had awoken *all* my good parts. Not to mention his massive hand cupping my hip, holding me to him protectively. Possessively.

And then there'd been the tiny detail hovering in the back of my mind that this festival was an event. A *public* event.

Which meant kissing was fair game.

I didn't have to be a genius to know that would be a colossally bad idea. My brain was already on the fritz simply from swimming in his flannel, his warm, woodsy scent something I couldn't escape.

Worse, I didn't *want* to.

"How long are you going to pretend to know where you're going?" Atlas asked as I led us through the corn maze.

His low, grumbly voice wasn't doing anything to assuage my not-so-newfound interest in him. And, great, just the sound of it had memories slamming into me, the filthy things he'd whispered in that same voice when he'd been inside me repeating on a loop.

C'mon, trouble. Show me how much you've missed my cock so I can slide so fucking deep and fill you up.

That reminder had me tripping over what appeared to be air but was most definitely a giant tree limb or something sticking out of the earth. Atlas reached out, quick as a whip, and steadied me. He stared down at me, his hands on my hips, his thumbs tucked under my shirt and brushing against my bare stomach. Even without his saying a word, I knew what was going through his mind. Every single thing that had been repeating in mine.

And that only stoked this fire between us even hotter.

I cleared my throat and stepped away, needing space from him. Not that it did me any good. "I do know where we're going. It's this way."

"Uh-huh," he said, his tone dry, but he followed anyway.

"Oh, like you know the way," I tossed over my shoulder.

"It's kind of part of the gig, trouble. This is the football team's fundraiser. Who do you think set this up?"

"You're telling me you willingly got involved in a town festival?"

"Again, not willingly."

I hummed, glancing over at this big, grouchy man who wore his grumpiness like armor. But in the short time I'd known him, I'd seen cracks in that facade... He liked to pretend a big game, but he actually cared. About a lot of things—this town, his players...me and my daughter.

"I don't know," I said. "I feel like the coach who happens to be a former pro football player could probably call the shots and say he wasn't going to do it if he thought it was stupid."

He grunted but otherwise didn't respond.

"And I actually heard a rumor at school yesterday. Some of the teachers were whispering about a certain someone who anonymously matches the football team's fundraising efforts and donates the same amount to every other sport, for the boys' and the girls' teams, *plus* all other extracurriculars." I turned toward him, studying his face. That tight clench of his jaw, the harsh furrow of his brow. Oh, he absolutely hated this. "You wouldn't know anything about that, would you?"

"What are you getting at, trouble?"

I shrugged. "Just that it's an awfully sweet thing for someone to do. And I'm not really sure why that certain someone would rather demand anonymity for something like that and instead prefer being called The Big Mean One and Coach Asshole. Hypothetically speaking, of course."

"Well, hypothetically speaking, that person might value his privacy and not want the entire town in his business."

Glancing over at him, I raised my brows. "Then you must really hate how much attention our little relationship is getting."

"If I were, it would only be because I'd rather keep you all to myself."

Our gazes were locked, so there was no way I couldn't see every ounce of sincerity and truth in that statement. I was so shocked by his admission, I tripped again, this time stumbling over a rogue corn cob in the path.

Atlas reached out to steady me, shooting me a scowl. "Jesus, trouble. If you don't quit trying to hurt yourself, I'm going to smack your ass. And then, I'm going to toss you over my shoulder and carry you out of here."

"Well, just so you know, that would be green."

His eyes heated as he stared down at me, his tongue slowly tracing along his bottom lip and leaving no doubt he was recalling the same thing I was—our night in the hotel. When I'd given him nothing but green, and he'd delivered.

Fuck me.

Why had I said that? All my words had managed to do was pour gasoline on this already smoldering fire between us. Now, it was nothing short of a raging inferno with no hope of being extinguished.

I hadn't realized Atlas was stalking toward me and I was retreating with every step until I backed into a wall of corn stalks. He didn't stop until my nipples brushed his chest with every inhale as he crowded me between the corn and his huge, hulking frame.

Standing so close, he blocked out everything else around me. I couldn't see anything beyond the wide expanse of his chest in that T-shirt, his shoulders looming above me, so broad and strong. And then there was his mouth and those eyes pinning me in place. Daring me to move an inch away from him.

But I was frozen where I stood, held still by the weight of his palm on my side, tucked beneath his flannel I still wore, those fingers digging into my flesh as if he could rip my clothes away with that pressure alone.

And, god help me, but I wanted him to.

He leaned down, his destination clear by how his gaze was locked on my mouth, and I was helpless to stop him. Didn't *want* to.

I knew this was fake between us. Had reminded myself of it on the hayride, but this—his body against mine, the heat of him seeping into me, his scent surrounding me and throwing me straight back to each time he'd been inside me— felt real.

It felt *real*.

And I wanted it. Was so tired of fighting it. I *needed* him to—

Raucous laughter broke through the pounding of my heart in my ears a second before Jackson and Clark, two kids from the team, stumbled into our path, jerking to a stop when they spotted us.

"Coach," Jackson said, looking like a deer caught in the headlights as his gaze pinged between Atlas and me. "Nurse Sutton. What are you two doing here?"

Atlas pinned them with a glare. "We're making sure little shitheads don't screw up the maze."

"He obviously wasn't calling either of you a shithead," I said, slipping under Atlas's arm and offering the kids a grin, even though my legs felt like jelly and I was pretty sure my panties were a lost cause.

"Yes, I was," Atlas said.

Clark held up his hands. "No shitheads here, Coach. We were just surprised to see you, is all. Didn't know you'd be here."

"Of course we're here," Atlas snapped. "It's a team fundraiser."

"And he dragged me along with him," I said

Jackson elbowed his friend in the side, then leaned in to whisper, "Told you they were together, man."

"If I'm not giving you enough work to do that you have time to gossip in the locker room about Sutton and me, I'll change that on Monday."

"N-no," Jackson said, shaking his head rapidly. "Coach, we're not— I mean, O'Reilly just mentioned—"

Before this kid could dig himself any further into the hole, I cut in, "It would probably be a good idea if you two headed out before you make things worse."

"Are you kidding?" Atlas said. "I'm not letting them run wild through here. We'll escort the two of you out."

It was over the top and unnecessary, but I read the intention behind it. Atlas knew as well as I did that if we'd had even thirty more seconds alone, I wasn't so sure those players wouldn't have stumbled on a scene that was much different, far dirtier, and completely inappropriate for their eyes.

All while we'd been tucked away in a maze without anyone around to perform for.

ATLAS HAD LACED his fingers with mine as he'd led us out of the corn maze and just...hadn't let go. I hadn't held hands with a man in longer than I could remember, and I'd forgotten how intimate it could feel. How we could have our attention diverted in different directions, each of us carrying on separate conversations—okay, it was mostly me chatting, while Atlas only scowled at anyone who'd been brave enough to talk to him—yet have this link tying us together. Anchoring us to each other.

I knew that wasn't what this was, even when my traitorous heart flipped at every squeeze of his hand against mine. It was just for show, our fake relationship on display for the entire town. I was used to the anonymity of a big city. What I was absolutely not used to were all of the not-so-subtle, nosy onlookers who didn't bother to hide their interest or appraisal.

"There you are," Mabel called from her station in front of a picnic table declaring a pie-eating contest. "I thought maybe you two snuck off to get in some *alone* time."

I didn't have to look at Atlas to know his gaze was on me. I could feel the heat of it on the side of my face, no doubt thinking about the alone time that had been interrupted in the maze. And what would've happened if it hadn't been.

I cleared my throat, desperate to steer the conversation in another direction. "We were actually just on our way out."

"Nonsense! You can't leave before the pie-eating contest. Atlas, you're a shoo-in!"

"No," he said without hesitation, his tone firm.

"Oh, come on," Mabel said. "It'll be fun, and it's to support your team! Wouldn't it be something if the coach won the whole thing?"

"Not happening."

"Don't be a spoilsport. Besides—" she shot a salacious grin our way "—I'm sure Sutton would give you a nice reward. *If* you win."

"Is that right?" Though he was responding to Mabel, his attention was on me. More specifically, my mouth.

I knew it would be a bad idea to kiss him. Possibly the worst idea in the history of the world, considering how worked up I was just from being in his presence. But I also knew we needed to sell this relationship to the town. And since my daughter's number one bucket list item was on the line, I was going to do everything in my power to make this believable.

Without second-guessing myself, I walked my fingers up his abs and his chest before hooking a hand around the back of his neck. I tugged him down, stopping when he was just a breath away from my lips.

"Winner gets a kiss," I murmured.

He released a rough sound. "There are more people than me entering this contest, trouble."

I let go of his neck and patted his chest, shooting him a grin. "Well then, you better win."

He stared at me for two beats before stalking over to Mabel without another word.

As I watched him take his place at the table amid others half his size and listen as Mabel recited the rules, I realized I'd really screwed myself when I hadn't thought this through.

And I also hadn't counted on how the sight of him devouring the pie as if it were as easy as breathing would remind me what it had been like to watch him devour *me*.

A shiver shot through my body, my clit tingling with the memory of his tongue circling it as he'd stared up at me from between my thighs. How many times he'd made me come against his mouth—again and again and again, as if he'd been starving for everything I could give him.

I was so lost in my memories, I didn't even realize the contest had ended or that Atlas had won and even had time to wipe the mess off his face. At least not until he stalked toward me, his eyes hot and hungry, his intent clear.

He was coming to collect his prize.

"I don't know what has you looking like you want to climb up and ride me right here where anyone can see, but it's time to pay up, trouble," he said once he reached me. "You promised the winner a kiss, and I'm cashing in."

I had no idea how many people were around. If anyone was even paying attention to us. If any eyes were on us at all. I should have been. That was the entire point of this fiasco— to make sure people *believed* we were a couple.

But in that moment, when Atlas hauled me against him with a hand on my ass, his other wrapping around my nape, I couldn't think of anything else but him. I'd made the stupid rule that only public kisses were allowed. I knew it was for the best—a definitive line in the sand.

I also knew I had no intention of wasting this opportunity.

Atlas didn't hesitate for even a second. As if he was just as desperate for this as I was. He lowered his mouth to mine, his lips hot and hungry, his tongue caressing my bottom lip before slipping inside to brush against my own. I wasn't sure whose groan I heard—his or mine, or maybe it was both of ours combined. I was too lost in the kiss to care.

Just like always when we were together, everything around me disappeared. The sounds of the festival melted away. The hum of voices and the feeling of everyone's eyes on us ceased to exist.

All I could focus on was Atlas—the grip of his hands tightening impossibly against my ass, the heat of his body seeping into mine, and the solid, immovable wall of him like a shield between me and everything else.

It was a heady feeling to get lost in—that I was his to protect. His to cherish. But that was nothing but a lie. What Atlas and I had was fake, nothing more than a ploy that would come to an end sooner rather than later.

No matter how much it felt otherwise.

CHAPTER TWENTY-SIX

SUTTON

EVEN THE PHYSICAL distance between us as I'd driven home in my car with Atlas following in his SUV hadn't been enough to dull this hum beneath my skin.

What I'd hoped would dissolve with time and space only seemed to intensify. It didn't matter if I lived in the guest cottage. It didn't matter if he was close enough to touch or if he disappeared for days at a time.

None of it mattered, because he was constantly on my mind, regardless.

If it wasn't the explicit memories bombarding me, then it was the smaller gestures he'd made since I'd moved here to Starlight Cove. The coffee and the delivered lunches and my always-full gas tank. But it was also the emergency kit he'd assembled for my car in deference to the upcoming Maine winter. And when he'd adjusted the thermostat to be warmer in the mornings after I'd come downstairs wrapped up like a burrito.

It was *him*.

Atlas didn't say a word as he followed me to the back door. Or when I pressed my fingerprint to the scanner. Or when the door unlocked and he reached around me to open it. Not a single syllable as the heat of his chest pressed into my back, his breath ghosting over my neck as he guided me inside.

He might not have *said* anything, but the way he stared at me left very little to the imagination. I knew exactly what he was thinking because it was written in every coiled inch of his body and in the hungry way he stared at me.

He wanted to bend me over this kitchen island and fuck me until we both saw stars. And I couldn't lie to myself and say I didn't want the same thing.

I blew out a breath and averted my gaze. "Don't look at me like that."

"Like what?" he asked, his voice low and rough, gravel coating his throat.

"You know *exactly* like what. Like you don't care that no one is around to witness it, or that my daughter is in her bedroom down the hall." I swallowed thickly, trying to put as much conviction into my words as possible. "Or that we've already established rules."

"The 'only in public' rule was yours, not mine."

"And it's a good one! You know sex between us will only complicate things now that Laurel and I are living here."

"We've already had sex, trouble. Several times. And if you think I don't spend half my day remembering exactly what it feels like to be inside you, you haven't been paying attention."

I leaned back, bracing my trembling hands on the edge of

the counter, and shook my head. "See? That's what I mean. I can't do this with you."

"No?" he asked, stalking toward me until he braced his hands on either side of mine. "So you don't want me to lift you onto this island, sit down on that stool, and dine on my favorite meal? Make you come over and over again against my tongue until you beg me to stop?"

I exhaled a shaky breath, my voice coming out in a croak. "No."

He hummed low, the vibration echoing from his chest to mine. "Just to be clear, you also don't want me to take you into my bedroom and give you every fucking inch your pussy has been aching for?"

"No," I breathed, the word just a whisper in the space between us.

Dropping his face to my neck, he traced along the column with his nose, the only part of himself he allowed to touch me. "Then I guess you also don't want me to use one of your battery-operated friends while I'm fucking you? Which kinds do you have? Would I be able to stuff your ass full of one while you took me inside your pussy? Or maybe I could press one of those little clit suckers against you while I filled up your perfect little cunt until you soaked me with your come?"

This time, I didn't even try to speak. Instead, I shook my head in response. Too worried that if I opened my mouth, I'd actually tell him, Yes, abso-fucking-lutely *yes*. I *did* want him to do that, along with everything else, multiple times.

Atlas's gaze pinged over my face, reading every subtle shift in my expression. With a single nod, he stepped back and tipped his head toward the steps. "All right, then. Let's go upstairs. I'll close myself off in my room and pretend you're not getting yourself off with your new little toy, and you can go into yours and pretend I'm not stroking my cock imagining it."

I WASN'T GOING to admit to Atlas that I'd done exactly as he'd suggested I would. I'd been so worked up, I hadn't even needed my toy to get me there. But I'd grabbed it anyway because I relished the idea of him imagining me doing so.

I'd fucked myself with it, the suction against my clit and the fantasy of Atlas standing in my doorway watching me sending me over the edge in less than a minute.

Usually, orgasms were my ticket to dreamland. If I was having trouble falling asleep, a quick fap session was my surefire way to get there. This orgasm, though? *This* only seemed to rev me up more, had me strung even tighter in the end.

I glanced over at the clock, the red 1:27 glaring back at me. *Taunting* me, just as it had for the past hour. Because I knew the answer to my problem of not being able to sleep was, in fact, another orgasm.

It just wasn't an orgasm by my own hand.

After tossing and turning for another seventeen minutes, I slammed my arms down on the mattress and huffed out a frustrated groan. Between an early morning wake-up, courtesy of the kitten, followed by a full day of patients at the clinic, and then a festival to top it all off, it had been a long-ass day. I was exhausted. Obviously sleep-delirious.

That was the only excuse I had for throwing off my covers, tiptoeing out of my bedroom and into the hall, and turning the knob on Atlas's door. Not even a creak broke the silence as I crept into his room, the hardwood floors cold under my bare feet.

This was a bad idea. An epic, colossally horrific idea.

He was probably sleeping anyway. All his talk downstairs had no doubt been just that—talk. He wasn't as worked up as I was. Didn't come up here and stroke himself off to the thought of me using my toy. Wasn't climbing the walls, thanks to this insatiable craving under his skin. A craving that just wouldn't go away.

He'd probably been asleep for hours and wouldn't even know I'd made this little slipup. I could just—

"Don't even think about leaving, trouble." Atlas's low rumble cut through the silence.

I froze mid-step, standing there in nothing but his flannel while I waited for my eyes to adjust to the darkness because I couldn't see a damn thing.

He, apparently, didn't have any such problem. "You think you can walk in here wearing my shirt and I'm going to let you leave before I find out what you have on underneath it?"

I swallowed thickly and turned back toward him. "That's pretty forward of you."

"Oh, are we going for subtle now? I thought you'd tossed that out the window when you opened my door." There was a rustle of fabric and then a soft click as the light from his bedside lamp softly illuminated the space.

While I'd been able to make out the vague shape of Atlas in his bed, now I had an unobstructed view of him. With his chest bare, the white sheet pooling low across his hips, he sat leaning back against the dark wood headboard, his gaze locked on me.

And my *god*, he was a sight.

He looked so fucking sexy sitting there, his hair in disarray, his eyes heavy—with sleep or lust, I wasn't sure. I wanted to stroke my fingers over the dark hair on his chest, wanted to trace that path all the way down to where that intimidating bulge taunted me from below the sheet. Wanted to use those massive shoulders for leverage as I sank down on his substantial length and rode us both to sleep.

While I'd been soaking in every inch of his glorious body, he'd been doing the same, his attention never straying from me. His gaze ghosted over me from head to toe, that bulge only growing more prominent as he did so, and I couldn't deny the heady feeling that gave me. Knowing I was affecting him.

It was all too intense. The fact that he was there, shirtless—arguably naked—and I was over here without any panties on like a fucking idiot. I'd come in here without any armor. Nothing keeping me from strolling straight over to his bed, climbing astride him, and taking that thick cock inside me.

In an effort to distract myself, I averted my eyes, my gaze bouncing around the room and cataloging everything in quick succession. The framed picture on his dresser of Atlas with three other men and a woman—his brothers and mom, no doubt—the well-worn baseball hat with the high school's logo tossed on the chair in the corner, and the familiar romance book on his nightstand, each giving a glimpse into the real him. The one he seemed to keep locked up tight.

"What are you doing in my room, and why are you still standing all the way over there?" he asked, his voice just a soft rumble in the otherwise quiet house.

Because it was infinitely safer this way.

Instead, I said, "I couldn't sleep. And I think a better question is, why do you have a copy of the book I'm reading on your nightstand?"

"Coincidence," he said without hesitation.

"Uh-huh." I breathed out a laugh and shook my head, narrowing my eyes at him. "You really weren't fucking with me that night out by the pool, were you? You knew exactly what chapter those four mobsters finally put her out of her misery and fucked her."

He grunted. "Now that we've cleared that up, come over here."

As if my body were controlled by his voice alone, I walked toward him, reveling in the way his gaze tracked my every step. My nipples pebbled under his scrutiny, the way his attention snagged on the hem of his shirt, making my clit throb.

And I hoped to god he was going to do something about that.

Once I stood next to his bed, he reached out, placing his rough palm against my bare leg, just below his shirt. "Here's what's going to happen, trouble. I'm going to slide my hand under this shirt of mine you decided to wear to sleep. If I find out you came in here with a bare pussy, I'm going to throw you down on the bed and put that sweet little cunt to good use."

My breath caught in my throat, and I had to force myself not to clench my legs together at the promise, knowing he'd feel my reaction.

"But," he continued, gaze never straying from mine, "if I find out you're wearing panties, I'll send you on your way. You can go back to your room, and we don't have to talk about this ever again. Deal?"

I should have told him no. Should've just turned around and walked out because I knew he wouldn't have stopped me. I should've headed back to my room, taken a gummy, and hoped it would finally lull me into sleep.

Instead, I said, "Let's say you don't find anything under this shirt... Aren't you worried about the rules?"

"Fuck the rules. Now, do we have a deal or not?"

CHAPTER TWENTY-SEVEN

ATLAS

WHEN I'D FIRST SEEN Sutton's frame outlined in my doorway, I thought I was dreaming. God knew I'd had enough featuring her over the past several weeks that it wouldn't be unusual.

But in my dreams, she was never hesitant. Never unsure about this thing between us. She always attacked me with the same urgency I felt.

So, when she'd started to turn, her intent to leave clear, I'd known she wasn't only in my imagination.

There was no denying how much she looked like a fucking wet dream, though, as she stood next to my bed. She stared down at me, wearing my flannel and what I hoped to god was nothing else.

It felt like half a lifetime passed in those three heartbeats of silence after I'd placed my deal on the table. When I'd given her an out, but also had given us an in.

Finally, she said, "Deal."

I didn't hesitate. Couldn't have held myself back if I tried.

I skimmed my rough fingertips up the outside of her thigh, slipped them under the hem of my shirt, and let out a long, rough groan when they met nothing but her soft skin.

I glanced up at her, meeting her heavy-lidded gaze. "Do you know what you coming in here with a bare pussy tells me?"

"That it was laundry day?"

"Nice try. It tells me I made this sweet little cunt all messy. Ruined your panties tonight, didn't I?" I gripped her upper leg, my hand spanning the width as I brushed my thumb over the silky skin of her inner thigh.

I didn't need contact with her pussy to tell how turned on she was. Her skin was damp, and the heat emanating from her cunt nearly tore a groan from my throat.

"You don't have to sound so smug about it," she said.

"But I am. I'm smug as hell, trouble. That I made this perfect slice of heaven weep without even touching it gives me that right."

"Maybe it was the toy."

"And maybe you're full of shit. Just like you were with the laundry-day excuse." I used my grip to tug her closer, forcing her to brace herself on my chest as she leaned over me. "You and I both know you could have slipped on another pair. But you were frustrated that I made you so needy tonight, weren't you? And decided to be a little brat about it."

"And if I was, what are you going to do about it?"

"Remind you exactly how I work that brat out of you."

"I don't know." She walked her fingers down my chest, her touch igniting every nerve ending along the way. "I'm just as needy as I was when I walked in here. Sounds to me like you're just talking a big game."

"Goading me isn't going to have the effect you're hoping for."

"It doesn't seem to be having any effect at all. Maybe I should go back to my bedroom and play with my toy again."

"Oh, we're going to play with your toy. And we'll see who makes you come harder."

I slid my hand around her hip and over her ass before slipping it between her thighs from behind. She let out a needy little moan when I cupped her soaked pussy, her eyes alight with interest. Then she yelped as I used my grip as leverage and tugged her into my bed. Right where I'd wanted her to be for weeks.

It didn't take long for her to acclimate to her position astride my hips. She braced her hands on my chest and ground that hot cunt against my cock, making both of us groan.

Without a doubt, I knew she was bound and fucking determined to make me lose my mind. And I wanted nothing more than to let her play. Allow her to rock herself over me, reach back and line up my cock with her pussy. Sink down and put us both out of our misery.

But she wanted to push the boundaries, and I was going to push back.

I pulled my hand away before bringing it down against her ass in a sharp smack. She let out a gasp of surprise before biting her lip, her eyes hooded as she stared down at me.

"You want to act like a brat, you're going to be treated like one. You don't get my cock just yet. First, you're going to straddle my face, hold on to the headboard, and ride my tongue."

She breathed out a laugh and shook her head. "That's not the punishment you think it is."

"We'll see about that." I eyed her wearing my shirt, looking so goddamn hot in my clothes it made my dick twitch. "Unbutton that first. I want to watch your tits bounce while you work that sweet little clit over my tongue."

Defiance lit in her eyes, as if she was deciding whether her desire to come overrode her inclination to challenge me. But her needy pussy must have been screaming at her, because in mere seconds, she'd worked open every single button and spread the shirt wide, revealing her gorgeous, perfect body.

Then, she gripped the top of the headboard, placed her knees on either side of my head, and grinned down at me. "Do your worst, big guy."

"You're gonna regret saying that, trouble."

Without allowing her even a breath to respond, I palmed both her ass cheeks and pulled her toward my waiting mouth. Both of us moaned at the first swipe of my tongue through her slit. She'd made herself come, all right, just like I knew she would. The taste of her arousal was so heady, it tore a groan from my throat.

Jesus, this girl was temptation personified. A fucking weakness I hadn't seen coming.

While I wanted nothing more than to swallow each drop of every orgasm I wrung out of her, I had a point to prove. So, I did my worst. Exactly as she'd challenged me to.

I flicked her clit relentlessly. Gripped her hips and made

her ride my tongue. Guided her to rock her cunt over my face until her pleasure dripped down my neck. Until she was *begging*.

I'd gotten her there countless times, only to pull back before she could peak. Despite her whines and pleas, I did this over and over, never allowing her to crest.

After the seventh time, she sagged against the headboard, rolling her forehead back and forth. "Oh my god, Atlas. I can't... I can't—" Her legs shook, tremors skating through her thighs as she pressed them against my head. And I fucking loved that tangible evidence of what I did to her.

I wrapped my hands around her waist, lifting her off me just enough so my lips brushed her pussy with every word. "What's the matter, trouble? Do you want to come?"

"God, yes. *Please*. Please, please, please."

I hummed against her, the vibration sending a shudder through her. "I love it when my little brat begs."

She let out a relieved cry when I pulled her back down against my mouth, swiping my tongue over her swollen clit. And this time, I didn't let up. I focused my efforts in the way I knew she needed, driving her toward the peak before pushing her straight over the edge.

Sutton came on a sobbed moan as she shook and shuddered, her entire body curving over my head as if she didn't have the strength to hold herself up even a second longer. I groaned into her flesh as I licked up every bit of her pleasure, loving her taste.

Loving even more that *I'd* been the one to make her fall.

Before the waves had finished crashing over her body, I flipped our positions, rolling her beneath me on the bed. I braced my hands on either side of her and glanced down at the fucking vision she made—hair spread out across my white sheets, my shirt open down the middle and pooling on either side of her body. Her tits were heaving as she tried to catch her breath, her nipples tight little peaks just begging for my mouth. And then there was her pussy—flushed a deep pink and so fucking wet, it took everything in me not to dive in for another taste.

I dragged my gaze back up to meet hers. "Do you think you deserve my cock yet?"

She glanced down at the appendage in question, jutting out from my body and pointed directly at her. Precome leaked from the head, proving just how fucking much I'd loved eating her out. But as much as I'd enjoyed feasting on her, it was the look of hunger in her eyes as she stared at my cock with open appreciation that nearly did me in.

"Probably not," she said. "But you do."

CHAPTER TWENTY-EIGHT

ATLAS

THIS WOMAN WAS GOING to be my goddamn downfall. And with the way she was looking up at me, her admission hanging in the air between us, it was as if she fucking knew it.

"After listening to you fuck yourself with that toy we both know is a piss-poor substitute for me? You're damn right I deserve it."

Settling on my knees between her spread legs, I draped her thighs over mine, taking a moment to appreciate the view. Her cunt was obscene like this, her clit swollen, her pussy lips soaked with her come. I gripped my shaft and slapped it against her clit, relishing in her sharp intake of breath.

"I *deserve* to slide into this tight little cunt, don't I? Deserve to sink so fucking deep since I made her slippery as hell just so she could take all of me."

"Yes, yes, I'm very wet thanks to you." She huffed out a breath. "Now, would you stick your dick inside me already?"

"In a hurry, trouble?" I ran my cock through her

drenched pussy lips, back and forth, tormenting us both. "You want me to fuck you bare again? Want me to fill you with my come?"

"I thought that was obvious." She gripped my thighs, her nails digging into my skin. I relished that sharp sting and the hunger in her eyes as she stared up at me. It meant I wasn't alone in this—she was just as far gone as I was. "You keep talking a big game, but my pussy's still empty."

I brought my fingers down on her clit in a soft smack, gauging her reaction. Just as I'd hoped, she gasped, arching her back as she stared up at me with need in her eyes. So I slapped it again, harder this time, forcing myself to hold out even though I was desperate to sink inside her.

"Good girls get my cock. Little brats get their clits spanked."

"How about you give me both?" She palmed her tits, arching her back and pinching her nipples as she rotated her hips. Teasing me. Taunting me. As if every fucking minute of every fucking day in her presence wasn't a temptation I'd been fighting against.

"You think I don't know what you're doing?" I slid the barest inch of my cock inside her before pulling out. Over and over, until her chest heaved with panting breaths, her nipples tightened so much they looked painful, and her arousal coated every inch of my dick.

"What am I doing?" she managed through panting breaths.

"Trying to get me to shove my cock so deep, you won't be mouthy anymore."

"You're right, so why aren't you doing it?"

I pushed in another inch, settling the head of my cock inside her snug little cunt. Then I braced my hands on either side of her shoulders, lowering myself until our noses brushed. "I like you mouthy."

With a nip to her bottom lip, I snapped my hips forward and sank deep in one thrust. Reminding myself in a single breath of everything I'd been missing. Everything I'd been craving. With *her*.

"Fuck, Atlas!" She gripped my shoulders, her nails clawing battle marks across my skin. "You feel *so* good."

"Not good, trouble. Fucking *perfect*. You're squeezing my cock so goddamn tight. Like this perfect little pussy was made for it. Made for *me*."

"*Yes*."

"Chapter thirty-one. Green or red?"

"W-what?"

"In the book." I cupped a hand around her neck, exerting the lightest pressure on her throat. "Green or red."

Desire sparked in her eyes before she wrapped a hand around my forearm and squeezed. "Green."

"There's my good girl."

At her consent, I tightened my grip on her, groaning when her pussy fluttered around my shaft. I didn't think it was possible, but my cock grew even harder inside her, throbbing with the desperate need to come deep. To fill her up so much, I'd be leaking out of her.

The remembered sight of exactly that when she'd been spread out on the desk made me clench my teeth, knowing when I saw it now, I wasn't going to wipe it away with a tissue. I was going to gather it up and shove it back inside where it belonged.

Then, I was going to fuck her all over again.

Her legs shook around my hips, and I knew she was close. Keeping my grip tight on her neck, I reached down with my other hand and pinched her clit, shifting my hips so the head of my cock hit her G-spot with every thrust.

"I can fucking feel you," I said, flicking her clit even faster as I squeezed her throat. "Now, let me have it."

"Oh my *god*." She sobbed out a moan, her eyes rolling as she shuddered and jerked, her pussy milking my cock.

"There you go," I said, sliding even deeper into her. "Don't expect me to go another fucking week without feeling this heaven. I'm not going a goddamn *day*. Not when it gets better every fucking time I sink balls deep. You hear me? I'm not playing around anymore, Sutton."

I slid my hand around to grip her nape and sat back on my heels, lifting her head and forcing her gaze down between us. "Watch us. Your perfect little cunt is wrapped so tight around my cock, isn't she? Taking me so fucking well. So fucking deep. You see how good we look together?"

"Atlas, please," Sutton breathed. "I need... I need—"

"To come again. I know you do. I made this sweet cunt so greedy, she can't help it, can she? Answer me first. Do you fucking see it?"

"*Yes*. Your cock looks so good inside me. Now make me come all over it." She clenched her pussy around my shaft, tearing a growl from my chest as I clenched my ass cheeks just to stave off my climax. I wasn't ready for this to end. Not yet.

Maybe not ever.

"Show me what a good fucking girl you can be, and do it, then." I brought my fingers down hard on her clit in three quick smacks, sending her straight off the cliff.

The second I felt her pussy clench around me, I clamped my hand over her mouth, trapping her scream against my palm. "That's right, baby, scream for me. Let me see how fucking much you love it when I show that brat how to be a good girl."

Her eyes were wild as she stared up at me, shudders racking her body while the pleasure coursed through her in seemingly unending waves.

But, still, I didn't let up. I couldn't. Not yet.

I sank deep over and over, loving the feel of her surrounding me, beneath me, clawing her marks into me. I was so fucking close to blowing, but I could tell she wanted more, her pussy desperate for another orgasm. And I was all too willing to deliver.

"You've got one more for me, don't you? I can feel how fucking needy you still are. Your pussy's gripping me so goddamn tight, just begging for my seed. Come on, trouble. Let go and give me what I fucking worked for."

Shoving my hand away from her mouth, she tugged me down and captured my lips with her own. Groaning into the kiss, she brushed her tongue against mine as she wrapped her legs around my waist. With her ankles locked at the base of my spine, she used that hold as leverage to take me deep.

Over and over, she rode me from below, taking exactly what she needed. And I fucking loved that she was taking it from *me*.

This time, her scream was trapped between us as I swallowed her keening cry. I slanted my mouth over hers, our tongues gliding together as she came around me. And I had no hope of holding back even a second longer.

Groaning her name, I settled deep, my cock emptying inside her as she held me tight in the cradle of her thighs.

I had no idea how long we lay like that, her legs locking me in place, fingers threaded through my hair, while she kissed me like I was the oxygen she desperately needed. And I couldn't do anything but reciprocate.

Jesus Christ, what had this woman done to me? She had me addicted to her after mere weeks, and I was tired of trying to stop it. Tired of fighting it with every fiber of my being.

So instead of sending her back to her room like I should have, I kissed my way across her jaw and down her neck. Forcing myself to pull away, I sat back on my heels, my cock slipping from her pussy, and stared down at her.

A sheen of sweat covered her, making her skin glow in the light. Her lips were swollen, her cheeks flushed, her inner thighs reddened thanks to my beard. And then there was the mess between her legs.

My come leaked out of her, mixing with her own pleasure, and I couldn't stop myself. I reached down, gathered every drop that had spilled out, and sank my fingers inside her, shoving my seed as deep as I could.

She gasped, her eyes locked with mine as I fingered her in slow, deliberate thrusts.

"I know you came in here hoping I'd fuck you to sleep, but I have bad news, trouble. You're not gonna be getting much sleep tonight."

CHAPTER TWENTY-NINE

SUTTON

ATLAS HADN'T BEEN LYING. There'd been absolutely no sleep happening.

I was sated but exhausted, draped across his chest while he traced his callused fingertips over my back. I'd lost count of how many orgasms he'd given me. I'd come so hard, tears had leaked out of my eyes. At one point, I was pretty sure I'd forgotten my name.

I didn't know what time it was and found I didn't have the strength to lift my head to look. Not when Atlas's heartbeat was thudding beneath my ear, his fingers tracing up and down my spine, that elusive sleep finally within reach.

At least until his phone buzzed on the nightstand, and he let out a muttered curse.

"I think you're the only person I've ever met who doesn't keep their phone on silent," I mumbled into his skin.

He reached over and glanced at the device before setting it back down. "Silent mode is when the disasters happen. There've been three water-related issues just this month."

"The cottage flooding is one... What were the other two?"

"My mom decided to play plumber and attempt to fix some leaky pipes by watching YouTube videos. That went as well as you're imagining."

I grinned into his chest, my mind conjuring up the kind of woman who birthed men as different as Atlas and Lincoln, not to mention her other two sons, and also got up to mischief with home improvement projects.

"Then the fridge at the bar shit the bed and leaked water all over, but Lincoln didn't tell me about it until the next day."

"Well, that was nice of him to try to handle it."

He let out a low grumble. "He *didn't* handle it. He left it to sit overnight. We're lucky we didn't have permanent water damage on the floors."

I scraped my nails through the hair on his chest, loving the almost involuntary sigh that left him at my touch. "So... what? You're always on call?"

He blew out a long sigh against the top of my head. "Pretty much."

I hummed in acknowledgment and glanced up at him. With the shades drawn, it was dark in his bedroom. But we'd been in this sleep cocoon for long enough that I was still able to make out his features. Could *feel* his gaze on me. "Let me guess. You're the oldest."

The corner of his mouth ticked up in the barest hint of a smile. "How could you tell?"

I shrugged and settled in again, nuzzling my face against his chest. "Pure luck. And the fact that you seem to take on the responsibility for literally everything."

"It's second nature by now." He cleared his throat, his words turning rough. "I take care of the people I care about."

For a brief moment, I wondered if he counted Laurel and me in that group. After all, he'd moved us in to his home when ours had become unlivable, and that showed a level of care most people wouldn't bother with.

"You do a great job of looking out for everyone else," I said. "But who looks out for you?"

He didn't answer, but his fingers stuttered to a stop against my back. That small reaction was enough to make me wonder, was there anyone? Had there *ever* been anyone? Or had Atlas always been an island all on his own—the strong one people never thought to check on?

Something fierce and protective unfurled in my chest, a sudden, overwhelming urge to be that person for him—to watch his back the way he watched everyone else's— slamming into me out of nowhere. I'd looked out for myself and Laurel for so long, never allowing another person close enough to enter that inner circle. I'd never even been *tempted* before.

With Atlas, though, I was. And the magnitude of what that might mean scared the hell out of me.

IT TURNED out Atlas hadn't meant that it was only that first night I wouldn't be getting any sleep. It was the following night and the night after that and the night after that as well. I'd never been so sated in my life. But that meant I was also exhausted to my bones.

Which was why it came as no surprise that I woke up after the fourth night of riding the King of Dicks with a migraine that was impossible to ignore. Usually, if one developed during the day, I could catch it early enough so it didn't make me bedridden. But all bets were off if one greeted me at dawn.

Every tiny movement sent a burst of pain through my head, throbbing in time with my heartbeat. After dressing in a pair of scrubs, I grabbed my sunglasses from my bag and slid them on in deference to the blinding sun. It didn't give a flying fuck about my migraine. The rays shot through the thin, white material of my curtains, illuminating the space like a solar flare.

Even brushing my teeth was painful, so I knew I wouldn't be able to suffer through taming my hair. Instead, I pulled it back, grateful it was finally long enough for a low, stubby ponytail.

Voices drifted up as I slowly made my way downstairs, Atlas's gruff tenor mixed with Laurel's softer, snarkier replies.

"There's a backlog on the materials for the cottage," he said.

"So?"

"So, you and your mom are going to be here a while longer." He didn't sound upset at that, more cautious. Like he was trying to get a read on how she felt about it.

I rounded the corner into the kitchen in time to watch him pull something from his pocket and slide it across the island to her.

"Use this for whatever you want."

She raised a brow and held up what looked an awful lot like a black credit card between two fingers. "Whatever I want?"

He grunted. "Within reason. I better not see a new car on the statement. But you can use it to buy shit for your room. You know, so it feels like home or whatever."

"Do I have a limit?"

"Do you need one?"

Laurel hummed, tipping her head to the side. "Probably not?"

"Am I supposed to feel reassured when that came out like a question?"

"So, no car. How about a motorcycle?"

"No."

"A scooter?"

"No."

"So just a pony, then."

"Do I *need* to give you a limit, kid?"

"C'mon, Daddy Grump, I'm just fucking with you." Laurel slipped the credit card into her pocket and shot him a grin. "I won't be an asshole, and you won't give me a limit."

"Fine."

"I hope you know how dangerous that is," I said, my voice just above a whisper as I braced myself against the counter.

He turned toward me, the heat in his stare replaced almost immediately by concern. He ran his gaze over me from head to toe, his brow pinching at whatever he saw. "Why are you whispering? And why the hell are you wearing sunglasses in the house?"

"It's just a headache," I mumbled.

Laurel snorted as she rinsed her bowl and put it in the dishwasher. "Right. That's just a headache like this is just a house."

Atlas turned toward her. "What's that mean?"

She lifted a shoulder in a shrug. "Mom gets migraines."

He snapped his attention back to me, his jaw clenching as he so easily clocked the tightness in my expression. "If you have a migraine, what are you doing down here? You should be—"

"Relax," I interrupted him. "I just took a magic pill, so I'll hopefully be fine by the time I get to work."

"Work?" he barked, causing an ice pick to stab me through the skull.

I cringed, closing my eyes through the reverberating throb.

He muttered a curse under his breath and pointedly lowered his voice, though there was no denying the command still behind it. "Absolutely not. You're not going to work. You're going to go upstairs and get back in bed."

"Can't. The sun shines directly on my bed."

"My room, then."

"But—"

"This isn't a negotiation, trouble." He plucked the phone from my hand and set it on the island before guiding me upstairs. "You go back to bed. I'll get Laurel to school."

"I have to call—"

"*I'll* call the clinic. You sleep this off, and let me worry about everything else."

Unable to argue, I shuffled into Atlas's now-familiar room, the light shining through the open curtains and making me cringe. I started toward them before I felt warm hands on my hips and his hulking form behind me.

"I'll get them." He led me toward his side of the bed instead of the one I'd been occupying for the past several nights before pressing a button on the remote sitting on his nightstand. A soft whir filled the room as the shades over his windows lowered, offering wonderful, blissful darkness.

I exhaled a deep sigh, my shoulders relaxing from the position they'd taken up below my ears. Then gently, so gently, he skimmed his hands under my scrub top and pulled it from my body. While I unhooked my bra beneath my tank top and tugged it out the arm holes, he slid my pants down my legs.

As if he didn't want me to suffer through even the effort of stepping out of my bottoms, he squatted in front of me and wrapped his hand around the back of my knee, lifting first one leg out, then the other.

Though I'd stood in front of him in much less than the panties and tank top I was currently wearing, this still felt far more intimate. I didn't allow many people to see my cracks. Didn't allow *anyone*, really, besides Laurel to witness me vulnerable.

It was something I'd learned growing up in the house I had—any weakness had been weaponized and used against me. When I'd left that house and my parents for good, I'd vowed never to allow anyone to do that to me again.

But as Atlas guided me into his bed and removed my

sunglasses before pressing a soft kiss on my temple, he didn't make me feel weak. Instead, I felt cared for. Cherished.

There, snuggled in his bed, wrapped up in blankets that smelled like him, I dozed off, not worrying about anything. Instead, completely comforted in the feeling of warmth that had settled over me.

CHAPTER THIRTY

ATLAS

WHEN I TOLD Sutton that I would worry about everything, I hadn't realized just how literal that would be. I'd spent the entire day glancing at my phone, hoping for an update, but I hadn't received anything from her. And I didn't dare call to see how she was doing. I didn't want to wake her up if she was sleeping. More than that, I didn't want the ringing phone to worsen her pain.

I stared at the whiteboard while my assistant coach ran through possible plays for the game against Westview on Friday. The X's and O's blurred together as my mind continually drifted back to the sight of Sutton curled up in my bed, her face pinched in pain. I fucking hated that there wasn't anything I could do about it.

"I was thinking we should run the Unicorn play. Westview won't know what hit 'em," Trey said, yanking me back to reality. He stood next to the whiteboard, arms crossed over his chest, brows raised expectantly.

Shit. He'd been talking to me for fuck knew how long

while my mind had been a million miles away. Or, more accurately, four miles away.

"Right." I cleared my throat. "Sounds good."

Trey's lips twitched. "You haven't heard a word I've said for the past fifteen minutes, have you?"

"'Course I have."

"Yeah? Then how about you draw up the nonexistent Unicorn play you just agreed to."

Fuck.

"I thought you said..." I trailed off, mentally flipping through the names of every other play in our book, but none even remotely sounded like Unicorn. "Something else."

He snorted and shook his head. "Man, I've known you for a long damn time, and your head's somewhere else today. Everything all right?"

"Fine."

My phone lit up with a notification, and I snatched it up, only to find another kitten name suggestion from Laurel, not a text from Sutton.

LAUREL:

Catalie Portman?

ATLAS:

No

Trey snorted, eyeing my phone as I set it on the desk harder than necessary. "Sure you are. That's why you've checked your phone seventeen times in the past hour. You're as bad as the kids."

I shot him a glare. "You counting now?"

"Don't get pissed at me for noticing. Bound to happen

when my usually laser-focused head coach can't stay on topic for more than thirty seconds." He dropped into the chair across from me, kicking his feet up on my desk. "Spill, Steele."

"Nothing to spill. And get your damn feet off my desk."

He grinned, linking his hands behind his head and not moving his feet an inch. "It's the new nurse in town, isn't it? The one who's staying at your place?"

"She has a name."

"I know...Alicia told me. Migraines can be a real bitch."

I snapped my gaze to his, narrowing my eyes. "How the hell do you know Sutton has one?"

"First of all, my girlfriend works with yours. Second, it's Starlight Cove, man. Heard about it when I grabbed coffee at the café this morning."

"Fucking small towns," I grumbled.

"Aren't they great?" He dropped his feet from my desk and stood. "Better get your shit figured out quick, Coach. I've got the HBCU Pipeline Program after school, so you're leading practice."

"I think I can handle it."

"Sure you can. Let me know how the Unicorn play goes." His booming laughter lingered even after he strolled out of my office.

LAUREL:

Help

ATLAS:

What's wrong? Where are you?

LAUREL:

Relax I'm hiding in the bathroom in the art
hallway

ATLAS:

Is someone bothering you?

LAUREL:

Yeah Aunt Flo

I need a tampon and some new jeans

Cami's sick today and I can't get ahold of
my mom

ATLAS:

Fuck. That's my fault. I left her phone in the
kitchen so she could sleep. Tell me what
you need, and I'll handle it.

LAUREL:

You're not going to freak out about touching
period products?

ATLAS:

I'm a grown ass man, Laurel. I can handle a
tampon. Just send me a list, and I'll take
care of it.

I COULDN'T REMEMBER the last time I'd left work in
the middle of the day. Hell, I didn't think I ever had. But I

hadn't hesitated when I'd received Laurel's text. Partially because I wanted to get what she'd asked for as quickly as possible. And partially because it gave me an excuse to check on Sutton.

For all the good it had done.

My room had still been dark when I'd cracked open the door, only the soft cadence of her deep breaths interrupting the silence. I hadn't wanted to risk waking her, so I left. But that hadn't stopped me from worrying.

It was midafternoon, which meant Sutton had been sleeping for more than seven hours. That was a hell of a lot longer than a nap. Was that common with migraine sufferers? I had no fucking idea, and I hated that I didn't know.

Now, I stood outside the bathroom in the art hallway after handing off the supplies to Laurel, waiting to make sure she had everything she needed.

After a few minutes, she strolled out, her backpack filled to bursting thanks to the clothes she'd changed out of.

"You good, kid?" I asked.

"Avoided a scene from *Carrie*, so yeah."

I held out my hand. "Give me that bag. I'll stash it in my office until after school."

She tugged it out of her backpack and handed it over with a raised brow. "You know I bled all over those jeans, right?"

"You know I coach football, right?" I tucked the bag beneath my arm. "Not the first time I've dealt with blood."

"All right. Well, thanks for being my period protector." She turned to leave, but I cleared my throat before she could walk away.

"Your mom was still sleeping when I picked up your stuff. Is that normal?"

Laurel shrugged. "Yeah. Happens sometimes, depending on how bad the migraine is. You don't need to worry about it."

I grunted in acknowledgment, but of course I was going to fucking worry about it. Especially when there wasn't anything I could do for Sutton.

Almost as if Laurel could sense I needed something to distract me, she said, "By the way, I pretended your phone number was mine this morning. So, if you get a text from some guy named Brad, that's why."

It took me a minute to catch up to the abrupt change in topic, but once I did, I crossed my arms over my chest, brow furrowed as I studied her. "Why didn't you just give him yours?"

"Because I didn't want to. Didn't want to give him any number at all, but he wouldn't leave me alone. He's been bugging me for weeks."

Jesus fucking Christ, what was wrong with the men in this world? Were their egos so fragile that they couldn't just take the L when a woman said no? It reminded me too damn much of the men Sutton had been dealing with. The fact that Laurel was sixteen goddamn years old only pissed me off more.

"What's his last name? Is it Prescott?"

"Don't know," she said. "But I'm pretty sure he's one of your players."

Considering there were only two Brads in the high school and the other one had a longtime boyfriend, I was pretty sure he was too. Also made sense, considering his mom was the one who hadn't picked up on my fuck-off vibes for five years. Brad obviously wasn't being taught consent at home. Which meant it was going to be my absolute pleasure to give those little fucks a teaching moment in the locker room.

"I'll handle it."

"Thanks, Daddy Grump." She patted me on the shoulder before heading past me down the hall. "Knew I could count on you."

Laurel's default method of communication was sarcasm, but I couldn't find an ounce of it in her tone. The realization that she *meant* what she'd said hit me square in the chest. She genuinely trusted me to handle it, without doubt.

I'd spent my whole life being everyone's problem-solver. The guy they called when shit went sideways. But her confidence that I'd take care of it without question felt different.

Heavier.

Not like a burden, but like an honor.

CHAPTER THIRTY-ONE

SUTTON

I HAD no idea what time it was when Atlas slipped into bed behind me. With the shades drawn, it was as dark as midnight in his bedroom, so it could've been 4 p.m. or 4 a.m.

With the gentle way he was trying to get into bed—a difficult feat for a man his size—I figured he was making an effort not to wake me. And as amusing as it was for him to attempt stealth, I decided to put him out of his misery.

I reached back until I brushed his skin and murmured, "What time is it?"

He exhaled what sounded an awful lot like a relieved breath and shifted closer, wrapping an arm around my waist. His bare chest was a welcome warmth against my back, and I snuggled into him. "Late. Are you hungry?"

Even the thought of food turned my stomach, and I let out a soft groan. "Not even a little. Tell me about your day."

"Not much to tell."

"No? How about we start with you giving my daughter unfettered access to your credit card?"

"It's just to get shit for her room since a fuckup on my watch caused half of her things to be ruined." He pressed his nose to the back of my neck and inhaled deeply. "I'd give you one, too, if I thought for half a second you'd use it."

Warmth bloomed in my chest at the realization of just how well this man knew me. Whether I had intended that to happen or not.

"Doesn't matter anyway," I said. "New shit keeps showing up in my bedroom, regardless."

"I don't know anything about that."

"No? Then we really need to have a talk with your grounds keeper, because I don't think it's appropriate that he's leaving panties on my bed."

"That was to replace the ones I ripped off you the other night."

"Okay, and how about the jersey with your name and number on it?"

"You need something to wear to the homecoming game."

"Uh-huh, and how about the—"

"Did you know some punk little shit won't leave Laurel alone?"

"What? Since when?"

"I don't know when it started—at least a few weeks. All I know is I'm putting a stop to it real damn quick." His words, though spoken softly, were firm, his resolve seeping into each syllable.

So...this was what contentment felt like.

I loved this little life Laurel and I had built. But there was no denying it got lonely. Would be even lonelier once she went off to college and I was by myself. I knew that was still two years away, and if my past was anything to go by, we wouldn't even be here when that time rolled around.

Still, a glimpse of my future flashed before my eyes—Laurel coming home from college to see me. But that home wasn't the cottage or some vague residence in some unknown town. It was *this* house. And it wasn't just me she was visiting. It was Atlas and the kitten of terror too.

That thought should have scared me more than it did. Should have sent me running. But I was too exhausted, my meds forcing me to suffer through what I referred to as a migraine hangover.

"How's your head?" Atlas murmured against my temple, tucking his legs beneath mine.

"Just a dull throb now. It should be gone in the morning."

He hummed and palmed my stomach, sliding his hand down until he tucked the tips of his fingers into my panties. "Maybe I can help you with that and get you back to sleep."

"And how do you plan to do that?"

"I heard orgasms relieve headaches."

"Oh, you heard that, huh?"

"I may have done a little research today."

"You have a lot of players who are migraine sufferers?"

"Something like that."

I breathed out a laugh. "While I very much appreciate the offer, being on the receiving end of one of your ground-shaking fucks is a surefire way to throw me right back into Migraineville."

"I wasn't talking about fucking you. Jesus, trouble, how selfish do you think I am?"

I lifted a single shoulder in a shrug. "You did say you didn't want to go a day without it."

"I say a lot of things when I'm drunk on your pussy. I'm not going to do anything that would make this worse for you." Lowering his voice, he grumbled, "God knows if I don't concentrate at work tomorrow, they'll probably fire me."

A smile curved the corner of my lips, and I rested my hand on top of his. "Are you saying you were distracted today because of me?"

He tucked his face into my neck, scraping his teeth along the sensitive skin. "I'm saying I want to make you come slow and easy so you can get some relief."

"What about you?"

"Don't worry about me. It won't be the first time this magic pussy has sent me to sleep with a hard-on. Now, are you going to let me make you come?"

"Nice and easy?" I huffed out a breath, knowing the likelihood of that was slim. I never got there nice and easy. "You can try."

He hummed against my skin, his voice a low rumble. "What did I tell you about that? I don't try, I just do."

Reaching down, he gripped my knee and tugged my leg back over his, opening me wide for him. Then he ran his hand down my stomach and slipped it into my panties. The first brush of his rough fingertip against my clit made me gasp and arch against him.

"Easy," he murmured. He ran his fingers up and down my pussy lips, softly stroking me until I relaxed back into him.

With relentless patience, he teased me in languid strokes,

his lips against the back of my neck as he slowly worked me up.

Finally, he pressed his palm against my clit and slid his middle finger the barest inch inside me, dragging a low moan from my lips. "See? Even soft and sweet, I can get this pussy wet, can't I?"

I hummed and reached down, gripping his forearm. Urging him to go faster, deeper. But that move also made me tense up, the answering pounding of my head reminding me why he was doing this in the first place.

"Relax. I told you I'd get you there, didn't I?"

I made a noise of agreement and once again melted into the warmth of him against my back.

"Good girl. You know I deliver on my promises, don't you? Know I can make this perfect cunt come for me however I want."

"Yes," I breathed.

There was no denying the truth of that anymore. Not when my clit tingled as heat bloomed low in my belly, that familiar peak within reach. A peak he'd gotten me to countless times before.

"I've got you," he murmured, pressing a kiss to my neck. "Trust me to get you there."

Mere months ago, that statement would have been laughable. I didn't trust easily, certainly not men.

But somehow, beyond all reason, *this* man had worked his way in. Busted through the walls I'd erected long ago, as if they were made of nothing more than tissue paper. And then he'd settled in beside me as if that was where he was always meant to be.

A whisper in the back of my mind wondered if this was a good idea. If getting involved with my landlord—the person who held Laurel's and my shelter in the palm of his hand—was in my best interest.

But before those worries could take root and grow into something I could no longer ignore, Atlas did exactly what he'd promised. With a soft circle around my clit and a scrape of his teeth at the sensitive spot behind my ear, I came.

"There's my good girl," he said, pure satisfaction in his tone.

This wasn't the earth-shattering climax of a tsunami I was used to with him—one that dragged me under whether I wanted it to or not. Instead, it was soft waves lapping at the shore, a rush of bliss rolling over me as tension seeped from my bones.

With his hand still cupping my pussy, his cock undeniably hard against my ass, he brushed a kiss against my neck. His voice was a low rumble when he said, "Night, trouble."

And just like that, I drifted off, snuggled into the only man I'd ever felt this safe with. Content with the knowledge that, for now at least, I was exactly where I should be.

CHAPTER THIRTY-TWO

ATLAS

THE LAST TIME I brought a woman home had been never, which was probably why my mom had lost her shit over the idea of me dating someone. And not just someone, but a Starlight Cove resident. Though she was eager as hell to meet my *girlfriend*, a sick librarian she'd had to cover for and a rogue raccoon causing trouble in the stacks had pushed this meet-and-greet back for two weeks.

Not that I'd minded. The longer I could put this off, the better.

"Meeting your family feels a little real for this whole fake dating fiasco," Sutton said as we stood in my mom's driveway, waiting for Laurel to get out of the SUV.

I glanced down at her—at this woman who was only supposed to be a means to an end but was turning out to be a whole fucking lot more than that. "Is that what this is? A fake dating fiasco?"

She tipped her head to the side, her gaze assessing as she studied me. "You tell me, big guy."

The problem was, I had no fucking idea. I was flying blind here, and I hated every minute of it. Hated that I didn't know what she thought about our arrangement. Hated that when I called her *mine,* it was just for show and not in response to the pull I always felt in my chest whenever she was around. Hated how much I loved that we'd taken our clear rules and broken every single one of them.

Before I could respond to Sutton—with what, I had no idea—Laurel stepped out of the SUV and shut the door behind her. Time was up.

I cleared my throat, leading the two of them toward my mom's back door. "Are you two ready for this?"

Laurel pointed at her blank expression. "My game face is on."

With a laugh, Sutton squeezed my tense forearm. "Relax. You worry too much."

I couldn't even deny that was true. Not when we were walking into the lion's den, and I couldn't do anything to stop it. Lincoln was going to flirt with Sutton just to piss me off. Declan was going to encourage him. And my mom—well, I worried she'd see right through this whole charade.

Worse, I was afraid I wouldn't remember it was supposed to be one in the first place.

"You gonna open the door, Daddy Grump, or are we supposed to eat out here?" Laurel asked, yanking me out of my thoughts.

"I'll give you a hundred bucks if you don't call me Daddy Grump in front of my brothers."

She raised a brow. "Make it a new DSLR, and you've got a deal."

"That's a hell of a lot more than a hundred bucks, kid." I pressed my finger against the scanner and unlocked the door, shooting a glance at Sutton. "Did you teach her how to be a hustler?"

Sutton held up her hands and shook her head. "Honest to god, she's been like this since she could talk."

Laurel offered me a serene smile so at odds with her personality, I nearly laughed. "Just one of my many talents, Da—"

"Fine," I cut in before she could finish. "We have a deal."

And I couldn't even be mad at her for it. Not when that serene smile turned into the self-satisfied one she usually reserved for her mom.

I opened the door and stepped inside, nearly running into my mom as I did so.

"Oh!" She jerked back before shooting a smile at the three of us. "You've been out there for so long, I was just coming to make sure everything was okay."

"We told her you probably had your hands full, dragging them in here against their will," Lincoln called from the dining room.

Mom spun around and pointed a finger at my shithead brothers. "You two, shut it."

"I didn't even say anything," Declan grumbled.

Ignoring him completely, Mom turned back to us with a beaming smile. "Come in, come in. You must be Sutton. I'm so happy to finally meet you."

Sutton held out her hand toward my mom. "It's nice to meet—"

Before Sutton could get the words out, my mom

wrapped her in a hug and squeezed. From the wide-eyed look Sutton shot me, I could tell exactly what was going through her mind. First, my mom was a lot stronger than she looked—her hugs were bone-crushing. And second, how the hell did a five-foot-nothing ray of sunshine birth a giant ogre like me?

Mom pulled back, holding Sutton at arm's length. "I am so happy to have you here. You can call me Holly."

"Thanks for having us, Holly."

"Of course, you're always welcome." She turned toward Laurel with a smile. "And Laurel, it's so nice to see you outside of the library."

"Um, yeah. Hi. Thanks."

Mom hooked her arm through Sutton's and led her to the dining room, seemingly oblivious to Laurel's stammering. But I wasn't. I caught Laurel's attention as we followed, raising a questioning brow.

With a roll of her eyes and an elbow in my side, she mumbled, "Shut up."

"Didn't say a word."

"I don't know how to meet my mom's boyfriend's parents, okay? I've never had to, so leave me alone."

Laurel's whispered admission nearly sent me stumbling. While I'd been contending with the fact that this was the very first time I had ever brought a woman home, it hadn't even entered my mind that Sutton had never experienced this either.

Something I couldn't quite name filled my chest as I stared at Sutton, watching her hold her own while my brothers did exactly what I'd known they would. While my mom laughed and Laurel smiled and everything just felt... right.

Perfect.

And when Sutton reached back to grab my hand, lacing her fingers with mine and tugging me to her side, I shoved aside the whisper in the back of my mind that reminded me this wasn't real.

SUTTON HAD HANDLED the pre-dinner small talk with an ease that was lost on me. Though that wasn't a surprise. She had a way of charming anyone who met her, and my family was no different.

Sutton sat to my right, Laurel next to her, as Lincoln smirked at me from across the table and Declan stared with disinterest.

When Mom strode in and placed a bowl of her homemade spaghetti in the middle of the table, Lincoln immediately reached for it. "Looks great, Mom."

With a quick slap to his hand, she said, "Guests first. What's the matter with you?"

"Yeah, Linc, what's the matter with you?" Declan parroted like he was ten years old all over again.

"It's Mom's spaghetti." Lincoln gestured to the bowl of pasta. "And I'm hungry."

"I'm sure Sutton and Laurel are too," Mom said. "I hope you both like spaghetti. I asked Atlas what your favorite meal was, and all he did was grunt before dashing out the door."

Sutton shot me an amused look before smiling at my mom.

"It is one of Laurel's favorites, so you made a good call. It's usually one of the first meals I make when we get settled in a new place."

"Atlas told me you're a traveling nurse. How do you like it?"

Sutton dished up a helping of spaghetti before passing the platter to Laurel. "It has its ups and downs like any job, but I'm happy with it. It's allowed us some adventures we wouldn't have had otherwise."

"And how about your next adventure? What are your plans for that?"

Sutton glanced over at me, an emotion I couldn't name in her eyes. Then she shot my mom a smile. "Haven't quite figured that out yet."

The thought of her and Laurel leaving at the end of her contract at the clinic made this boulder in my stomach sink even deeper. But maybe that was exactly what I needed—a reminder that she'd never intended to stay.

Before my mom could poke any more and ask the questions I was afraid I already knew the answers to, Sutton said, "Atlas told me you all get together for a weekly family dinner. It's nice you're able to do that."

"Isn't it? I wish Xander didn't live so far away, but you have to let your babies fly. I'm sure your parents feel the same."

I stiffened, my gaze darting to Sutton. I knew enough about her relationship—or lack thereof—with her parents to realize she probably wouldn't want to discuss it. And definitely not at first meeting.

But her expression was calm, her body relaxed as she

said, "I'm actually not sure. I haven't spoken to them since Laurel was born."

Mom split a glance between the two. "Ah. That must've been hard. I'm sorry."

"I'm not." Sutton leaned her shoulder into Laurel. "We make a pretty good team."

My mom smiled. "And now a trio with Atlas."

"That's been a nice surprise. I hadn't been counting on him when we moved to town."

"*I* hadn't been counting on him looking like he was going to murder someone in the bar," Lincoln said before shoveling a forkful of pasta into his mouth.

"I wasn't going to murder him," I grumbled. At least not in front of all those witnesses.

"Looked kinda like you were, man."

Sutton laughed. "He *does* have that look about him, doesn't he?"

"Always has," Mom said, the fondness in her voice unmistakable. "So, how are you two liking Starlight Cove so far?"

Laurel stuffed her mouth full of spaghetti and gave a noncommittal shrug. Smart kid, that one.

"She's being a bit of a teenager about it," Sutton said with a smile. "It's different from what we're used to, but we're settling in. You sure do have a lot of festivals, though, don't you?"

Dec snorted. "Too fucking many, some would say."

"Declan!" Mom snapped. "Not at the table in front of guests. And a child, at that!"

"Please," he scoffed. "Laurel's what, sixteen, seventeen? I guarantee she said worse before first period today."

Considering she'd been running around the house that morning wondering aloud where the fuck her shoes were, that was an accurate statement.

Laurel lifted a single shoulder in a shrug. "He's not wrong."

Mom raised her brows, splitting her gaze between Laurel and the not-at-all-surprised-by-that-information Sutton. "Oh. Well, then. I guess we do have a lot of fucking festivals here."

Laurel barked out a surprised laugh before clapping a hand over her mouth, her eyes wide as she darted her gaze around the table.

"*Mom*," Lincoln said in a scandalized tone. "Not around the child!"

Mom waved him off. "Hush, you."

Grinning, Sutton picked up her glass of wine and lifted it toward my mom in a silent toast. "I like you, Holly."

"Well, let's just hope you keep liking this son of mine." She tipped her head toward me with a smile. "He's not exactly the most easygoing guy, is he?"

Sutton smirked. "That's putting it mildly. I don't know if you know this, but he's a little bit of a grouch."

The two of them laughed like they were in on some joke, and my traitor brothers joined in. Even Laurel, the little shit.

"I'm not that bad," I grumbled.

Sutton glanced at me with raised brows. "You remember when I told you the kids call you Coach Asshole, right?"

"Oh my god, is that true?" Lincoln asked, splitting his gaze between Sutton and me. "Please tell me that's true."

"It's true," she confirmed with a nod.

"So you don't have fans *everywhere*, I guess," Mom said. "Thank god, or the fan mail would be even worse. By the way, I brought home the most recent deliveries for you to go through tonight."

Sutton snapped her gaze to me, her eyes bright. "I want to go through your fan mail."

"No."

Fuck no, actually. I didn't want Sutton to see half the shit the jersey chasers sent me, let alone Laurel.

"Oh, come on," she said. "It'll be fun."

"For *you*."

"Exactly." She rested her chin in her hand and shot me a soft smile. The same one she gave me after I made her come. Evil little temptress. "Don't you want me to have fun?"

I stared at her, and she stared back, a glint in her eye that told me she knew exactly what she was doing. And she was going to win.

"Fine." I shoved back from the table and gathered our plates. "But I'm not going to watch. You shouldn't either, Laurel."

"Yeah, I'm totally going to watch," Laurel said with a shrug.

Without a word, I stalked into the kitchen and tried to ignore the murmured conversation in the other room. It was damn difficult, especially when my brothers listed off some of the more...interesting...pieces of mail I'd received loud enough for me to hear.

Too distracted by Sutton's laughter, I didn't realize my mom had joined me until she laid a hand on my forearm.

"Need any help?" she asked.

"I'm good."

"You are, aren't you?" She smiled as she studied my face. "It's nice to finally see you happy."

I shot her a scowl as I loaded the plates in the dishwasher. "I'm always happy."

Pressing her lips together to hide a grin, she nodded once. "Of course, my mistake."

After closing the dishwasher, I braced my hands on the counter and huffed out a breath. "Can't believe you brought up my fan mail around Sutton."

"You thought you could hide it from her forever?" She laughed. "Besides, I don't think it's going to faze her. You two make a good match."

"We couldn't be more opposite."

"Maybe that's why it works." Mom bumped her shoulder against my arm. "And why you should let it happen."

I glanced into the dining room. Sutton's head was tossed back in laughter as she clutched an envelope to her chest and leaned into Laurel's side. Lincoln was chuckling along, and even Declan was smiling, which was usually rarer than a solar eclipse. Sutton and Laurel fit so perfectly here. With them. With *me*. As if they belonged.

There was only one problem.

"I'm just not sure it's real," I admitted quietly.

Mom hummed. "Well, I see the way Sutton looks at you when you're not watching her. Which, by the way, isn't very often. The only time you've taken your eyes off that woman is to glare at your brothers."

"They're being shitheads. They deserve the glare."

"And you deserve to be happy, Atlas." She squeezed my arm and waited until I met her eyes. "Start by trusting it's real."

That was easier said than done. Especially with a painful past that had a way of sneaking up on me.

The family we'd had with my dad had felt real too. We'd had laughter and fights and connection and compromises. With a rock star father, we'd never been a typical family, but we'd been a family, nonetheless.

Or so I'd thought.

But after a decades-long relationship with my mom, after having all four of us boys, after being in our lives for years, he left.

Walked away and never looked back.

While he'd still been around, he'd taught me a few things. To look out for my mom and brothers when he was busy chasing his next thrill. To be a rock for my family to lean on because he'd been nothing but quicksand. To stand as a shield, protecting the people I cared about most from his unforgivable deceit.

But the lesson that stuck with me the most was that nothing lasts. Not love, not family. Sure as hell not promises.

Everything was temporary.

In a blink, the people you loved without exception could decide you didn't matter anymore. And there wasn't a damn thing you could do about it.

After that, how could I trust anything to be real? No matter how desperately I wanted it to be.

CHAPTER THIRTY-THREE

SUTTON

MEETING ATLAS'S family hadn't been nearly as scary as I'd been expecting. His mom was vibrant, easygoing, and clearly loved each of her sons beyond measure. She was everything I'd wished a thousand times I'd had in a mom.

Lincoln was the same charming flirt he'd been that first night I met him. Though now I knew he did it solely to get a rise out of Atlas, and it definitely had. I'd lost count of how many times Atlas had growled at his brother to *knock that shit off*.

I hadn't been sure what to expect with Declan, considering what I knew of Atlas and Lincoln. But it sure wasn't the motorcycle-riding tattoo artist covered in ink he turned out to be. He definitely leaned closer to Atlas's gruff personality than Lincoln's laid-back charm, but he wasn't quite as serious as my fake boyfriend.

And why did that accurate descriptor have my stomach twisting in knots? Even though it was the truth, it didn't feel quite right. I wasn't sure it was reflective anymore of this arrangement that had begun as make-believe.

After saying good night to Laurel, Atlas and I headed upstairs. Even though I had spent every night for the past several days in his bed, I didn't want to be presumptuous, so I headed toward my room.

Before I could make it a step into the guest bedroom, Atlas hooked an arm around my waist and tugged me back into his chest. Without conscious thought, I melted into his warmth, releasing a deep sigh at how right it felt.

He lowered his head until his lips brushed my ear. "Don't even think about it, trouble. You sleep with me."

Then, he dropped his hand from around my waist, swatted my ass, and guided me into his room.

I wasn't going to complain. I'd gotten used to having a furnace at my back each night, not to mention the whispered conversations between us that always seemed to come a little easier in the dark. I'd also gotten used to him fucking me to sleep or waking me up with his mouth on my pussy. I was truly living the dream.

Atlas hadn't been lying—barring extenuating circumstances like a migraine from hell, he meant what he'd said. We hadn't gone more than twenty-four hours without him inside me, and I definitely didn't mind.

"Was tonight better or worse than you were expecting?" I asked as I headed into the en suite.

Atlas leaned against the doorway, arms crossed, as he watched me grab my toothbrush from the spot next to his, an unmistakable surge of male satisfaction sweeping across his features.

With my toothbrush in my mouth, I met his gaze in the mirror and raised a brow. "You gonna answer or just keep watching me like a weirdo?"

The corner of his mouth twitched—a full-blown cackle in Atlas-speak—and he walked to his sink before grabbing his toothbrush. "Went pretty much how I figured it would. I knew Lincoln would flirt with you to piss me off. I knew Dec would egg him on. And I knew my mom would love you and Laurel."

"I loved her too." I rinsed my mouth and set my toothbrush down. "And your brothers weren't all bad."

He grunted in what I took to mean, *yes, they fucking were, but I don't want to argue about it.*

"Lincoln did make a good point, though. When he said that you looked like you were going to murder Doug at the bar."

Atlas spat water into the sink, his hard eyes locked on mine in the mirror. "I don't know why that's such a fucking surprise to everyone. He's a—"

"Stalker." I rolled my eyes. "Yes, Atlas, you've said this before. Which made me wonder about the fact that Doug just left and you just let him, and that was it. You didn't dig any more into it?"

"Of fucking course, I dug into it."

"How?"

"Had my PI look into Pillow Humper."

My mouth dropped open as I stared at him. "Oh my god, Atlas, that's such an invasion of privacy."

"Are you kidding me?" He spun around to face me rather

than watching me in the mirror. "I don't give a shit about his privacy. He sure as hell didn't give a shit about yours."

"Fair point. Well, first of all, did you find anything good?"

"Besides some questionable and, quite frankly, disturbing emails between him and his mom? No," he grumbled, as if he'd been hoping for something worse just to have an excuse to go after Doug. "I think he's an idiot, but ultimately harmless."

"That's what I've been saying."

"Didn't stop me from letting him know that if I ever saw him in Starlight Cove again, I was prepared to go to jail."

I breathed out a laugh and shook my head. "I hope you didn't threaten him in an email."

"'Course not. But it wouldn't have mattered if I did. He wouldn't dare come after me or what's mine."

Those words had come so easily, so naturally, it was almost as if Atlas didn't even realize he'd said them. Or what kind of effect they'd have on me. My stomach flipped as I watched him, this mountain of a man, so casually claiming me as his.

But the real question was if it was all part of the act.

"What was second of all?" he asked.

"Huh?"

"You said first of all when you asked about Pillow Humper."

"Oh, right. You said you had your PI look into it. You do so much investigating that you have someone on retainer?"

"Not a lot," he answered gruffly. "But some."

"That sounds like there's a story there."

In the blink of an eye, Atlas's entire demeanor shifted. His body tensed up, the muscle in his jaw ticking. I'd clearly hit a nerve, though I had no idea why.

"Never mind. That's a story you don't want to tell." I tried to keep my voice light and airy, but I had no idea if I succeeded.

Mostly because it felt like this bubble we'd been in all night—the one where I'd glimpsed what a real relationship with him could look like—was losing air, and I didn't know how to stop it.

Needing something to do, I gathered the makeup I'd left strewn across the counter and stuffed it back into my bag, avoiding Atlas's gaze.

"Trouble."

Still pretending to be *oh*-so busy, I answered without glancing at him. "Hmm?"

He stepped up behind me and stilled my hands with his. Our gazes met in the mirror, and the turmoil reflected in his eyes nearly knocked me off-balance.

"Mitch has been with me since my twenties," Atlas said. "I've used him for typical pro footballer bullshit. Checking out anybody suspicious. Basic, boring stuff."

Which absolutely did not explain the haunted look in his eyes.

"That's not much of a story."

"No," he agreed. "But the reason I started using him in the first place is."

Trying to bring some levity to the situation, I said, "Is there a baby mama out there you haven't told me about? Or maybe someone pretending to be a long-lost relative to cash in? Or a—"

"I hired him to look into my dad."

Those words landed like a cement block, so much gravity in them I knew they meant more than just what was on the surface.

After spending hours at his mom's house, I hadn't seen photos or heard even the mention of a father, so I'd been curious. I'd been tempted to ask Atlas about it, but Laurel had been in the car, and I figured that was probably something better done with just the two of us. And considering his reaction, I'd been right.

I turned around, resting my hand on his chest, and looked up at him. This strong, steady man whom I'd never seen so much as a crack in, but who now looked like he was about to break wide open. "I'm sorry if I overstepped. You don't have to tell me anything."

"I want to," he said, his voice low and rough.

"Okay." I sat on the counter, hooking my legs around him and pulling him as close as he could get. "As much or as little as you want."

He stared down at me, his mouth pressed in a thin line as if he was fortifying his resolve to share. After taking a deep breath, he said, "I had a wild childhood. Spent my first fourteen years all over the world while my dad and his band toured. When I went into high school, everything changed. Don't know how or why, but we moved to Starlight Cove. My parents were both from here, and my mom's always loved it."

"And your dad?" I asked, sensing he needed the prompting.

Atlas shrugged. "He made it work. Bought the bar. Tried to do the typical dad things he'd never done before. But he still left for weeks at a time. He'd fly to LA to get his fix of the lifestyle he missed. Then, a couple of years after I was drafted, his band went on a reunion tour."

My stomach twisted, the uncertainty of what came next weighing heavily on me, and I couldn't help but anticipate the worst. There had been an accident—a plane crash, maybe—or he'd had a heart attack on stage. Something devastating and permanent that would take him away from his family. Make it difficult for them to even speak about him.

"He went on the three-month reunion tour across the country," Atlas said. "And then he just...never came back."

I gasped, unable to hide my shock. Though I wasn't sure why I was surprised. I knew better than most just how shitty some parents could be. But knowing what I did of Atlas and his brothers...of their mom? I couldn't imagine someone leaving them behind.

I wanted to tell him exactly that, but I knew the second I interrupted him, he'd stop. Clam up and put an end to this sharing session. And I wanted to know all I could about this man I'd grown to care for so deeply...so unexpectedly.

So, instead, I sat quietly, my hands resting on his hips. My silent reassurance that I was here for him.

"Three months turned into six months. Then a year... then two. That was when I'd had enough. I hired Mitch to find out what the hell was going on. My dad went no-contact. Just fucking disappeared. We didn't know if he was dead or alive. My mom was trying to hold it together, but I could see how it was wearing on her. And I wanted to fix it. Instead, I just fucked it up more."

"No, Atlas," I said, unable to bite my tongue. "I'm sure you didn't make anything worse."

He huffed out a breath and shook his head. "I made *everything* worse. I never told anyone I was looking into him. Figured it would be better that way...just in case."

"In case you uncovered something too painful..."

"Yeah. But I never thought the *just in case* contingency would be the PI finding him...along with his new wife and two little girls. He didn't leave us for his music career. He left us for another *family*. That whole time, he was in a small town in California, living the life my mom had tried to build for them here. And he was doing it without a care in the world, like he hadn't left anything or anyone behind."

Atlas's words slammed into me, each one piercing my heart and leaving me stunned. My god, not only had his dad abandoned him—abandoned *them*—but he'd made Atlas feel like their whole family was unworthy. Like he and his brothers and their mom weren't good enough.

Wrapping my hand around his neck, I pulled him down until our foreheads rested together. He closed his eyes on a heavy exhale, the weight of the world in that deep sigh. I didn't know how to help. Didn't know what to say to comfort him.

So, instead of struggling with the words that wouldn't come, I pressed my lips against his, reminding him that I was here with him now. Thanking him without words for sharing something so deeply personal with me. For trusting me enough to do so.

Of course, the soft, sweet kiss I'd intended didn't last long. Atlas tightened his grip on my hips, holding me to him as if he were afraid I'd disappear without the anchor of his touch. But that was fine with me, because I couldn't get close enough.

I wrapped my legs around his waist, locking my ankles at the base of his spine, and held him as tightly as I dared.

Even though our bodies were pressed together, his tongue brushing against mine in an all-consuming kiss, I still wanted —*needed*—him closer. Wanted to feel every inch of his skin against mine. Wanted him inside me, as close as two people could possibly get.

As if Atlas read my mind, he cupped my ass and lifted me off the counter before carrying me to his bed. We didn't speak as he shed his clothes before ridding me of mine. Not a word whispered as he kissed me all over, getting me ready with his fingers and his tongue. And only a soft moan from me and an answering groan from him when he finally slid inside.

He hooked my legs over his hips, his hands everywhere, his mouth never leaving mine. Over and over, he sank into me in slow, deep thrusts. As if we had all the time in the world.

As if he never wanted this to end.

I wasn't so sure I wanted it to either. I would have gladly stayed forever in this cocoon with him, his body rocking into mine, our lips pressed together as we breathed the same air.

But the crash was inevitable. It always was with Atlas.

I was just grateful that, this time, when I came apart in his arms, pulling him with me, he slanted his mouth over mine. His kiss capturing the three words I'd been so tempted to speak aloud. Words I knew I couldn't say.

Not when I didn't know if this was real or if we'd both gotten too good at make-believe. Finding out the latter would crush me. I just didn't know which would hurt worse—hearing him confirm what I feared...that this was all pretend. Or realizing I was the only one who'd stopped pretending.

CHAPTER THIRTY-FOUR

ATLAS

I NORMALLY HATED the pomp and circumstance of a Starlight Cove homecoming game. There was too much bullshit all around. All I wanted to do was coach some goddamn football. But I couldn't deny there was something worthwhile about experiencing it through Sutton's eyes.

I'd been on edge all day, and only partially because of the town. But being on edge whenever I wasn't near Sutton had become my baseline. If I could wear her around like a backpack, I would.

Besides that, I worried how she'd handle all this. Starlight Cove was a whole fucking lot on the best of days. But this town became an entirely different beast during homecoming.

I didn't want her to feel singled out or alone, so I'd asked my mom to sit with her during the game. It could have been the charge I felt in the air, or it could have been that I kept glancing over at the stands every two minutes, but I noticed immediately when Sutton arrived. Those fears that she would be left out were instantly squashed.

She hadn't been able to walk more than five steps without someone stopping her. Where that kind of interaction would have only pissed me off, Sutton met each interruption with a bright smile. Seeing her here, in my town, being welcomed by the people I'd known more than half my life, all while wearing a jersey with my name on it, did something to me. Made me want to climb to the top of the bleachers and yell to the entire stadium that she was *mine*.

I only wished it were true. Now, more than ever.

Especially since the other night when I'd cracked open my chest, baring my heart to her. Other than my brothers and mom, Sutton was the only other person in the world I'd shared that information with. Considering the aftermath that had followed once my family had found out, I never thought I'd be able to.

And then Sutton had come into my life, shifting... everything.

My gaze was on her when she finally sat next to Laurel, giving her daughter a quick hug. Seeing them here together, for me? I hadn't realized how much it would mean to have the support of my girls.

"Holy *shit*," Trey said. "Is that a smile?"

I immediately wiped the expression from my face and shot him a scowl. "I don't smile."

"I don't know, man. Looked like a smile to me." He elbowed me in the side. "You were thinking about the Unicorn play again, weren't you?"

"Fuck off."

And even knowing Trey's attention was on me, I couldn't

stop myself from glancing in Sutton and Laurel's direction once again.

"I *knew* it." He clapped me on the shoulder, a broad grin on his face. "I fucking knew it."

"You didn't know shit." I glanced at the countdown clock. "And why the hell are the boys still stretching? You should've shifted them to isolated position drills already."

"I'm on it, Coach. You keep making googly eyes at the pretty nurse. I'll make sure we win the football game."

I glared at him. "Stop looking at her, and don't call her pretty. Unless you want me to tell Alicia what you think of another woman."

"There's the vicious Steele I know and love. Knew that smile was a fluke."

Except, as Trey blew the whistle, calling for the players to group with their coaches, I couldn't stop my attention from drifting back to my girls. Nor could I stop the smile as I watched them be welcomed into the place I called home.

• • •

SUTTON

I HADN'T KNOWN what to expect for Starlight Cove High's homecoming game. But I knew, without a doubt, whatever I would have imagined would have paled in comparison.

The entire town went all out for this thing. Every storefront on Main Street was decorated in the school colors, the café had renamed all its breakfast sandwiches after football plays, and more than half the people in the stands had their faces painted blue or gold or both.

Thank god Atlas had given me a Starlight Cove Sharks jersey with his name to wear, and that he'd picked up a shirt for Laurel from the student store. Otherwise, we would have been woefully out of place.

The game wasn't scheduled to start for another thirty minutes or so, but it was already crowded. Luckily, Atlas had saved us a spot in the first row of the bleachers, or we would've been in the nosebleed section.

I'd never been one for football. Or sports in general. I'd never even given athletes a second thought. But I couldn't deny how hot Atlas looked standing out there on the field. He wore a dark blue Sharks half-zip, his arms crossed over his chest, brows drawn down, a scowl firmly on his face while he studied the players warming up.

I was all too aware of what it was like to be on the receiving end of all that focus. My *god*, the things I wanted to do to this man. More than half of them were probably illegal in at least fifteen states.

"You know everyone can see you, right?" Laurel said dryly.

I snapped my gaze to hers. "What? Why?"

"Um...because we're in public?"

"No, I mean, why would you say that?"

"Because you're staring at Daddy Grump like he's a Double Stuf Oreo."

"Really? Only like he's a single cookie? I thought I was looking at him more like he was the whole damn package."

"Gross," she said, though the word lacked heat.

With a quick glance around to make sure no one was within hearing distance, I leaned into Laurel's side and lowered my voice. "I'm starting to question if this thing between Atlas and me is actually fake."

She rolled her eyes. "Only starting to? I figured that out weeks ago."

"You did? Why didn't you say anything?"

"Because I didn't want you to get all in your head about it. Historically, you and relationships haven't gotten along very well." She shrugged. "And I thought this one deserved a fighting chance."

"You do?" I asked, unable to keep the interest out of my voice.

"Whatever. Don't make a big deal out of nothing."

"It's not nothing. As you've pointed out many, many times, I don't have the best track record when it comes to men. I'm second-guessing myself a little bit on this one. You see this way better than I ever do. So I want to know what you think."

"I think..." Laurel blew out a long sigh. "He rescued a kitten, even though he hates cats. He brought me tampons at school and handled my bloody jeans like it wasn't a big deal. He took care of you when you had a migraine. He scared off guys who wouldn't take no for an answer—for both of us. I think...he's actually one of the good ones."

"Really?"

"Yeah."

I breathed out a relieved sigh, reassured that, for once, my instincts hadn't steered me wrong this time. Glancing out at Atlas, I found his gaze already locked on me. That simple eye contact made my stomach flip, even from twenty yards away.

"See?" she said.

Before I could respond, someone shouted Laurel's name from behind us. I turned around, finding Cami and several other kids Laurel had become friendly with a few rows up.

With a wave, Cami said, "Hi, Sutton! Can I steal your daughter?"

"Steal away." I turned back in my seat and wrapped my arm around Laurel's neck. Tugging her close, I pressed a kiss to her forehead. "Thank you, Lolo. Now, go have fun. Holly will be here soon, and Quinn's going to stop by. Text me when you want to grab your bag for your sleepover."

"All right. I'll let you know when we're gonna leave."

"Stay sexy—"

"—and don't get murdered," she finished before heading toward her friends.

Laurel had been gone for less than a minute when someone called my name.

"Sutton, hey!"

I glanced over to find a very pregnant Addison Lockhart —formerly Addison McKenzie—striding my way with Quinn by her side. The two of them were sisters-in-law, and though Addison was the youngest, far tiniest—even with that basketball bump—and only girl in the McKenzie family, it was obvious this little force of nature was the boss of the whole crew.

"Hey, Addison." I smiled at her. "How are you?"

"Good." She sat down on my right while Quinn took the spot to my left. "I'd be even better if you told me you ripped up that six-month contract and decided to stay *forever*. It's my literal dream to have an all-female health clinic. You can't give me that for a little while and then take it away! After dealing with male incompetence for the majority of my life, I'm over it."

"Real subtle, Addison," Quinn said, and I could only laugh.

Addison shrugged. "Subtlety has no place in my life and definitely not when it comes to this."

"All I'm saying is, I've been going with the cool and calm method," Quinn said.

"Is it working?" she asked.

Quinn eyed me, pursing her lips to the side. "Too early to tell."

Addison turned toward me, her eyes bright. "How about I—"

"Addie!" Chase, Addison's husband, yelled from a few spots down the row. "Quit harassing the new nurse."

"But I need to get Sutton focused on the prize," Addison called back, gesturing to me.

I snorted at her deadly serious tone as Quinn breathed out a laugh beside me.

Her husband just shook his head and pointed to his lap. "What you need to do is get your cute ass over here before I eat the mini donuts I bought for you."

Huffing, Addison stomped her foot, and I smothered a laugh behind my hand. "That sneaky bastard knows all my weaknesses."

"The good ones always do," Quinn said.

"Work on her for me. I'm counting on you," Addison said

to Quinn before heading over to Chase, who pulled her straight into his lap.

I turned back to Quinn with one brow raised. "Is this where you beg me to stay?"

"If I thought it would have any effect on you? Definitely. We both know you make decisions on your own timetable. But just so we're clear, I *absolutely* want you to stay."

Mere weeks ago, I was certain my response would have been a resounding no. But now, hearing my kid's laughter behind me and feeling the weight of Atlas's stare at my front, I wasn't so sure. I was beginning to love this town.

Not to mention on my way to the same with a certain someone in it.

Before I could seek Atlas out, Alicia strolled up and took Addison's vacated seat. Her locs were tied back with blue and gold ribbons, and shimmering gold eyeshadow highlighted her eyes. "You ready for this? They take their superstitions very seriously."

I glanced toward the field as our players lined up along the sideline, several ribbing Atlas, who stood still as a statue, his focus solely on me. "As much as I'll ever be."

"Good, because we're up."

"Try to keep it PG this time," Quinn offered as I strode away with a laugh.

Alicia and I made our way down to the field as people cheered in the stands, many students following us as they headed toward their partners.

I strolled up to Atlas, feeling the weight of a thousand stares on my back, and raised a brow at him. "When you told me about this, you conveniently left out that the entire town would be here to watch."

He stared down at me, his gaze straying to my lips before lifting back to my eyes. "Thinking of backing out, trouble?"

"No. Just wondering if you're going to grope my ass like you have during every other public kiss we've shared."

"Figured I'd save that for home."

His casual use of the word home in reference to me made my belly swoop, and that only intensified as he stepped closer until our bodies were flush. Instead of gripping my ass, he cupped my face and leaned down, pressing a soft, gentle kiss against my lips, his eyes open and locked on mine the entire time. And somehow, that felt like more of a claim than anything else could have.

As the catcalls grew louder around us, Atlas started to pull away. But before he could get far, I pressed up on my tiptoes, wrapped a hand around the back of his neck, and tugged him down toward me.

"Good luck, Coach," I said against his lips. "How about I promise we can celebrate tonight if you win?"

He gave me another kiss as he squeezed my hip, the tips of his fingers brushing my ass. "With that on the line, there's no *if* about it."

That was exactly what I was hoping for.

By the time I made it back to my seat, Alicia was down at the concession stand grabbing us drinks, and Quinn wasn't even trying to hide a grin.

"What?" I asked.

"Nothing. That was just tame compared to the other public kisses you've shared."

"I know. He didn't even slip me any tongue." Even I could hear the pout in my tone.

She laughed. "I'd make him pay for that if I were you."

I turned to her with a raised brow. "I'm taking suggestions."

She shot me a smirk. "If Ford leaves me hanging—like he did this morning—I text him something naughty while he's at work and can't do anything about it."

I bit my lower lip, knowing her suggestion would absolutely be playing with fire. But as I watched Atlas in his element, standing there all competent and confident while he barked orders and did whatever it was football coaches did, I decided it was worth the burn.

SUTTON:

> Laurel's staying at Cami's tonight, which means we have the house to ourselves. Was thinking about taking out my new toy for a little fun. Wanna play with me?

Almost immediately after I sent the text, he pulled his phone from his pocket. I knew the moment he'd finished reading my message, because he snapped his head up, his gaze immediately seeking mine, that furrow in his brow more defined than usual.

Probably because he was shifting on his feet, no doubt feeling the *restriction* of being on the field. I pressed my lips together to hide a smile, realizing belatedly what a bad idea that had been. Not just teasing him, but doing so while he was standing in front of hundreds of people with a veritable spotlight on him. And considering what he was packing, that would make hiding his...substantial enthusiasm a bit difficult.

ATLAS:

You're going to pay for that when we get home.

SUTTON:

I sure hope so.

CHAPTER THIRTY-FIVE

ATLAS

I STRODE into the bedroom behind Sutton, her ass swaying the entire way. Taunting me, just like she'd been doing all night. Just like she'd been doing since the day she walked into my life.

"So, you decided to be a brat tonight. Is that right?"

"I don't know what you mean," she said, tossing me a smile as she sat on the edge of the bed. "I went to the homecoming game, kissed my boyfriend in front of the entire stadium, and cheered for the home team."

"Uh-huh. And then you sent that boyfriend a text that made him think about your pretty cunt stuffed with a toy while he stood out there in front of half the town."

She braced her hands behind her and tipped her head to the side as she stared at me. "Should I not have done that?"

"I could've gone the rest of my life without my assistant coach seeing the outline of my cock in my pants, but you made that impossible."

"Sorry?"

"Was that a question?"

"Kind of. Because I'm not actually sorry, but I feel like you *really* want me to be."

"What I want you to be is begging. And you're going to be by the end of the night. Go get your toy."

She raised a brow at me. "If you want to play so bad, you go get the toy."

This fucking woman was going to make me lose my goddamn mind.

I strode to my closet and pulled out several ties before tossing them on the bed. "Chapter forty-seven in the book you read last week. Green or red?"

She darted her gaze down to the pile of ties before lifting her eyes to meet mine, and there was no denying the interest in their depths. "Green."

"I was hoping you were going to say that."

I reached behind my head and grabbed the neck of my half-zip before tugging it off and tossing it aside. I couldn't lie and say I didn't enjoy how her gaze raked across me, the hunger unmistakable in her eyes.

My body had always been built for function. I'd worked hard for it, crafted it into a finely tuned machine in order to perform my job better. But even earning a multimillion-dollar paycheck had nothing on the feeling in my chest when Sutton looked at me like I was the best thing she'd ever seen. It made every ounce of hard work worth it a thousand times over.

"You've got two choices tonight, trouble." I braced my hands on either side of her hips and leaned forward until our noses were nearly touching. "You can be a good girl for me and be undressed with your arms above your head by the time I get back in here."

"And if I don't want to be a good girl tonight?"

I caught her bottom lip with my teeth, tugging until she let out a soft whimper. "If you're not undressed, I'll take that to mean you want to continue being a little brat. In which case, I'm going to use every single toy in your arsenal until your entire body feels like a live wire and you can't take any more. I won't stop until you're fucking begging for it."

She hummed, her eyes dancing with mischief. "That's quite a decision I need to make."

"What's it going to be?"

She lifted a single shoulder in a shrug. "Go get my toys, and you'll find out."

Except I didn't have to find out. I already knew what she was going to choose. I could tell by the spark of challenge in her eyes. But I couldn't say that I would mind. Not when she was wearing a jersey with *my* name on it. It wouldn't exactly be a hardship to fuck her in it.

I strode into the guest bedroom, headed for the nightstand, and pulled the top drawer out completely. She didn't have a ton of battery-operated friends—a small bullet vibrator, a clit suction toy, a combination G-spot/clit stimulator, and a vibe meant for double penetration.

When I made my way back into the bedroom, I found her exactly how I expected. Sitting in the same place, her hands braced behind her on the bed, a smirk shot in my direction. The little shit hadn't even taken off her socks.

"I was hoping you'd choose this." I tossed the drawer onto the bed, making the mattress bounce, Sutton's tits jostling with the movement. "I won't feel so bad about what I'm going to do to you tonight."

"Promises, promises."

Slipping my hand under her jersey, I glided it up her abdomen, my fingers meeting nothing but bare skin. I brushed a thumb over her nipple before tugging it hard enough to draw a gasp from her.

"Bare tits again, trouble? That tells me you were planning on being a brat before you even left the house."

"The thought crossed my mind." She hooked a leg around me, tugging me into the cradle of her thighs. "Now, what are you going to do about it, big guy?"

"Have some fun." I slipped my arm from beneath her shirt and pressed against her chest until she collapsed back on the bed.

She stared up at me with a coy little smile that made my dick even harder than it already was. "That doesn't sound like much of a punishment."

I pulled off each of her socks before undoing her jeans. I tugged them and her panties down until she was lying there with nothing but my jersey rucked up around her hips. "I said *I* was going to have fun. You, on the other hand, might shed some tears by the time I'm done."

I made quick work of the ties, binding her hands together above her and securing them to the headboard, her legs spread and hooked to the bottom corners of the bed.

And still, she smirked. "I'm surprised you left the shirt on."

I stood at the foot of the bed, the drawer of toys within reach, and glanced up the length of Sutton's body. To her strong legs, that already wet pussy, those lush hips, and then the rest of her hidden beneath a jersey bearing *my* name. "I want to know you're wearing my name when I'm making you come for the tenth time."

She breathed out a laugh and shook her head. "Ten is a little ambitious, even for you."

"We'll see."

The first one came easy. She was so worked up, she shot off in under a minute when I pressed the bullet vibrator straight against her clit.

Two, three, and four came from my fingers and my tongue, unable to stop myself from licking up the evidence of her pleasure.

Five and six came from the clit suction toy, a handy little thing I was going to love using on her while I was inside. I knew it couldn't compare to my mouth. But it would allow her the best of both worlds without inviting someone else in, because fuck knew I'd never share.

Seven, eight, and nine came from the double penetration vibrator, the larger curved end deep in her cunt, and the smaller, shorter dildo buried in her ass.

"There you go," I said, feeling like a goddamn king as I watched her come apart for me again. "Did that feel good?"

"Atlas, please," she rasped. She'd screamed her way through so many orgasms, her voice was rough and low, the sound only making my cock harder.

"Please, what?" I asked, pulling the vibrator from her before tossing it into the drawer with the others.

"I need..." She trailed off, shaking her head as much as

she could with her arms bound above her. "I don't know. I just *need*..."

I stood from the bed, undoing my jeans before shoving them and my boxer briefs off. Climbing back on the bed, I settled between her spread legs and rubbed my hand over her drenched pussy, absolutely loving the whimper she couldn't seem to help.

"You feel how messy I made you?" I used the wetness I'd gathered on my hand to grip my cock, stroking down to the base before circling the head. "I could finish just like this. Jerk off with every drop of your orgasms and paint you with my come."

She whimpered again, but this time, I heard only disappointment in the sound.

"What's the matter, baby? You need something?"

"Your cock," she said, her eyes locked on it as I stroked my fist up and down the shaft.

I'd been hard as fuck for almost two hours while I'd tortured her, and I was ready to blow. But I had no intention of coming anywhere but deep inside her snug little cunt. "The toys are nice to play with for some fun. But they don't give you what you need anymore, do they? They don't fill you up like I can."

"No, they don't. *Please*, Atlas."

"You're lucky I'm desperate to make you come for that *lofty* tenth orgasm on my cock, all while you're wearing my name." I scooted forward on my knees, draping her legs over mine, and pressed my cock against her, gliding it through her slit. "And I already told you, I love it when my brat begs."

Unable to wait even a second longer, I guided my cock down to her entrance and thrust deep, groaning at the hot fist of her pussy.

"Oh god," Sutton choked out as she arched beneath me.

Curling my body over hers, I slid my hand up to cup her throat and brought my face down to hers. Her panting breaths swept across my mouth, her gasps music to my ears.

"It better be *my* name you say tonight, trouble. Not God's." I tightened my grip on her throat, using it as leverage to fuck into her faster, deeper, the bed rattling with my efforts. "It's not God who's going to make you come on his cock, is it?"

"No," she breathed, her eyelids fluttering closed as her hands twitched above her. As if she wanted to reach for me. As if she needed to feel me like I had the pleasure of feeling every inch of her.

I sank inside her over and over as I brought my lips down to her ear. Against it, I murmured, "Whose cock are you going to come on?"

"Yours," she said on a moan, her pussy already tightening around me, her legs shaking against my hips.

"That's right. My bratty girl is going to do exactly what she said she wouldn't, isn't she?"

Her only response was a whimper, her breaths growing more ragged each time I filled her.

"Give it to me. Let me feel this perfect cunt come around me. And it better be my name you scream as you do it."

I thrust deep, grinding against her clit, and she detonated, doing exactly what I'd told her to. The sound of her screaming my name echoed off the walls while her pussy pulsed around me, her body quaking with the waves of her orgasm.

But I wasn't done.

As desperately as I wanted to fill her up, to come as deep inside her as I could, I also wanted to prove that not only could I get her where she didn't think she could go, I could go even further.

I released my grip on her throat before untying her bound wrists from the headboard. Immediately, she held me tightly, tugging my face down for a kiss while I continued rocking into her.

After pulling her onto my lap, I reached back and untied her ankles, allowing her to wrap her legs around my waist. She rolled her hips, soft and subtle, just the barest of movements, thanks to how I'd wrung out her body tonight.

She held me as close as she could, pulling away just long enough to whisper, "I want you to come for me."

"You first." I gripped her hips, guiding her forward and back in my lap, working her swollen clit against me with every motion.

"No, Atlas." She shook her head, exhaustion and need warring in her eyes. "I... I can't—"

"You can." I kissed across her jaw, scraping my teeth over her earlobe. Against the shell of her ear, I murmured, "You're doing so good for me, baby. Just one more."

It said a hell of a lot that instead of pushing back or fighting me about it, she simply melted into my touch. She allowed me to move her exactly how I wanted, her nails digging into my back as I bounced her on my cock.

Her cunt squeezed me like a vise grip, tightening around me until I wasn't sure how much more I could take. Wasn't sure how long I could balance on the precipice while I was buried inside the sweetest heaven I'd ever known.

"Fuck," she choked out before reaching a hand between us, rubbing fast circles on her clit. Seeming just as desperate as I was, she ground down hard, taking me as deep as she could, and let loose a low moan.

"There's my greedy fucking girl. Show me how much you want my come."

"*Yes.*" She locked her eyes on mine, bringing our lips together as she whispered, "Come with me, Atlas."

I growled against her mouth, holding her tight as I drove upward to meet her frantic movements. The sound of her ragged breathing combined with how tight she was squeezing me only pushed me that much closer to the edge, my muscles tensing in an effort to hold back.

With a loud cry, she tossed her head back as she shattered around me, and I finally let go. I gripped her hips, working her up and down my length in a few quick strokes, before exploding inside her.

Minutes passed as we stayed tangled together, our skin cooling in the aftermath. I pressed my lips to her temple, tasting the salt of her sweat and the tears she hadn't been able to hold back, breathing in the scent that was uniquely hers. Loving that my whole fucking bedroom smelled like it.

I used to like my space. Used to like that I came back to this empty house, by myself. That no one was here to bother me. But in a few short weeks, all that had changed.

Now, I wanted Sutton in my bed every night. I wanted to

eat breakfast with her daughter every morning. I didn't want my space. I wanted *them*.

And that was a fucking problem.

CHAPTER THIRTY-SIX

SUTTON

A COUPLE OF WEEKS LATER, I sat at the kitchen island, laptop open in front of me, while Laurel ran around like a chicken with her head cut off.

What had once been a pristine space—beautiful, but not really lived-in—now had touches of chaos everywhere. Atlas was order and routines. Laurel and I were...not. Half a dozen scrunchies decorated several doorknobs around the house, a pair of fuzzy slippers lay haphazardly next to the couch, and one of Laurel's textbooks was open on the island, her notebook and pencil next to it.

But he hadn't said a word. Actually appeared to *enjoy* how much we'd changed his space. He seemed almost too good to be true.

"I thought you said the party didn't start till eight," I called toward my daughter's bedroom. "Why are you running around like there's a bomb about to go off?"

"It doesn't start till eight, but I wanted to get there early because Cami is freaking out that Jordan might be coming.

Apparently, he and Madison broke up, which means he's available. *Finally.* And she's wondering if it's too soon to make a move, or if she should take the signs that he's been giving her at lunch that he's actually into *her* and has been for weeks."

"Wow, that is a lot of high school drama."

"That's not even the most dramatic part—Madison broke up with him because he said Cami's name when he fell asleep in class on Tuesday, and it was all over school by lunch. Madison was *mortified.*"

"I have never been more glad to be out of high school than I am right now in this moment."

"Yeah, it's a real shitshow."

"Same as it was when I was in high school. Romantic drama makes the world go round. Speaking of, anyone sparking your interest?"

"For the thousandth time, Mom, no," Laurel said, storming into the kitchen with a bag slung over her shoulder. "Besides, wouldn't it be pretty convenient for me to find someone when my class literally has seventy-two people in it?"

"I'm not saying you're gonna find the person you're going to marry. I just thought maybe you'd like to do some kissing."

"I think you're doing enough for both of us," she said dryly with a roll of her eyes. "I know you think since you two are upstairs and clear across the house, it means you're in some sort of soundproof booth, but you're not. I had to put on my noise-canceling headphones last night just to fall asleep."

I pressed my lips together to hide a smile. "I don't know

what to tell you, Lolo. We've had this talk before—when two people care about each other, they—"

"Save your old-person sex speech."

My mouth dropped open as I huffed out an incredulous breath. "Excuse you. I am not old."

"Twice as old as me," she said, not giving my feelings a single ounce of care.

"That was rude."

She shrugged before darting into the family room, picking up and tossing the obscene number of blankets strewn across the couch, clearly looking for something. On her way back toward me, Laurel picked up the kitten and nuzzled her. "Have you seen my favorite hoodie?"

"You mean *my* favorite hoodie?"

Laurel groaned. "I don't have time for this argument again. Have you seen it or not? There's going to be a bonfire tonight, and I need it."

"Check the dryer. I think Atlas threw it in last night."

"Love that big grump," she mumbled as she set the kitten on the island and headed toward the laundry room.

I reached out and scratched the sweet girl under her chin, smiling at her soft purr. "I really hate calling you 'the kitten' in my head. I wish your dad would just pick a name already. Personally, I thought Pawdrey Hepburn was a winner. But what do I know?"

Giving Not-Pawdrey one more scratch, I turned my attention back to my laptop. Laurel mentioned the photography club adviser had sent an email with an opportunity for her, and I wanted to look it over before I inevitably forgot.

Unfortunately, the kitten was a real attention whore and didn't appreciate any time she was ignored. Clearly pissed that I'd taken my scratches away, she pounced on my hand, jumping on the keyboard as she did so.

"Oh my god," I said with a laugh as I picked her up and held her in front of me. She was bigger now than the one-pound thing Atlas had found all those weeks ago, but not by much. The white fluff ball still fit in one of his giant hands, and she was damn adorable. Especially when she curled up on his chest and purred. Even more adorable was how he pretended to hate it but was clearly in love with her. "You are a menace."

I set her down on the floor and turned back to my laptop, ready to search for what I needed when the email on the screen stopped me in my tracks. The kitten's keyboard mischief must have pulled up an unread email, because I definitely hadn't seen this before.

It was from the hospital I'd interviewed at in Boston. My gaze darted across the screen as several key phrases jumped out at me.

Original hire didn't work out...very impressed by your credentials...would love to discuss this opportunity...looking for replacement by mid-November.

Exhaling a deep breath, I sank back in my chair, my mind spinning a million miles an hour. This was the job Laurel had begged me to take in the first place. The one I thought would have been the better fit for us—a bigger city, more like what we were used to, and a position in the ER, which meant a nonstop pace I used to crave.

My thoughts drifted back to what Quinn had said at the

homecoming game—that she'd been ready to hire me permanently from day one, and I'd been the one to put on the brakes. Even then, I hadn't been ready for anything other than what we'd agreed to. Hell, I wasn't sure I was now.

So much of my life here was uncertain, especially whatever was happening between Atlas and me. Was I willing to reroute my life—to give up a great-paying job with a two-year contract—for a guy I didn't know where I stood with?

I needed to talk to Quinn. If for nothing else than to get my head on straight and decide what the best course of action was. She might've wanted me to stay, but she'd be unbiased in her advice—it was one of the things I loved most about her.

I typed out a quick reply to the email, asking for a bit of time to get back to them, my mind spinning the entire time.

"Found it," Laurel said as she rushed into the room. "Come on! Hurry up, hurry up."

After clicking send, I rolled my eyes and stood from the island. "Don't even try to pretend that I'm the one who was holding you up."

"Whatever, let's go."

I threw on one of Atlas's hoodies and grabbed my purse before Laurel and I headed out. He had a few things he had to do tonight and wouldn't be home till later, so I'd planned to curl up with my latest book and gather some inspiration for our night in an empty house.

Instead, I made a detour to Quinn's to hopefully make sense of the clusterfuck that had become my life.

ATLAS

AFTER HELPING my mom with another project gone awry, I stepped through my back door. I expected to find Sutton curled up on the couch with a paperback or her e-reader as usual, but she wasn't there. The house was still and silent, except for the soft meow that came from the kitten lying on the kitchen island, her head resting on Sutton's open laptop.

"Trouble," I called out.

Her car hadn't been in the garage, but that didn't always mean anything. Not with a sixteen-year-old in the house. When I didn't get a response, I pulled out my phone and sent her a text.

ATLAS:

I finished early. Where are you?

Almost immediately, the bubbles at the bottom of the screen danced before her reply came in.

SUTTON:

Change of plans. I had to talk to Quinn about something important. I'll be back soon.

My brow furrowed as I read over her message. I'd talked to her just a couple of hours ago, and she hadn't mentioned anything important.

ATLAS:

Everything okay?

While I was waiting for her reply, a text from Laurel popped up.

LAUREL:

Pandora?

I snorted and didn't even try to stop my small smile. Shaking my head, I glanced over at the kitten. "I have no idea where she comes up with these." I scrolled back through our texts and began reading them off. "Clawdia, Jinx, Pawdrey Hepburn, Mitts, Purrsephone, Mayhem."

When the kitten didn't so much as twitch, I said, "See? I knew you'd hate them. Probably hate this latest too. What kind of name for a cat is Pandora?"

Before I could type out the automatic "no" to Laurel, the kitten scrambled to her feet and pounced on the keyboard.

Phone in hand, I looked at her with my brows raised. "Really? Pandora?"

If I thought her reaction had been a fluke, the way she did zoomies on the island, dashing across the laptop once more before leaping to the back of the couch, proved otherwise.

"Fuck. I guess that's a yes."

ATLAS:

Fine

LAUREL:

Knew you'd cave. I've had that one picked out since the first day. I just had to wear you down first.

Huffing out a laugh, I strolled around the island, intent on closing Sutton's laptop so Pandora didn't cause any trouble with it. But as I reached to do just that, words on the screen caught my attention.

Job opportunity. Impressive credentials. Mid-November. Boston.

All the air left me in a whoosh as I dropped into the seat, unable to tear my gaze away from the screen. Or the reply she'd sent.

Thank you so much for this offer. Could I have a couple days to get back to you?

I'd been tackled by some of the biggest, meanest football players in history, but not even those had felt as jarring as this. She was...leaving?

My phone buzzed with a text, Sutton's name popping up on the screen.

SUTTON:

Can we talk when I get back?

Talk about her moving to Boston. Probably wanted to know if I'd let her out of her lease early so she could make that November start date.

The pain that shot through my chest caught me off guard. I shouldn't care this much—not when the entire basis of our relationship had been built on a lie. But the thought of Sutton and Laurel walking out of my life hollowed me out in a way I couldn't explain.

I rubbed at my sternum, trying to ease the tightness there. Boston would be good for them—more opportunities, better schools, more pay. This was the smart move, and Sutton always had Laurel's best interests at heart. I'd be a selfish prick to stand in her way...to ask her to stay. For what? This small town? Me?

She deserved better. They both did.

SUTTON:

ATLAS:

No need. Pandora stepped on your keyboard, so I saw the email.

SUTTON:

Pandora?

ATLAS:

The kitten. The name was your daughter's idea.

SUTTON:

We can talk about that too. I'll be there soon.

ATLAS:

I meant what I said. There's no need. It sounds like a great opportunity for you. I bet Laurel will love the bigger city. And don't worry about the lease.

I'd let my guard down with Sutton. Allowed her to glimpse the parts of me I'd never shared with anyone else. I had no interest in repeating that mistake. Letting people in was something I couldn't afford—not when they always ended up walking away.

CHAPTER THIRTY-SEVEN

ATLAS

I HADN'T BEEN able to leave fast enough, needing to get out of my home before Sutton returned. I'd fled to the workout room in the high school, but there'd been no escape for me. My mind kept spinning back to what I'd known from day one.

Sutton wasn't the kind of woman who stuck around.

She'd built a career on being temporary. I'd just been the fool who'd deluded himself into thinking she might stay. All while ignoring the voice in the back of my mind reminding me that the people I cared about always left.

Running ten miles didn't do shit to clear my head. Hopefully some alcohol would.

It was after eleven when I stepped into One Night Stan's, not bothering to return the greetings tossed my way from the patrons inside. Instead, I walked behind the bar, ignoring Lincoln's questioning glance, and grabbed a bottle of Blanton's Gold Edition and a tumbler.

Sitting down on a stool as far from everyone else as

possible, I slammed the glass down on the bar top and poured a double shot. I swallowed it down without hesitation, then poured another.

I was a big guy, and it took a hell of a lot for me to even feel a buzz. To get me drunk enough so I could forget this day would take a fuck-ton. I just wished there were something that could make me forget the past two months.

Before I could lift the third pour to my lips, Lincoln set a hand on my forearm. "You in a race to see who can get shit-faced first? Considering you're the only one in it, I think you can slow down. You're winning."

"Fuck off," I said without heat and brought the glass to my lips. This time, I sipped the liquid, feeling the burn of the first two glasses already working their way through my system.

Linc pulled out his phone, his thumbs flying across the screen before he pocketed it and braced his hands on the bar top. "Part of the gig of being a bartender is people usually tell me why they're drowning their sorrows in a bottle."

I didn't respond. Couldn't. I was nowhere near numb enough for that.

Instead of pressing me, Lincoln just let me be, keeping an eye on me while serving other customers. I had no idea how much time had passed when Declan set his helmet on the bar top next to me, only that I was finally starting to feel a little of that numbness I'd been so desperate for.

"What the hell is this about?" he asked.

He got nothing but silence from me, just like Lincoln had. But it didn't matter, because Linc strolled over, all too happy to fill Declan in.

"Don't know. The asshole won't talk to me. I *do* know he's drunk more than his share of that three-hundred-dollar bottle of Blanton's, though."

"Right," Declan said. A pause followed, and I could feel the weight of his attention on the side of my face. Then he spun to face the bar and boomed, "We're closing early. Time to get the fuck out."

"What the hell are you doing?" Lincoln asked.

Declan turned back to him. "You think anyone else in Starlight Cove needs to see him like this? Mabel's probably already on her way over for an interview."

"I don't disagree," Lincoln said. "I'm just saying you could have used a little tact."

"That's your job, not mine."

"Yeah, no shit," Lincoln grumbled before stepping out from behind the bar. "Sorry, everyone, burst pipe in the bathroom. Regulations say we've got to close up until we get it fixed. Should be up and running tomorrow, so we'll make it up to you with two-for-one drinks."

It didn't take long before the hum of voices faded, leaving nothing but the music pouring from the speakers until even that was cut off.

"The discount for those two-for-one drinks is coming out of your cut, not mine," Declan said to Linc.

Lincoln braced his arms on the bar top and snorted. "Are you kidding? It's coming out of this idiot's cut."

If he was hoping that would provoke a response from me, he was sorely mistaken.

"Jesus Christ," Dec muttered. "Enough with the silence. I

didn't get called over here on a DEFCON 1 alert for you to sit there like a toddler refusing to talk."

"Nothing to say."

"Well, something made you think coming over here was a good idea," he said.

As he probably intended, his words only made me think about exactly what had sent me here in the first place.

I tipped my nearly empty glass toward myself and mumbled, "She's leaving."

"Who?" Lincoln asked, surprise clear in his voice. "Sutton?"

"Knew she was trouble from the second I saw her," I said.

A weighted silence descended, and then Lincoln asked, "Did she actually tell you that?"

"The email with the job offer in Boston and her reply asking to get back to them said enough."

"I'm not asking about a couple of emails. Did you *talk* to Sutton?"

"I didn't need to. I saw the evidence."

"A couple emails aren't evidence. Jesus, man, are you serious? I get, like, fifty emails a week telling me how to enlarge my dick. Doesn't mean I'm going to do it. Or need to, for that matter."

"This isn't a fucking joke," I growled.

"I'm not joking." Lincoln leaned back against the counter across from me and raised a brow. "I'm illustrating what an idiot you're being. If she's moving to Boston—and that's a big fucking *if*—the correct response from you is to start looking for coaching jobs in Boston. Not drowning your sorrows in the family bar."

"Why the hell would I leave?"

Lincoln and Dec shared a glance before Declan said, "Why the hell wouldn't you?"

"You two don't know what you're talking about." I drained the rest of my glass before reaching for the bottle to pour another.

Declan snatched it away before I could grab it. "I think you've had enough."

"And I think you should mind your fucking business. What good is having a bar if I can't drink all the alcohol I want?"

"What good *is* having a bar?" Declan shot back. "It's the same thing I've been asking for ten fucking years."

"Yeah, well, maybe you're right," I snapped. "Maybe we should just sell this fucking place so neither of you are tied down anymore. You can leave just like everybody else."

"Dude, what the fuck?" Lincoln said.

"Don't pretend to be confused now. You've been bitching about how you're drowning here, and Dec can't go a week without saying we should sell the damn thing. So, let's do it."

"You're a fucking idiot," Declan said, his face impassive even when I pinned him with a glare.

"Fuck you both. I don't need this shit. I came here to drown out everything, not have more bullshit shoved down my throat." I pushed to stand, but Declan shoved me back into my seat, illustrating just how off my game I was. I had two inches and fifty pounds on the guy, but I dropped back onto the stool like a sack of bricks.

"Dec's right," Lincoln said. "And you need to listen. Yeah, I've been complaining about drowning, but that means

I want to open the circle of trust a little bit. You know, promote a couple people who've been with us for years to managers, so one of us doesn't have to be here at all times? Not give up the whole place. And you know Dec only spouts off about selling the bar when the hot librarian has pissed him off that day. He's not going anywhere."

My shoulders slumped, the fight seeping out of me. "Well, Sutton is."

"And if she is, you should be figuring out how to go with her, not sitting here talking to us."

"I'm not looking for advice. I don't need you two to fix this."

"You sure about that?" Lincoln asked. "Because from where I'm standing, you could use a little fixing."

"*I'm* the one who fixes problems. I don't bring them to others and make them deal with my shit."

Lincoln snorted. "Yeah, and doesn't that get fucking exhausting?"

I didn't respond because I didn't know what to say. It was complicated. Yes, it was exhausting—being the only one who held things together, the one everyone counted on, the constant rock for people to lean against. But it was also a privilege I took seriously, needing to prove my worth to the family I'd let down while only trying to protect them.

"Fine, you don't want to talk? I'm going to talk," Lincoln said. "Here are some things I know that are objectively true—one, you downed more alcohol tonight than I've seen you drink all year. Two, you're mumbling some nonsense about Sutton leaving without actual proof. And meanwhile, three, she's texting me, wondering where the hell you are."

I snapped my head up, searching his expression for any sign of a lie.

"Yeah," he confirmed with a nod. "And your dumb ass is here, while she's waiting for you at home."

I pulled out my phone, my chest tightening at the number of notifications I'd missed from her. Anger, fear, and something that felt a hell of a lot like heartbreak all swarmed inside me, and I had no idea which would win out.

I'd spent forty years building walls no one could breach. But somehow, this woman had not only slipped through, she'd also made herself at home while she was at it. The thought of watching her walk away was fucking unbearable.

Unbearable but inevitable.

"It doesn't matter anyway," I said, the fight draining out of me. "Even if she's not leaving now, she'll leave eventually."

Both of them were quiet for long moments until Lincoln's voice broke through the silence. "You sure it's not you who's leaving first?"

"I'm here, aren't I?"

"Physically, maybe," Declan said. "But you checked out the second you saw that email."

"She deserves better than me anyway."

Declan shrugged. "Probably. But for some reason I will never understand, she chose you."

"I don't understand it either," Lincoln said. "I'm clearly the hottest Steele brother. And Sutton and I had a connection that night of the book fair. Before you—"

"Shut the fuck up," I growled, even though I didn't have a right to. I'd *never* had a right to—not when Sutton had never truly been mine—and that only rankled more.

"Linc's not the only one in town who's interested," Declan said like he wasn't tearing out my heart with each word. "I know half a dozen guys who are ready to shoot their shot."

"Shit, man, I was joking," Lincoln said. "That's not helping anything."

"You got any other ideas on how to get through his thick head? Because you and I both know where this is coming from."

Lincoln shook his head. "Don't say it."

"Why not? You know as well as I do, this all boils down to the asshole who left us with nothing but this bar. We're still here, while he's out there living—"

"Don't bring Dad into this," I growled.

"I didn't bring him into anything," Declan shot back. "He's been in it since the day he walked out."

I shoved my stool back and stood. "I'm done with this conversation."

"You might be done with it, but it's clearly not done with you," Dec said.

Clenching my hands into fists, I took a step toward Declan, who stood and met my glare with one of his own. Before I could land the punch I so desperately wanted to, Lincoln stepped between us and shoved us apart.

"Let me break up this little dick-measuring contest. *I* have the biggest. Both of you need to cool down." He turned to me and clapped a hand on my shoulder. "But Dec's right. If your first instinct wasn't to go with Sutton and instead just assume she'll leave, you need to deal with that shit. Before it ruins the best thing that's happened to you."

CHAPTER THIRTY-EIGHT

SUTTON

I GLANCED at the clock hanging on the wall for the hundredth time, the hands reading 12:22 mocking me. At least it was in good company, along with my phone, which had remained silent despite the texts and calls I'd sent to Atlas after his dismissive bullshit earlier tonight.

It sounds like a great opportunity for you. I bet Laurel will love the bigger city. And don't worry about the lease.

His immediate dismissal of me and what I'd thought we had was like a punch to the gut, knocking the wind straight out of me. It was proof in black-and-white that these past several weeks clearly hadn't meant to him what they'd meant to me.

Meanwhile, I'd been talking to Quinn about the possibility of making my position permanent. When Laurel and I had first moved here, I hadn't been sure Starlight Cove would be the right fit for us. But now, after building a life here—one that felt fulfilling in a way it never had before, for not just me, but her too—it was hard to imagine us anywhere else.

Taking a permanent position would be a huge leap for me. Laurel and I had traveled my entire career, and I thought it was something I'd always do. Would always *want* to do. But things changed along the way.

Of course, I never could've guessed what I actually wanted was a former pro football player who was built like a bear and just as protective as one.

I also never could've guessed that same man would throw me away with seemingly little thought.

I'd spent all night flipping between hurt and anger, the bubbles of nervousness and excitement I'd felt earlier after talking with Quinn long gone. Turned out I didn't need to try to figure out how to ask Atlas if he wanted the same thing as I did—namely, permanence and not a fake relationship crafted only as a means to an end.

He'd already decided what we had was over.

The back door lock disengaged, and I snapped my head up at the sound, steeling myself for what was coming. I heard a car drive away—probably one of Atlas's brothers—as Atlas strode in, head down and footsteps heavy, stopping suddenly when he spotted me on the couch. He looked like hell, with rumpled clothes and disheveled hair. Nothing like the stoic statue of a man he was known for being around town.

"You're still up," he said, his voice rough.

I huffed out a humorless laugh and threw off the blanket, careful to avoid Pandora, who was curled up on the couch. Standing, I crossed my arms over my chest and met his stare. "It's a little hard to sleep when the guy you're supposedly with ends the relationship in a text without bothering to have a conversation."

"Why do we need a conversation?" He scrubbed a hand over his face and heaved a sigh. "I already told you I saw the email."

"Yeah, and you also told me it's a great opportunity and that I shouldn't worry about the lease." The anger that had been simmering all night flared bright. "You decided what I was doing without my even saying a word."

His mouth tightened, his shoulders as tense as ever, but that was the only outward sign of emotion he showed. Just as still and immovable as ever.

I shook my head, a bone-deep exhaustion washing over the anger that had sparked inside me. I'd thought Atlas was different. Thought this relationship was different. But he was only more of the same.

"I thought getting involved with someone eight years older than me meant I might be getting some maturity instead of the bullshit I'm used to. Thought you might actually have a conversation like a grown-ass adult."

"What's there to talk about? You got a job offer in Boston."

"And you assumed I was taking it without even discussing it with you!"

"Why would you? That's what people do in real relationships. And you and I both know what we had was fake."

Getting stabbed repeatedly in the heart would've hurt less than those words coming from his mouth. As desperately as I tried to keep my emotions at bay, I couldn't stop the tears from welling. My eyes stung as Atlas blurred in front of me, and he made a gruff noise, a tiny crack in his facade. He took a step toward me, but I held up a hand to stop him, desperate to maintain whatever distance between us I could.

"Fake," I said. "Right. I'm glad we cleared that up. Otherwise, I would've made a fool of myself if I'd told you I went to see Quinn today to talk about a permanent position at the clinic because I was considering staying."

Surprise followed quickly by hope flickered in his eyes, but it was too little, too late. "Sutton—"

"No. You don't get to talk right now. You had your chance earlier when I asked you to have a conversation. You had your chance when I called and texted you half a dozen times, trying to figure out where you were and what the hell was going on. Instead, you disappeared for hours, all because you convinced yourself I was going to leave."

He opened his mouth to speak before snapping it shut, his jaw clenching tightly to keep in whatever he refused to say. His silence was deafening as the scent of bourbon hung in the air between us. It only served as a reminder of what he'd chosen to do instead of talking with me.

This man who'd always been a mountain for everyone else couldn't—or just plain didn't want to—weather a tiny storm with me.

"You've been waiting for me to leave since day one, haven't you? That must be why this is so easy for you to throw away—you never believed it was real in the first place."

"It was never supposed to be." His voice was hard, like if he spoke with enough conviction, what he said would be true. His words and the resignation in his tone only sparked my anger that had receded, stoked my pain because he hadn't even given us a chance. He'd given up without a fight.

And I deserved someone who would fight for me.

"Maybe not at first. But I thought, somewhere along the way, we'd moved past that. That what we had actually meant something. That *I* meant something," I said, hating how my voice broke. "I was clearly wrong."

Unable to spend another second in his presence, I strode toward the stairs. Tears had pooled in my eyes, but I wasn't going to allow him to see them fall.

"Where are you going?" he asked, as if he had a right to know.

"To pack a bag. I'll stay in the cottage."

"But it's not done—"

"It has four walls and a roof. It'll do."

"You don't have to go back there. You can stay—"

I turned to face him from halfway up the stairs, running my eyes over the man I'd come to care so much about, despite my best efforts otherwise. The man I'd come to love.

"No, I can't. Because every time I look at you, I'm going to remember this feeling in my gut. And it'll just remind me that the one time—the *one* time—I found somewhere I wanted to stay and someone I wanted to stay with, he was holding the door open for me to leave all along."

CHAPTER THIRTY-NINE

SUTTON

SUTTON:

Come to the cottage when you get home.

LAUREL:

Why are you at the cottage? Daddy Grump
said it'd be another six weeks at least.

SUTTON:

I'm not here because it's finished.

LAUREL:

???

SUTTON:

I moved back.

LAUREL:

You WHAT?

SUTTON:

Atlas and I had a fight.

LAUREL:

Whatever happened he was definitely in the
wrong

Obviously

But please I'm begging you do not make
me move back into that cottage in its
current state.

Have you seen my bedroom in his house? It
has its own bathroom!

And a huge walk-in shower! It feels like I'm
washing my hair in a rainstorm!

Have I mentioned the heated floors?

SUTTON:

I'm not saying you have to stay here while
it's still a construction zone, but you will
eventually. I'm just saying I couldn't stay.

LAUREL:

Cami's bringing me home, be there in five.

IT WAS ACTUALLY LESS time than that when my
daughter came strolling through the front door of the cottage,
her face displaying her disgust at the living situation.

"Lawn chairs? Seriously, Mom?"

"Well, it's no twenty-thousand-dollar couch, but on the
plus side, there are no dumb boys over here."

She blew out a heavy sigh, walked straight for me, and
wrapped her arms around me in a tight hug. "What the hell
happened?"

"You should sit down for this." I gestured to the other lawn chair next to mine. "It's kind of a big deal."

"Oh shit. Are we moving again?" she asked, the distress in her voice surprising.

"I don't know," I said honestly. I thought I'd had it all figured out, and that had only blown up in my face. "I got a job offer yesterday. For that position in Boston you wanted me to take."

"Seriously?"

"Seriously. I asked for a little time to get back to them, and then I went to talk to Quinn. About making my position here permanent."

"Like...*permanent*, permanent?"

"Yep."

"As in, we'd stay here, and I'd graduate from Starlight Cove High?"

"Yeah. I wanted to talk it over with Atlas first—and you know how that went," I said, gesturing to me sitting in a lawn chair in the half-finished cottage. "And you, of course. What do you think of Starlight Cove? And don't pull your punches now."

"You know I never do." She was quiet for long moments as she studied me. "I hated it when we first got here."

"I remember," I said dryly.

"But now..." She blew out a sigh. "I don't know. It's different than we're used to. Everyone knows everyone, and I thought I'd hate that. But I actually sort of...like it? And the friends I have feel like actual friends, you know? Ones I can count on, not just people I hang out with."

I felt similarly about Quinn and the women she'd

introduced me to. Her sisters-in-law and her other friends. The pool of people in town was small, but it was a tight-knit community that looked out for its own. And it had started to feel a little like Laurel and I were included in that.

"Plus, I like hanging out with you more. And how happy you've been here." She poked my foot with her own. "Tell me what happened with Atlas."

I exhaled a heavy breath, my chest squeezing painfully all over again. "He saw the emails about the Boston position and assumed I'd take the job. Told me it was a great opportunity and not to worry about the lease here."

"Okay, but he, like, *talked* to you about it, right?"

"No. He texted me what amounted to *see you around* and then went to One Night Stan's and didn't answer my calls or texts."

"Oh my *god*. Seriously?"

"Yep. When he finally showed up at home, we got into it. He said what we had was fake. That it was never supposed to be real."

Her mouth dropped open as she stared at me. "What a *dick*."

"Not the worst thing I've called him in the past twelve hours."

"You know what's going on, right?"

Yeah, I knew what was going on. I'd fallen for the one guy who was more emotionally unavailable than I was, and look where that had gotten me.

"What's going on is I'd begun to think what we had was real, and he'd been banking on it being fake the entire time."

She huffed out a breath and shook her head. "Not even a little. That man is terrified to lose you."

"He didn't *lose* me. He pushed me away."

"*Because* he thought he was going to lose you. I've seen this play out in, like, a hundred romance books. The brooding hero who pushes the heroine away because he's afraid of getting hurt? Then, eventually, the big, dumb dummy realizes what an idiot he was and grand gestures the hell out of her."

I shot her a small smile. "Unfortunately, I don't think there's going to be a grand gesture this time. Our life isn't a romance book."

"Isn't it? We're basically living in a trope factory over here—grumpy/sunshine? Fake dating? Forced proximity? *Hello?*"

I laughed, unable to stop myself and looked over at my wise-beyond-her-years daughter. "You're pretty smart, you know that?"

"I do," she said solemnly. "I've clearly spoiled you with my intelligence, so you're not used to having to deal with people who fuck up. And—to be clear—he definitely fucked up."

"No argument from me."

"But I also get why he was running scared. And I think you do too."

I did. Especially knowing what I did about his father and what he'd done to Atlas and his family. But that didn't stop the fact that I refused to be with someone who wouldn't fight for me or what we had. Who spent the entirety of our relationship waiting for the other shoe to drop. I wanted someone who was completely invested, without exception.

"So, are we staying in Starlight Cove or not?" she asked, her tone tentative.

"I had to override your vote on the last move because I didn't have a choice. I don't want to do that this time. So, you tell me...do you want to stay in this tiny town with too many festivals and without a mall for that future point in time you might like to go to one? Or do you want to head to Boston, where you begged to go in the first place?"

She sat quietly for a few moments, no doubt weighing the pros and cons of each. "I can't believe I'm saying this, but...I want to stay. I like this town with goats that roam across the street and old ladies who peddle me smut."

"Mabel?" I asked.

"Mabel," she confirmed with a nod.

I blew out a laugh and squeezed her hand. "Does your answer change if Atlas isn't in the picture?"

"No. Same answer with or without him. But for the record? I think he's going to come around."

"Don't hold your breath, Lolo."

She pressed her lips together like she had more to say but was holding it in. Eventually, she said, "You didn't tell me what your vote is. Are we staying?"

Pushing down the uncertainty that had been simmering under the surface for weeks, I took a leap that was equal parts terrifying and exhilarating. "We're staying. I'll let Quinn know I want to accept the position and tell Boston Medical Center I'm no longer interested."

A huge smile swept across her mouth, and the sight made the ache in my chest recede just a bit. "This is, like, a *huge* step, Mom."

"I know. We should celebrate tonight with some PB&J's because that's pretty much all I have over here."

She laughed. "Deal. Should I tell Atlas that we're sticking around? I mean, I'm going to be staying at his house until this place is finished, so it's not like I can avoid him."

"You don't have to lie to him if he comes out and asks, but I'm not volunteering the information. He needs to figure this out on his own."

She stood and grabbed her bag before pressing a kiss to the top of my head. "And you need to have a little faith that he will. Be back later for dinner."

I wanted to have as much faith in Atlas as Laurel seemed to have, but I couldn't. Not when I'd been a front-row witness to just how easily he'd cast me aside.

If he wanted me like she claimed, he'd have to show me that. Prove that he wanted a life with me—with us—and that he was willing to go all in. To put his heart on the line because I was worth it.

But I wasn't going to sit around and wait, hoping he'd figure shit out. I was going to continue building the life Laurel and I deserved here in Starlight Cove. With or without him.

CHAPTER FORTY

SUTTON

THESE PAST FEW DAYS, I'd gotten a glimpse of what my life would be like once Laurel went off to college. And I could say with complete certainty that I absolutely hated it.

Not only did I love my kid, but I actually *liked* her. I genuinely enjoyed spending time with her and wanted to soak up as much of that as I had left. But I also wasn't going to force her to move into a dilapidated space without actual floors just because I was too stubborn to stay in the home of the man who'd broken my heart.

The clinic closed late tonight, and Laurel had plans, which meant I was once again alone for the evening. I figured it was the perfect excuse to eat cereal for dinner and attempt to read my current book. In actuality, I'd probably end up doomscrolling on my phone instead until I fell asleep and dropped it on my face.

I couldn't seem to concentrate on anything—least of all reading—which was really unfortunate, considering I could use an escape now more than ever.

"The last patient is gone, and Alicia headed out, so it's just you and me." Quinn strolled into the back room and grabbed her coat. She shrugged into it as she ran an assessing gaze over me. "You said Laurel's studying with Cami tonight, right?"

"Yeah, she's got a big test tomorrow and has been freaking out about it all week."

"Perfect."

"Exactly what I was thinking about my cereal-for-dinner plan, followed by doomscrolling."

"Nope, not happening," Quinn said, tucking her arm through mine as she led us toward the front. "A few of us are getting together tonight, and you're coming."

I was shaking my head before she'd even finished speaking. "Oh no, I don't want to intrude on your plans."

And I wasn't sure I was fit for company anyway.

"My *plans* included you, but you kept dodging me—again." She shot me a look out of the corner of her eye, and I could only duck my head because...yeah, I had definitely been doing that. "Plus, Luna's bringing a friend who's new to town, so you guys will have that in common. They're meeting me at—"

"If you say One Night Stan's, I'm definitely out," I said, unable to stop myself.

I just couldn't go there. Not yet. I didn't know how I was going to navigate that while living in Starlight Cove, considering the best place to grab burgers, drinks, and generally hang out with friends was owned by my ex-not-even-real boyfriend.

I'd worked hard the past few days to avoid running into

Atlas, but that wouldn't last forever. Not when I lived in his backyard and worked in the same building once a week.

All I knew was, I wasn't ready to tackle that today. It was a problem for future me to figure out.

Quinn's brows lifted. "I was going to say they're meeting me at my place, but your reaction only proves just how much you need this. Come on. Addison's bringing enough tacos to fill a truck, and you obviously could use a night with some friends."

I could, actually. Desperately needed one, even if it had always been in my nature to retreat when I had shit to deal with. I always managed to work things out on my own eventually because I'd always been forced to. But I couldn't deny how nice it would be to be surrounded by girlfriends. And hadn't that been one of the reasons I'd decided to stay?

"All right. I'm in."

Ten minutes later, Quinn and I strode into her newly renovated house. Though she and Ford had moved in recently, no one could have guessed that with how cozy and warm their home was. The two-story Cape Cod had been a fixer-upper when they'd purchased it, but Ford was handy with a hammer and saw. His work was evident throughout, from the floor-to-ceiling, built-in bookcases and stone fireplace in the family room area to the custom-built island on the kitchen side of the great room.

"Finally," Addison groaned as she poked her head around the open refrigerator door. "I'm starving. I hope you're hungry, Sutton."

"Sutton! So glad you're here," Luna called from the other side of the kitchen as she dumped a blender full of what looked to be margaritas into a pitcher. Then, to Addison, she said, "Don't think I didn't see you inhale one of those tacos already."

"Lay off me!" Addison gestured to her stomach. "I'm eating for two here."

"Please, come in," Quinn said dryly. "Make yourselves at home."

"Chloe and I were going to wait outside." Luna tipped her chin toward a blonde I'd never seen before. "But Addison forced us to come in."

Chloe shot a bright smile from her perch on the couch and waved. "I just go where they tell me to."

"Well, I wasn't going to hang out in here all by myself," Addison said with a roll of her eyes.

"That's funny." Quinn shrugged out of her coat before taking mine and hanging them up. "I don't remember giving you a key."

"I had to pee like a racehorse, so your husband let me in." Addison shut the fridge, arms overflowing with food. She made her way to the family room and unloaded what looked like the entirety of the Mexican restaurant in town onto the coffee table. "After I made Ford grab the chips off the top shelf for me, I shoved him out the door because his services were no longer needed. He said he was working on a project anyway, so he'd be back later. Before he left, my absolute shit of a brother tried to give me a play-by-play of what he was going to do to you tonight. I shut him up when I threatened to throw an avocado at his head."

"I can verify that." Luna nodded, carrying the pitcher and several glasses into the family room. "She kept her brothers in line before, but now, with the pregnancy? They're *all* scared of her. Even Brady, though he'll deny it to his dying breath."

"They *should* all be scared of me," Addison said, dropping down into a chair and ripping open a bag of tortilla chips.

I followed Quinn into the family room and took a seat next to Luna. I didn't know how or why, but she had a naturally calming vibe that always seeped into me each time we hung out. And god knew I could use a bit of that tonight—could've used it all week.

She turned to me with a smile and passed me a margarita. "I'm so glad Quinn talked you into coming."

"Me too."

"Of course, I always want to see you," she said, bumping her shoulder into mine. "But I also wanted to introduce Chloe to some friendly faces."

"Then why did you bring Addison?" Quinn said, laughing when her sister-in-law lobbed a chip at her.

"How dare you," Addison said. "I'm only mean to my brothers. And they deserve it."

Chloe grinned, accepting a margarita from Luna. "I know I'm new, but Addison won points with me with how fast she laid out this spread."

"I don't have time to fuck around. I've got about twelve minutes before I'll need to run to the bathroom again." Addison leaned back in the armchair, her plate full of tacos, guac, and chips balanced on her round stomach as she dug in.

I offered Chloe a warm smile, remembering just how

overwhelming, albeit well-meaning, this group of women could be. "How long have you been in town?"

"Not long. Luna kept talking about how gorgeous it was up here in the fall, and I was itching for a change." She shrugged. "So, here I am."

Luna tipped her head toward Chloe. "This one's like a tumbleweed, just rolling wherever the wind blows her."

Chloe rolled her eyes. "I'm not that bad."

"If you say so," Luna said with a smile.

I took a long sip of my margarita. "How do you two know each other?"

"We worked at the same massage studio in North Carolina," Chloe said.

"You're a massage therapist?" I asked.

"Yes..." she said, trailing off.

Luna laughed and shook her head. "She means 'Yes, and...'"

"What kind of code language is that?" Addison asked, splitting her gaze between Luna and Chloe. "Pregnancy brain is a real thing. Don't make me feel dumber than I already do."

Chloe laughed. "Luna just means I'm not *only* a massage therapist."

"What else do you do?" Quinn asked.

"What *doesn't* she do?" Luna said, bumping her shoulder into Chloe's.

"Guilty as charged." Chloe grinned. "I've been a personal chef, a dog walker, a makeup artist, an au pair for a count in Monaco, a photographer, and a bunch of other things that only lasted a month or two."

Luna tipped her margarita glass toward Chloe. "And don't forget about the artisanal soaps."

"How could I?" she said with a laugh. "I still have all the supplies somewhere."

I glanced at her with raised brows. "Wow, that is an eclectic resume."

She shrugged. "I get bored easily. Besides, I don't have any commitments tying me down. So I figure, if I don't do this now, when will I? Starlight Cove is so cute, though! I think I'll stay for a little while," Chloe said.

"You'll probably fall in love like everyone else."

"I wouldn't count on that, but it'll be nice while it lasts," she said. "You just moved here a couple of months ago, too, right?"

"Yeah." I nodded, ignoring the memories those first days in town conjured up. "Quinn happened to have an opening when my last contract ended, so it was a little serendipitous."

"Not to mention Mabel scored you that sweet place." Addison waggled her brows. "How is it living in that mansion? Atlas's house is *gorgeous*."

"Oh, like you're one to talk." Quinn rolled her eyes. "Your former pro-hockey-playing husband literally built a secluded mountain lodge to your specifications."

"Not because I asked him to!" She threw her hands in the air. "I didn't even know about it when he was building it."

"Exactly," Quinn said.

"Addison's not wrong, though," Luna said, turning to me. "It *is* a gorgeous house."

That was undeniably true—I'd thought the same when I'd first seen it. But I'd had no idea just how much that gorgeous house would grow to feel like a *home*. Or how bad it would hurt to have it ripped away.

I forced a smile, though I felt like doing anything but. "It was nice while it lasted, but I'm back in the cottage for now."

"The cottage?" Quinn asked, her brows furrowed. "I thought it had to be completely redone. It's not finished already, is it?" She narrowed her gaze on me, and I could practically see the gears working in her mind. "And why would you move back there anyway when you and Atlas are together?"

I shrugged, grateful as ever that Luna hadn't skimped on the tequila, and took another sip of my margarita. "I'm not so sure we're together anymore."

"*No*," Quinn said, her disappointment seeping through.

"Yeah," I confirmed.

"God*dammit*," Addison said, slapping a hand down on her leg. "Why do they *always* fuck it up before they figure out how to fix it?"

"Seriously." Luna shook her head. "Every time."

"Yeah, well..." I downed the last of my margarita, already eager for another. "I'm not so sure he's going to be able to fix this. Or even try to."

"Men can be really stupid," Luna said. "We all know this. But sometimes they pull out a win when you least expect it."

Quinn nodded. "She's right. I don't know the ins and outs of your relationship, but I've seen how he looks at you. And I can safely say that man is head over heels. Don't give up on him just yet."

It was another version of what Laurel had already told me. I wanted their words to be true, desperately. Wanted to believe them, but I couldn't bring myself to. Laurel had seen behind the act, but Quinn had only witnessed the show Atlas and I had put on. Everything we'd done in public had been pretend.

I offered Quinn a smile, not bothering to correct her assumption. Because what could I say? *I'm devastated, but oh, by the way, the whole thing started as a lie.* Yeah, I wasn't going there. It would only lead to more questions I wasn't prepared to answer. Didn't *want* to answer. Because there was no way I could tell them what Atlas and I had was all fake without each of them seeing my pain.

They'd know exactly how hard I'd fallen for a man who'd just been waiting for me to leave.

CHAPTER FORTY-ONE

ATLAS

ALCOHOL HADN'T BEEN the answer. Neither had baring my soul. And watching the woman I loved more than anything move back in to a construction zone hadn't done much for me either.

It had been more than a week since Sutton had last been in my bed. Since I'd held her in my arms, kissed her, heard that soft, sultry laugh I loved so much. And I still wasn't any closer to figuring out what the hell I needed to do.

The only thing this time apart had managed to solidify for me had been my worry that I wasn't good enough—not just for Sutton, but Laurel too. Because they were a package deal, and I knew a thing or two about the effects of having a shitty father.

I'd never forgive myself if I messed up like that with Laurel.

She was a good kid, so much like her mom it had been bittersweet to have her staying over here while Sutton was in the half-finished cottage. But her being around had also given me purpose, something to focus on.

I went through the motions each day. I started my morning by trying and failing not to be a creep, the pull of glimpsing Sutton for the brief moment when she left for work too impossible to resist. Then I busied myself with whatever I could find—playing Daddy Grump taxi for Laurel, logging extra hours at work, pushing myself as far as possible in the gym. All in the hopes that I could close my eyes without seeing Sutton's stricken face when I'd told her this wasn't real.

Unfortunately, none of it had worked.

"Seriously?" Laurel snapped, jerking me out of my thoughts.

"*Jesus.*" I fumbled with the battery I'd charged last night for her DSLR, and it clattered to the counter. "Most people start with 'good morning.'"

"And most people would've pulled their head out of their ass by now, so I guess it sucks for both of us."

Brow furrowed, I glanced around. I couldn't lie and say I'd been on my game since Sutton had left, but I'd been managing. The team shirt Laurel wanted to wear for the game this weekend was already washed and folded on the arm of the couch. The report she'd needed printed out was in her backpack. Her camera was now ready to go. But she was still looking at me like I'd fucked up.

"What's the problem?" I asked. "Cami can't pick you up for school anymore?"

"Oh my *god,*" she groaned. "I'm not telling you to pull

your head out of your ass about *me*, you big, lovable idiot. I'm talking about my mom."

I blew out a heavy sigh and rubbed my fingers against my chest, where an ache had settled and wouldn't go away. "Your mom and I—"

"Are being idiots. Yeah, I got that." Laurel opened the fridge, the happy little hum she made when she saw the fancy French yogurt she liked at odds with the scowl she shot me. She pulled a spoon out of the drawer and pointed it at me like a weapon. "I don't like it when my parents fight. And this custody situation is bullshit. I'm splitting my time between this glorious home with my beautiful bedroom and the heated floors and everything that you've spoiled me with, and that construction zone my mom's living in because she thinks it's better than sleeping in the room next to you."

"Maybe she's better off without me."

"Says who? All I said was that she'd rather sleep in a construction zone than next to you because you're being a big, dumb boy."

"*I'm* saying it. I'm not good enough for her. I've got a lot of shit I need to deal with that I haven't."

"And?"

"What do you mean 'and'?"

"I mean, look around. Everybody's dealing with shit. You are, I am. You think my mom's not? She had me when she was sixteen and then emancipated herself from parents who never thought she was good enough. And now you're showing her she's not worth fighting for."

Her words hit me like a ton of bricks, the force of them crashing into me as I sank onto the stool. "Fuck."

"Am I starting to get through?"

"I never intended to make her feel like that."

"Yeah, well, impact matters more than intention."

"That's exactly what I'm worried about. I didn't have a great role model. What if I fuck this whole thing up? I'm already doing it."

"For the past nine days? Yeah, you haven't been doing great. But are you really trying to say you weren't good for us? Have you forgotten about the weeks before this mess?"

"What about them?"

Laurel dropped her head back and groaned toward the ceiling. "Are all guys really this oblivious? Or is it, like, a football player thing?"

"I don't know, but I'm begging you to let me in on the secret, kid."

"Fine, let me lay it out for you." She settled on the stool next to mine and turned toward me. "You moved us in here after our home was flooded. You set me up in that sweet-ass bedroom with my own bathroom. You gave me a credit card with an unlimited spending limit to buy whatever I needed to make myself feel at home. You brought me tampons and a change of clothes when I bled all over myself at school because my period likes to show up whenever the hell she wants. You made every player on the football team sit through a two-hour lecture about consent, all because that asshole wouldn't stop harassing me for my number. Am I getting through yet?"

"None of that was a big deal. Anyone else would have done that."

"No, Daddy Grump. That's what I'm telling you. No one

else would do that for us. No one else ever has. I've watched my mom go through shitty boyfriend after shitty boyfriend. And now I'm just supposed to accept that when she finally found a good one, he can't pull his head out of his ass to make things right?"

Before I could form a coherent thought in response to Laurel's words, the back door lock disengaged, and my mom poked her head in. "Knock, knock."

"Oh, thank god," Laurel said, relief in her tone. "Maybe you can talk some sense into your son."

I shot Laurel a scowl, a little offended at just how quickly she sold me out. "Really? We couldn't keep this between us?"

She looked at me with raised brows. "I've kept it between us for nine days. It's time for a few reinforcements."

"So you called my *mom?*"

"Don't get mad at Laurel," Mom said. "She didn't call me. She didn't have to. Your brothers told me about your little meltdown in One Night Stan's."

"It wasn't a meltdown," I grumbled.

"Well, all of Mabel's social media accounts, the *Gazette*, and the talk around town say otherwise."

That would explain the looks I'd been getting around town and why people had been jumpier around me than usual.

"You know that's just Mabel stirring shit. It's what she does."

My mom poured herself a cup of coffee before standing at the island. "And what *you* do is distract and avoid. Like you're doing right now. I gave you time to get this figured out. But enough is enough. I'm not going to sit back and let you throw away the two best things that have ever happened to you." She shot Laurel a wink before pinning me with her unimpressed mom glower, a look usually reserved for my younger brothers.

"Mom, it's not—"

"Do not insult me by telling me that what you and Sutton had wasn't what I thought it was. I've known from the first moment I saw you together that you had something special. Something worth fighting for."

"You're only saying that because Sutton helped you choose all the fan mail to share with the book club, and she didn't pull any punches."

Just the thought of her smiling that night, and the memory of how right it had felt to have her as part of my family—a family that had been fractured but not broken—made my chest tighten, that persistent ache thrumming harder.

A secret smile lifted her lips, and she shook her head. "That wasn't the first time I saw you two together."

I snapped my gaze to my mom's, a dozen possibilities flipping through my mind, each one more horrifying than the last. I could think of countless times Sutton and I had been together—in public—that I didn't want my mom to have any knowledge of.

Before I could ask her what she meant, she pulled her phone out of her purse, navigated to something, and slid it across the island toward me.

It was the Instagram feed for the Portland Punishers with a post featuring a bunch of photos taken the night of the charity gala. But instead of the ballroom, this black-and-white image had been taken in the bar. Marino, Wilkins, and Sharp, all former teammates of mine, stood together, drinks in hand, smiling at the camera.

But that wasn't what caught my attention.

It was Sutton and me in the background. And just like that, I remembered that moment. It was after she'd shifted my entire world with that kiss. I held her against me, lifting her right off the floor as if she was meant to be there. As if it had been as natural as breathing.

And that feeling was written across every inch of my face.

"See?" my mom said. "*That's* when I knew. It just took a bit for you to work your way back together. As... *unconventional* as that path has been."

I stared at her in shock, not quite able to believe what she was saying. "Are you telling me you've known all along that this was fake?"

"Oh shit," Laurel whispered, but I couldn't tear my eyes away from my mom.

Mom laughed and leaned over the island, resting her hand on mine. "Oh honey, no. I'm saying I knew all along it was *real*. I was just waiting for you two to catch up."

"Double shit," Laurel whispered.

I glanced down at the picture again, enlarging it until just Sutton and I filled the screen. Since the morning after that night, I'd been lying to myself. Pretending I hadn't felt what I did with Sutton. But I couldn't continue to lie when the evidence was staring back at me in literal black-and-white.

"We make a good team, don't we, Laurel?" Mom said.

"Thank god for that," Laurel said. "Maybe now he can finally do his thing."

I tore my gaze away from the picture and met Laurel's gaze. "What thing?"

"You know, where shit happens, and you just handle it," she said with a shrug, like it was the most obvious thing in the world.

Fuck, that *was* what I did. What I'd been doing my whole life. And while sometimes it got a little heavy knowing I was the one people counted on, I also enjoyed taking care of people I loved.

And I'd fallen down on the job when it mattered most.

"I handle things like plumbing issues and shopping for custom refrigerators and dealing with a cottage flooding. I have no idea how to fix this, kid."

"Come on, Daddy Grump. You're a smart guy. You can figure it out. Just think about what my mom loves and go from there."

My mind was already spinning, a dozen possibilities popping up, but I disregarded each one as soon as they came. None of them was good enough. None of them proved that I was in this for the long haul. That I loved Sutton. That I wanted her and Laurel by my side for the rest of my life.

I glanced around, hoping for inspiration—something, *anything*, that would help—when my gaze landed on a stack of books I'd ordered for Sutton before everything had happened. And a spark lit in my mind.

"Did you figure it out?" my mom asked, clearly reading the determination in my expression.

"Not yet, but I'm getting there."

CHAPTER FORTY-TWO

SUTTON

EVERY DAY that went by without Atlas choosing us over his fears was another day in which I lost a little more faith that what Laurel and Quinn had said might possibly be true.

Fortunately, my daughter had kept me occupied all weekend, so I couldn't dwell on the fact that the singular man I'd ever loved couldn't be bothered to put up a little fight for me. Yesterday, we'd visited every antique store and flea market within a fifty-mile radius before grabbing dinner at the sushi place she loved. It had been well after dark by the time we'd gotten back. But instead of retreating to her cozy bedroom in Atlas's house, she'd stayed in the cottage.

Thankfully, my mattress had been high enough off the floor that it hadn't been ruined in the flood, so she'd slept with me, reminding me of when we'd done that when she was younger.

We set up her laptop between us and binged the latest serial killer documentary before finally falling asleep at 3 a.m. But her activities hadn't stopped there. She'd filled today as well, making me try on every piece of clothing I owned that hadn't been ruined and make piles to keep or donate.

Four hours later, I was exhausted and just wanted to veg for a while.

"Seriously, Lolo, I love you so much. You are the light of my life. But for the love of god, I don't want to do *anything*. I just want to sit and eat chips and scroll through mindless nonsense on my phone. Can we do that? *Please?*" I asked, collapsing into one of the lawn chairs in the living room.

She blew out a long sigh and took a seat next to me. "Fine. I was just trying to get your mind off this shithole you call a home."

"First of all, I didn't call it a home. You're not here, so at best, it's four walls and a roof. And second, it's not *that* bad."

"Are you kidding? It's worse than the apartment in Schenectady."

I thought back to that place—the first apartment I'd rented on my own after scoring my first contract. I hadn't even started paying off student loans, so I couldn't afford much. There was no denying it had been a dump.

"I can see the resemblance with the lack of finished walls," I said, glancing around. "But I think it's cute in here."

Laurel rolled her eyes. "Be for real, Mom. You think sitting on lawn chairs with a plastic tablecloth covering the subfloor is *cute?*"

"Well, it's better than the alternative."

Laurel tipped her head to the side and raised a brow at me. "Is it, though?"

"Is it better than living with a guy who decimated my

heart?" I asked. "Yeah, I think so. He's just like all the rest, except this time I got in too deep."

"I thought I told you, Atlas is different."

"I don't know. It doesn't feel very different from where I'm sitting."

"Give it a little bit and keep an open mind," she said, throwing back words I'd told her countless times when we'd first moved here.

"Those words sound familiar."

"Yeah, well, they worked, didn't they? I love it here in this stupid little town with too many fucking festivals. Where else could we possibly live where I could go to the library for a study group, swing by a book club meeting while there, *and* buy a vibrator from the local sex toy dealer?"

"Oh no," I said, shaking my head. "Please do not let Mabel talk you into her special this month. You need to start small, Lolo. Maybe a bullet vibe—"

"Jesus, Mom, I didn't literally buy a sex toy. It was just an example."

I blew out a breath and sank back into my chair. "Okay, well, I'm just saying... Masturbation is totally normal, and it's fine if you want to explore—healthy, even. And there are definitely worse places to get a toy hookup than from Mabel."

She stared at me for several long moments, her expression broadcasting loudly just how little she wanted to be discussing this with me. "Okay, well. I've had enough of this conversation. And I've also had enough of this depressing-ass construction zone." She stood and held out a hand to me. "Come on."

I placed my hand in hers and allowed her to pull me up. "Where are we going?"

"Don't worry about it. We're just leaving these four walls and a roof for a little bit."

My shoulders sagged, and I blew out a deep sigh to the ceiling. As much as I wanted to do what I'd just told her—namely, a whole lot of *nothing*—I couldn't deny that this was sort of helping. These were the first two days in many when my heart didn't feel like it was constantly being pulverized, and that was solely because of Laurel's distractions.

Unfortunately, I knew as soon as I lay in bed tonight, alone, with nothing but my thoughts to keep me company, I would sink right back into that heartache. The one that had been a constant companion since I'd walked out Atlas's door and he hadn't stopped me.

Laurel grabbed her coat before tugging it on and stepping outside into the chilly early-November evening. Slipping on my jacket as well, I trailed after her, having no idea what her current plan was but knowing I'd follow her wherever she led.

"Lolo, what are we—" I stopped short in our trek across the backyard when I spotted Atlas pacing at the back door, Pandora perched on his shoulder.

He stopped mid-step, his gaze locked on me, drinking me in as if he'd been starved for the sight of me.

"What's happening right now?" I whispered to Laurel without taking my gaze off the man I loved with my entire soul.

And with how my heart thundered at just the sight of him, every cell in my body seeming to recognize him as *home*, there was absolutely no denying that was where I was. Where I *still* was, no matter how much I'd wished otherwise these past two weeks.

She hooked her arm through mine and tipped her head to rest on my shoulder. "Remember what I said—just keep an open mind, okay? I meant it when I told you he's not like all the other ones. And I think you know that too." She squeezed my arm once before stepping away, jingling my keys at me. "I'm stealing your car to stay at Cami's tonight. And when I get back tomorrow, my parents better not still be fighting."

"Your par—"

"I said what I said!" she yelled, cutting me off before shutting the driver's side door.

With a quick wave, she pulled out of the driveway, and then it was just Atlas and me and this chasm between us.

Even the distance I tried desperately to maintain didn't deter him. He ate up the space between us, his gait purposeful, determined. But I had come to see behind the facade he put on for everyone else. I immediately noticed the tension around his eyes, the lines bracketing his mouth, the uncharacteristic way he ran a hand through his hair as if he couldn't help it. And I realized with a start that he was... nervous. *Atlas*—aka the Mountain—was nervous to talk to me?

Once he stood only an arm's length away, he darted his gaze all over my face, soaking in every bit of me as if he couldn't get enough. As if he'd been lost without me.

"I've missed you," he said on an exhale. Then he immediately grimaced. "Shit, I wasn't supposed to say that yet."

Seeing this giant of a man who was normally unshakable stumble through his words was pretty damn endearing, no matter how tender my heart was.

"Did Laurel tell you not to start with that when you enlisted her help?"

"She volunteered," he said. "Actually, she threatened me with bodily harm if I didn't get my shit together and fix this."

Despite myself, I breathed out a laugh. "Sounds like her. And Pandora?"

He reached up and scratched the kitten where she was curled up on his shoulder, like that little curve against his neck was better than any plush bed could have been. I remembered that curve, remembered how solid and sure it had always felt beneath me, and I couldn't say I didn't agree with her.

"She's been my emotional support, but she's a shitty listener. Claws the fuck out of me if I'm not completely focused on her. Hopefully she lets me say what I need to."

I studied him in the quiet night, unsure if I should guard my heart or hear him out. Unsure if I could handle choosing wrong. This man had already hurt me once, and I didn't know if I was strong enough to go through that again.

But from the way he was looking at me, like I was his whole fucking world, hope bloomed bright in my chest. So, I took a leap.

"What do you need to say?"

His shoulders sagged on a relieved exhale. "I fucked up," he said without hesitation. "I *know* I fucked up, but I didn't know how to fix it. For a while, I wasn't even sure I should. I really did want you to go to Boston if that was what *you* wanted."

Tears clogged my throat, the reminder of him so willing to let me go just as painful now as it had been the day we'd fought. "And I just wanted you to tell me to stay."

He made a rough sound in the back of his throat, the pain I was feeling reflected in his eyes. "I'm sorry. Like I said, I fucked up. But I still wouldn't have given you what you wanted." He stepped up to me, running a callused finger from my temple to my jaw, my entire body lighting up at the soft touch. "I never want to hold you back, trouble. Never want to be the reason you can't be everything you want to be."

His words hit me like a physical force, stealing my breath and any response I hoped to have. My chest ached with a longing so fierce, I was afraid it might crack right open. Just split, straight down the middle.

I'd run from people trying to stifle me, trying to control me. My parents had always wanted to shove me in a tidy little box, uncaring about what *I* wanted. About what my dreams were. I'd lived with that my entire life. And now, Atlas's words had soothed a wound I hadn't even realized was still raw after all these years, showing me he wanted me to soar, even if it meant watching me fly away.

"Atlas, I—"

"Shit, I wasn't supposed to get to that part until later." Atlas scrubbed a hand down his face, muttering a curse under his breath. "Can we go inside for a minute? I need to show you something."

"I'm not sure that's a good—"

"Please, Sutton," he said, his voice low and sincere, a thread of panic woven through at the possibility of my walking away. "Five minutes."

I wanted to say no. Definitely should have said no. Part of me was yelling at myself to walk away now while I still could. To not give him a second chance at breaking my heart. But the other part—the larger part—couldn't help but see the earnestness in his eyes. The sincerity. The pain that mirrored my own. Couldn't help but want to see what exactly he had planned.

Before I could stop myself, I nodded once. "Five minutes."

With a relieved breath, he led us into the house, Pandora still perched on his shoulder like a tiny little bodyguard. I wasn't sure what I'd expected when he'd asked me to come inside, but it wasn't leading me through the house and up the stairs until we stood outside the closed door of the guest bedroom.

I didn't think I'd been gone that long, but it now smelled different in here—like paint and fresh wood. That scent had always meant new beginnings for me, and my stomach swooped at the thought that this might be *our* new beginning. If I did what Laurel had told me and kept an open mind.

"Are you ready?" he asked, lifting Pandora off his shoulder and setting her on the floor.

"I guess that depends on what's behind that door. Did you get help with this part too?"

"Some. But it's still not done. Turns out, it doesn't matter how many zeroes I offer to add to a check, it doesn't produce more hours in a day." He swept his gaze over me from head to toe, that single glance reminding me exactly how good it had been with him. "But I couldn't wait anymore."

"Wait for what?"

"You." With that, he opened the door to my old bedroom, but it wasn't the gray walls, generic white bedding, and furniture that could've belonged to anyone that I'd been expecting. It had been completely transformed in the short time I'd been gone.

I gasped as I stepped inside and looked around at what had once been his guest room, but was now well on its way to becoming—

"A library?" I breathed, taking in the warm and vibrant space.

The walls were a deep, rich teal, and a ridiculously girlie chandelier cast rainbows around the room. Enough floor-to-ceiling bookcases lined the perimeter to house triple my entire collection, and I wouldn't have any problem reaching the higher shelves thanks to the freaking *rolling ladder*. Between that and the reading nook stacked high with pillows that hadn't yet been arranged, I was in love.

"Yeah," he said. "A library."

I glanced at the stacks of books piled on the floor, noticing many, *many* familiar titles. "I spot an awful lot of my favorites in here."

"You should spot *all* of your favorites in here."

"You bought all *my* favorite books for *your* library?"

"No, trouble. I bought all your favorite books so I could read the endings, see how those swoony motherfuckers turned shit around, and get a clue about how to win you back."

Something warm and tender unfurled inside me, catching me off guard with its intensity. Unsure if I could trust the hope that seemed to grow with every second, I swallowed it down. "Is that what you're doing?"

"I guess it depends on if it's working or not."

"It's a very nice library—a little girlie for you, but—"

"That's because it's not for *me*. It's for *you*."

I stared at him in stunned silence for a moment, the reality of what he meant crashing into me. "Atlas—"

"*Fuck*," he said, reaching into his pocket and pulling out two keys. "I was supposed to give you these before I told you that, but you distracted me with how gorgeous you looked walking in here."

I breathed out a laugh and shook my head, so endeared by how he continued to fumble this when his entire career had been spent executing perfect plays. "What are those?"

"Your future. *Our* future, I hope." He swallowed hard, holding up a key hanging from a keychain that simply read *home* and placing it in my hand. "This one is for here—this house that never really felt like a home until you and Laurel moved in." He held up the second key before setting it in my palm next to the other. "This one is blank because it can be for wherever you want to go. Boston, San Francisco, Chicago. Anywhere."

"Anywhere?" I asked, that hope faltering as I wondered if this was his way of letting me go.

"Anywhere," he confirmed. "But you should know that while I'll always support whatever decision you make, there's no way in hell I'm not going with you if you decide to leave. I love Starlight Cove, but it's not my home. You and Laurel are."

Tears blurred my vision as the reality of what he said crashed into me. He was choosing me—choosing us—no matter where that led. As long as we were together, it would be perfect.

"That was a lot of words for you," I said through a clogged throat.

"Don't expect it all the time. But it was worth it if you take at least one of the keys." He cupped my face, leaning down until we were eye level. "I want you to be *mine*, trouble. For real. No more bullshit excuses about how this was supposed to be fake. It hasn't been for me for a long time. I was just too fucking scared to admit it."

"You're not the only one who's scared. But I need us to be scared *together*. I can't handle it if you push me away again."

"I won't. I swear. It's going to be hard as hell sometimes, but you're worth it. You're worth *everything*."

I smiled, unable to hold it back a second longer. "See, I told Laurel you needed to figure this part out on your own. It would've ruined everything if she'd admitted that we're staying."

"If she—" His words cut off, his eyes intense as he darted his gaze around my face, trying to get a read on me. "You're staying? In Starlight Cove?"

I reached up, wrapped my hands around his wrists, and nodded. "We're staying. In Starlight Cove." I tossed the blank key over my shoulder before holding up the *home* keychain between us. "With you."

He exhaled a heavy sigh and wrapped his arms around

me, lifting me straight off my feet. With his face buried in my neck, he murmured, "Thank fuck."

I breathed out a laugh, wrapping my arms around him and holding him as tightly as I could. "If you'd given me the choice of keys before showing me the library and I'd chosen the blank one, were you just going to keep this library from me?"

He pulled back and met my gaze, giving a quick shake of his head. "No, trouble. I was going to build you one wherever you let me follow you to."

CHAPTER FORTY-THREE

IT TURNED out the mountain of a man who'd been immovable in so many ways could surprise me after all. Between the library he'd built for me, the future he'd given me with those keys, and, most importantly, his words, Atlas had crashed through every defense I had.

The way he held me to him, his mouth soft but urgent against mine, reminded me of exactly what we'd almost lost. Exactly what I was so desperate to reclaim. And he was right there with me. He didn't break the kiss as he strode with purpose toward his bedroom—*our* bedroom—clearly feeling this need just as intensely as I was.

"I broke my promise to you," he murmured against my lips.

I tightened my arms and legs around him, loving having him this close after being without for too damn long. "What promise?"

He set me down on the bed and braced his hands on

either side of my hips. "I've spent more than a day without being inside you. I've spent more than a *week*."

"Try two."

"You don't have to remind me, trouble. I've been thinking about it every goddamn day, barking orders at Ford to move fucking faster."

"So that's why Quinn was grumbling about her husband never being home this week?"

"I'm not sorry about that," Atlas said without an ounce of fucks to give. "He's going to be able to take her on a monthlong vacation to a private island with how much I paid him to make this happen."

I cupped his face, making sure he saw the sincerity in my eyes. "I didn't need the library, Atlas. I just needed the words. Needed to know you were in this with me. As deeply as I've been."

"I am. And you may not have needed the library, but you deserved it. Hell, you deserve a library in a dozen houses across the world if that's what you want."

"What I want is *you*," I said, tugging his shirt from his body. Needing to feel him, skin to skin. "And what I deserve is a partner who's going to fight for me. Who's going to open up, even when it's scary. Who's in this with me until the end."

"For the rest of my life," he swore, his words feeling like a promise. An oath.

The weight of his declaration hung in the air between us, the raw emotion in his voice giving way to pure need. He moved with deliberate purpose then, stripping away my clothes with the same intensity he'd stripped away my doubts.

There weren't any more words as he sank to his knees at the side of the bed, yanked me toward the edge, and tossed my legs over his shoulders.

He groaned against me at the first swipe of his tongue through my pussy, and I was a boneless pile of limbs at his mercy. How I'd gone the vast majority of my life without knowing the pleasure of Atlas's mouth was a travesty. But he reminded me exactly how talented he was with that tongue as he licked me to my first two orgasms without even breaking a sweat.

As the last aftershocks quaked through me, I gripped his hair and tugged, pulling him up until he braced himself above me, his mouth wet from my pussy. "While I always appreciate your dedication to the number of orgasms I have, I need you inside me. *Now*."

Thankfully, we were on the same page, because Atlas shed the rest of his clothes with focused efficiency before climbing into bed and pulling me astride his hips.

Tipping his head back to rest against the headboard, he breathed out a long groan as I settled myself over him. "Come on, trouble. Don't make me wait another second. Put me out of my misery and put my cock inside your sweet little cunt. I've been fucking lost without it. Lost without you."

His words lit me up from the inside out, his sincerity ringing true. I rocked against him, sliding his cock through my slit, the pleasure he'd coaxed out of me easing the way. Atlas gripped my hips, holding me up as I guided him to my entrance, a breath leaving me at that first delicious stretch. It didn't matter how well he'd prepped me or how hard I'd come on his fingers and tongue, that first slide of him inside was always a challenge.

I braced my hands on his shoulders as I sank down, taking him inch by impossibly thick inch. With our foreheads pressed together, we both stared down between us, watching as my pussy swallowed him whole.

"Christ, you feel so fucking good, baby. Dreamed about this. Dreamed about *you*. Every goddamn night."

"Tell me about them."

He darted his gaze all over my body, drinking me in, his grip on my hips firm and solid. Unrelenting. As if he were afraid I'd disappear. "I could've fantasized about having you anywhere in the world. But do you know where I always, always fucked you in my dreams?"

"Where?" I asked, riding him with slow, languid rolls of my hips. Taking him deep enough to steal my breath.

"Here in my bed—*our* bed—right where you belong. I thought about you in every position imaginable, but you were always here. On these sheets. And no matter how dirty or hard I fucked you, I always ended the same way."

"How?" I asked, my breaths growing ragged, my pussy tightening the closer I got to my peak.

He slipped one hand between us, swirling his thumb around my clit. With his other hand, he cupped the back of my neck and tugged me forward until our breaths mingled in the space between us. "I filled this sweet little cunt that was made just for me. And I did it while telling you over and over how much I love you."

At his words, my breath caught in my throat, the last

remnant of the wall surrounding my heart completely obliterated. "Atlas..."

"That was what I hated most about waiting for your library to be done," he said, his thumb guiding me toward my peak with unerring precision. "And I couldn't do it anymore. Needed to say it to your face instead of just in my dreams."

"Tell me," I begged, even as my legs began to quake.

He played my body as if he'd been born to do just that, everything inside me tightening...tightening, so desperate to fall.

"I love you so fucking much, trouble. And I'm going to tell you that every day for the rest of my life. Every day. You hear me?"

"*Yes.*" I nodded, my movements growing erratic, my orgasm so close I could taste it. "I love you too, Atlas. So fucking much."

A growl of pure, male satisfaction rumbled in his chest before he captured my lips with a kiss, his thumb speeding against my clit. "That's what I wanted to hear. Now, be a good girl and come on my cock so I can give you what we both need."

He kissed across my jaw, down my neck, and scraped his teeth against the juncture where it met my shoulder. That, combined with his attention to my clit, the feel of him so deep inside me, and I was flying. I cried out his name as pleasure crashed through me, each pulse more intense than the last.

"There she is," he said with a groan. "There's my good girl. Such a good fucking girl for me. Gonna make me come so hard."

He tightened his grip on my hip, his fingers digging into

my flesh as he held me to him. He thrust deep, his cock pulsing with his release as he groaned my name.

I didn't know how long we sat like that, with Atlas's forehead pressed between my breasts, his heavy breaths ghosting over my skin, but I wasn't in a hurry to move.

In fact, I couldn't think of anywhere else in the world I'd rather be than right here, wrapped in his arms. Knowing, with complete certainty, that this feeling of belonging, of connection, was worth fighting for.

And now that I had it, I was never letting it go.

ATLAS

I'D SPENT my entire adult life building a playbook for every situation. Every minute had been about strategy and control. About protecting myself. And then Sutton Sinclair had stumbled into my life, dropping her book at my feet, and blown my best intentions to hell.

Baring everything to her last night had felt like throwing a Hail Mary pass in the last seconds of a game. There was no guarantee it would work—in fact, the odds were stacked against me. But somehow, beyond all hope, it had.

The woman who'd stormed her way into my world and dismantled every defense I'd built over the past forty years had chosen to stay.

She'd chosen *me*.

By the time Laurel made it home the next morning, Sutton and I were lounging on the couch. She was tucked into my side while she focused on a book, and I focused on her. Or focused as much as I could with Pandora curled up on my chest, demanding attention.

Laurel walked in the back door, set the car keys on the counter, and split a gaze between Sutton and me. "I see we've finally gotten over this bullshit between you two. Can we agree to no more fights?"

Sutton laughed and glanced up at me before turning her attention back to her daughter. "You know that's going to be impossible, Lolo. Just this morning, Atlas and I fought about whether pineapple belongs on pizza."

Yeah, and she may have thought she'd won that one, but I'd spread her out on the island and feasted on her for breakfast just to put an end to the argument. So who was the real winner here?

"Fine," Laurel said with a sigh. "Fighting is okay. Moving in to a place without real walls or floors when you're mad at each other is not."

Sutton dipped her chin in a nod. "I promise I won't storm off in a huff and move in to another residence, temporary or not."

I tugged Sutton into my side and pressed a kiss to her forehead. "And I promise I won't make her."

"Good. Maybe now things can get back to normal around here." Laurel headed toward her bedroom before turning back to us, her eyes narrowed. "Unless this means there will be little rug rats running around."

Sutton tipped her head back, glancing up at me, and I met her gaze with a raised brow.

"Your call, trouble. I want what you want." I lowered my

voice so only she could hear. "I'll take you upstairs right now and start practicing, or I'll call on Monday and schedule a vasectomy."

"I've already gone through the terrible twos and the tyrant threes. I don't need to do it again."

"Second option, it is," I said.

Sutton rested her hand on my stomach, heat flaring in her eyes as she caught her bottom lip with her teeth. "I'm definitely not opposed to the practicing part, though."

With a groan, Laurel tossed up her hands. "Control yourselves for five minutes, please."

"Sorry, kid," I said.

"No, you're not."

"You're right. I'm not."

She crossed her arms over her chest and leveled her stare on me. "Since there won't be any children running around, I would like to negotiate something else."

"What's that?" I asked warily, already sensing I was in trouble.

Laurel's chin tipped up the slightest bit, and she stared down her nose at me like the confident little shit she was. "I want another cat."

"Absolutely not," I said without hesitation. "I hate cats."

"Clearly." She rolled her eyes, gesturing to where Pandora was curled up on my chest. "Come on, Daddy Grump, I'll even let you name the next one."

"The *next* one? I named this one!"

Her laughter rang out as she walked away, tossing over her shoulder, "Sure you did."

As I watched her head toward the bedroom she'd made

her own, something unfamiliar settled in my chest. A warmth that had absolutely nothing to do with the tiny menace purring against my sternum.

My house had always been just a space to escape to when I needed solitude and privacy. Now, it was a home. Filled with the absolute chaos of two strong-willed women, both of whom had somehow become essential to my existence.

That should have terrified me. Instead, it felt like I'd finally found the missing pieces to a life I hadn't realized was incomplete.

"I love that little hustler," I murmured, brushing a kiss against Sutton's temple.

She tipped her head back, smiling up at me. "She loves you too."

Not long ago, the knowledge of that would've shaken me to my core, worried I'd fuck it up. But now, with Sutton in my arms and Laurel making this house her home, I finally felt like everything had clicked into place.

I pressed my mouth to Sutton's, grateful I had the privilege of doing so. That she'd let me back in. That she wanted me to be hers.

The kiss was gentle, unhurried. Just a slow meeting of lips and tongues, the rest of the world fading out as we enjoyed each other without the urgency that had weighed on so many of our encounters before.

Because, it turned out, we had all the time in the world.

EPILOGUE
ATLAS

I COULD SAY with absolute certainty that the past few months had been the best of my life. And that included the months I'd won the Big Game. But there really was nothing better than knowing Sutton and Laurel were mine forever.

The first family dinner after Sutton had really, *truly* moved in with me, my mom had been smug as hell, giving me that *what did I tell you?* stare. And I didn't even mind. Why would I, when what she'd told me had given me the kick in the ass I needed to get back the woman who had my entire fucking heart?

Sutton and Laurel fit right in with my family, just like they had since the first night I'd brought them over here. Not to mention, my mom loved adding two more girls into the former testosterone-overload zone.

"Sutton, that book for book club came into the library, so I grabbed it for you," Mom said.

"Thank you." My gorgeous girlfriend smiled, accepting

the book from my mom. The cover featured a shirtless man wearing a Ghostface mask holding a bloody knife.

Raising a brow at her, I murmured in her ear, "Discovering a new kink, trouble?"

"Maybe. Probably not knife play, but I definitely wouldn't be opposed to you in that mask." She bit her lip as she trailed her gaze down my body, and fuck if my cock didn't twitch behind the fly of my jeans at just that look.

You bet your ass I was going to order that mask just as soon as we got home. And when the fuck would that be anyway? We'd already eaten dinner, and now we were just waiting for my brother to show up.

"When the hell is Xander supposed to get here?" I asked, shifting in my seat.

Sutton shot me a smirk, as if she knew *exactly* what my problem was. And I had no doubt she did.

"Any time now," Mom said. "Just need to have a little patience. No one's more anxious than I am!"

"I very much doubt that," I grumbled under my breath, earning a snort from Sutton.

"Well, I'm excited to meet him," she said.

Mom beamed. "I'm excited too. Like you wouldn't believe."

She was excited for my girlfriend to meet my younger brother? That was weird, but that was Mom.

"Oh, Laurel," Mom said, "I grabbed a couple of books for you too. One of the college girls who was home last weekend went on and on about how good the series is." She leaned forward, lowering her voice. "Though I'm not sure how spicy your mom lets you read."

Laurel snorted and slid a glance to Sutton. "The one I finished last week had three dudes and two women in it."

"Oh!" Mom stood up straight, her eyes wide as she darted them to my girlfriend.

Sutton shrugged. "I'd rather have her read sex written by women that explores consent, pleasure, and sexuality than have her look to mainstream porn that generally only focuses on the man's satisfaction."

"Good point." Mom nodded. "Well then, perhaps this one won't be spicy *enough*."

"Damn, I didn't know they had all *that* in them," Lincoln said, brows raised. "Can you hook me up with one of those, Mom?"

"If you think you'll read it," she said, as if she didn't care one way or the other, but I saw the self-satisfied smile before she turned around.

"How long is Xan staying?" Declan asked. "He hasn't responded to a text in, like, two weeks."

Lincoln rolled his eyes. "You're a fine one to talk."

"Fuck off," Declan said without any heat.

"Watch your mouth, Declan," Mom said. "We're having a special guest tonight."

Lincoln snorted. "Xander's not special, Mom."

"As for how long he's staying, you can ask him yourself," Mom said, staring out the window as she wrung her hands. "He just pulled up."

I removed my arm from around Sutton and pushed to stand. "I'll go help him with his bags."

"Sit down," Mom said, her voice sharper than usual. "Just let him come in on his own."

"Yeah, you don't see either of us getting up to help, do you?" Lincoln said.

"Never do," I shot back.

"Like Xander needs it," Declan said.

"Seriously." Lincoln nodded. "If he has more than a carry-on with him, I'll delete my dating apps."

Sutton shot him a smile. "I'm gonna hold you to that."

"You won't need to," Declan said. "Xan packs like a minimalist."

"Sounds like someone else I know." She leaned into me and shot me a smile.

"I have a system," I muttered.

While my brothers and Sutton joked about my grocery shopping system—who had time to fuck around with that shit? Efficiency was key—Mom headed into the kitchen. She grabbed a plate of cookies and set them on the counter before pulling out a juice box from the fridge—Jesus, was Lincoln making her buy those again?

Then the back door opened, and she hurried toward it, disappearing from my sight. Her voice was soft and gentle as she said something I couldn't make out, Xander's deeper tone following. I kept glancing toward the doorway, but neither of them seemed in all that much of a hurry to come in here.

I wished they'd get on with it already. *Some* of us had a sex mask to order.

"What the hell's taking so long?" Declan said.

"Seriously. I want some of those cookies Mom said we couldn't have till Xan got here." Linc rubbed his stomach. "I'm starving."

"You're always starving," I said.

Before Lincoln could respond, Xander and Mom finally appeared in the doorway. It hadn't been that long since I'd seen Xan, but he looked...different. Exhausted. Dark circles hung under his eyes, and there was tension in his shoulders he didn't usually carry.

But that wasn't what shocked me.

It was the small figure partially hidden behind his legs.

A little girl with dark hair pulled up into a lopsided ponytail clung to Xander's jeans like a lifeline, peeking out at us.

"What the hell?" Declan murmured, perfectly voicing my thoughts.

"You didn't tell me he had a little girl," Sutton whispered, so low only I could hear.

"He doesn't," I murmured back.

"Hey," Xander said, his voice rough. "Sorry for the radio silence. Things have been...complicated."

"Who's your friend?" Lincoln asked.

Xander inhaled deeply before blowing it out. Then he placed a hand on the little girl's head and glanced down to her.

"Everyone, this is Emma." He swallowed hard, his gaze darting to each of us. "My daughter."

His fucking *what*?

THANK YOU FOR READING THE GRUMP NEXT DOOR!
Want to know if Atlas orders the mask to make Sutton's
fantasy come true? Or if Laurel talks him into another kitten?
For the sexy and swoony bonus chapters spanning six years
delivered straight to your inbox, scan the QR code below!

ACKNOWLEDGMENTS

This book is what it is because of a bunch of really smart women I'm lucky enough to call friends.

Thank you to Zoe York, Annika Martin, Selena Blake, and Molly O'Keefe for our daily Zoom rooms. Honestly, it's a wonder I ever got work done before we started our little virtual office. Having a second (or third or fourth) brain when I'm stuck in the depths of writing despair is invaluable to my #34 Ideation ass. (lolsob)

And then Galveston happened! Thank you, again, to Zoe, Annika, Selena, and Molly, plus Skye Warren and Sophie Andrews, for talking through my Bleeding Edge and helping me craft this into the showstopper I wanted it to be. Plus, margaritas on the beach. 'Nuff said.

Thank you to Molly for swooping in like a fairy plotmother when I just could *not* figure out the ending for Atlas and Sutton. You weave some kind of magic when you read and critique, I swear.

Thank you to Lisa for reminding me exactly what kind of hero I write (because, yes, *obviously*, Atlas would claim Sutton in front of her creepy ex!). You always make my words shine.

Thank you to the amazing Queen B's for your excitement and enthusiasm for these brothers and this book.

Thank you to all my readers, some of whom have been with me for twelve (!!) years, and some of whom have just recently found me. You are the reason I'm able to do what I do, and I can't thank you enough for turning my dream of writing for a living into a reality.

But this job doesn't come without a cost, as much as I wish it did... Thank you to my surgeon, my physical therapists, and my massage therapist (and friend!) because without you all, I wouldn't have working arms in order to produce this (or any) book. (Side note: fellow writers, learn from me. Do your stretches, wear your braces, work in ergonomic conditions, and dictate as much as you can.)

Last but never least, to my guys. You make me want to write nothing but Happily Ever Afters because it's all I know thanks to you. I love you more than I can say.

ABOUT THE AUTHOR

Award-winning *USA Today* and *Wall Street Journal* bestselling author Brighton Walsh spent a decade as a professional photographer before taking her storytelling in a different direction and reconnecting with her first love—writing. She likes her books how she likes her tea—steamy and satisfying—and adores strong-willed heroines and the protective heroes who fall head over heels for them. Brighton lives along the shores of Lake Michigan with her real life hero of a husband, her two kids—both taller than her—and her dog who thinks she's a queen. Her boy-filled house is the setting for dirty socks galore, frequent dance parties (okay, so it's mostly her, by herself, while her children look on in horror), and more laughter than she thought possible. Connect with her online at <u>brightonwalsh.com/quicklinks</u>.